"He wants to build a prototype first to demonstrate the potential and then present the idea to a group of investors."

Max Brita is an angel investor who sponsors a "Designing the Future" contest to support small businesses, inventors, and innovators who need financial support to get their ideas off the ground. In the pile of proposals, he finds detailed plans by Alexandra Schultz for a lighter-than-air cruise ship that will revolutionize leisure travel. Their collaboration, both in business and romance, leads to many new and profitable uses of the material graphene and to ventures in many different businesses. Alex's work as a structural engineer and designer, coupled with her family's Hindenburg history, make her an ideal person to revive airship travel with new materials and modern techniques. Her success also makes her a frequent target of sabotage. As her luxury airships traverse the globe, her team faces danger and scrutiny, often problem-solving for safety while flying hundreds of passengers.

Rhodes' novel illuminates the design process from idea to prototype to logistics and beyond through the work of Alex and her team. The financial demands and building processes are detailed and thoroughly explained. The relentlessly inventive mind of Alex showcases the wonder of science and imagination combined to create futuristic modes of transportation and even floating cities that seem only possible in movies. With the right materials and scientific support, things never dreamed of before become possible. Alex boldly embodies this spirit with her intelligence and determination. She fearlessly imagines the future and finds ways to build it. This modern story contains the beginning of jetpack/pod travel and floating cities but feels very of the moment rather than far off in the future. Matter-of-factly, Rhodes lays out the process with such authority and certainty that the creations don't even seem speculative. Fans of speculative fiction with a focus on novel inventions and travel may find this book meets their criteria.

- US Review of Books

I0695062

GRAPHENE

LARRY RHODES

ISBN
979-8-88945-245-4 (Paperback)
979-8-88945-246-1 (eBook)

Brilliant Books Literary
137 Forest Park Lane Thomasville
North Carolina 27360 USA

Table of Contents

1

The End of an Era

Naval Air Station Lakehurst, New Jersey, May 6, 1937

George Schultz stomped his feet to bring some circulation back. He was a member of the air station ground crew waiting for the Hindenburg airship to arrive. It was over six hours late due to an unseasonably cold and wet weather front that covered most of New England. The ground crew alternated between waiting at the mooring tower and trying to stay warm in the hangar. The Hindenburg had been forced to deviate from its predetermined course and circle the landing field, waiting for the weather to clear enough to allow the huge ship to attach to the mooring tower and winch its way to the ground. Schultz was only nineteen and had been in the navy for a year. This was a temporary position until new naval vessels under construction were completed, and he could join one as a seaman.

The weather cleared some, and the crew received word the huge ship would land soon. They quickly resumed their pre-appointed positions near the tower and waited. Schultz was far from an expert on lighter-than-air vessels, but the rapid turns the Hindenburg was making as it neared the tower seemed excessive. Surely the Zeppelin Company's experienced flight crew knew what they were doing.

Schultz watched a new storm front looming on the western horizon and hoped they could complete the landing before it arrived. Someone yelled, and he glanced up at the ship. Was that a fire on the top? Maybe it was St. Elmo's fire? Suddenly, a huge fireball appeared near the tail of the ship, and pieces of flaming debris rained down on the waiting ground crew.

Most of the crewmen scattered, but Schultz saw someone dangling on one of the mooring ropes. He knew he had to help the people on board if possible. The flames were now spreading quickly to the midsection of the ship, and it turned nose up just before the tail section rammed into the ground.

He saw some passengers breaking windows, and he motioned to them to jump. They were less than twenty feet from the ground; but, in a panicked state, they probably believed they were much higher. A young boy saw him and jumped. Schultz caught him and ran away from the ship. He saw others trying to jump and returned several times to help drag people away from the burning debris still raining down on them.

With a final groaning noise, the huge ship slowly settled on the ground. Most of the ship's structure was now visible as the outer skin, and the "gas bags" holding the hydrogen had burned off. Diesel leaking from the engines was now burning, and several small explosions completed the tragic crash of the once enormous vessel.

Schultz didn't even notice his shirt was on fire until someone covered him in a blanket. He passed out. The next morning, he woke up in a hospital, to the relief of his fiancée, who filled him in on the terrible loss of life. She told him there was a rumor he would receive a citation for the lives he saved. When he told his fiancée he would have quite a tale to tell their children, she was so relieved she cried.

2

Designing the Future

Max Brita settled into a comfortable high-back chair in his well-appointed Manhattan office for a long afternoon. Longtime friend and business colleague Tom Babineaux entered with a cup of gourmet coffee and another stack of proposals submitted for his biannual "Designing the Future" contest. The winner would receive every inventor's dream, a presentation to an interested room full of investors, hoping to receive funding to build a prototype, or make the next big step in increasing the size of their company. Fortunately, the contest proposals were limited to ten pages, including drawings, so Max hoped to make it through the last batch of entries and still make it to dinner with Jill Thornton.

As an experienced angel investor, Max had seen thousands of proposals from early concepts to small operating companies, hoping for funding to take them to the next level. Max breezed through most of the proposals. He had seen similar proposals countless times, and few offered the possibility of the next big thing that would make the lucky investor and the angel investor fabulously wealthy. The minimum expectation for an angel investor was at least a quick ten-to-one return on investment.

As he neared the bottom of the stack of last-minute proposals, a drawing caught his attention. It was a colorful 3-D rendering of a lighter-than-air airship with such detail it almost seemed to pop out from the page. Most of the proposal dealt with the engineering aspects of the ship, rather than the business purpose or profit potential. Normally, he would have tossed the proposal onto the large reject pile, but it had piqued his interest enough to search the Internet for more information about the lighter-than-air concept.

While Max would consider almost any technology, he was most comfortable funding new types of materials, information technology and biotechnology proposals. This was so far outside the range of projects he normally dealt with that he wanted to know more. He highlighted the author's name and contact information and looked at his watch. He realized he might be late; traffic in Manhattan was always a challenge. He quickly stuffed the proposal in his briefcase and hurried to meet his girlfriend. She didn't like it when he was late.

3

The Concept

Max Brita and Tom Babineaux arrived without fanfare at the headquarters of Armstrong Aeronautics in Clear Lake City, near Houston. Founded by a group of ex-NASA engineers, Armstrong Aeronautics specialized in the design of small-to medium-size business jets. Normally, Max would have been escorted directly to the president's office and treated almost like royalty. Besides his angel investments, he also managed a huge hedge fund that was the second largest stockholder in Armstrong Aeronautics, after the founder Jack Armstrong. Vice presidents of the company jostled to meet him and shake his hand. More than once, he had steered a potential client their way who later became a major customer. They owed him.

Today, Max was just another visitor. Tom Babineaux had made the arrangements in his name, and only a few people at Armstrong knew him. Upon their arrival, they were informed that Alex Schultz was still in a meeting and would probably not be available for another hour. Tom was embarrassed that Max had to wait, but he waved off Tom's apology with a magazine and settled into a large comfortable chair in the visitor's lobby.

Jeanne Wellman, the secretary of the design department, soon appeared to fetch them to Alex's office. Always observant, Max noticed that, while Jeanne wasn't someone you would easily pick out of a crowd, she had a nice smile, expressive large green eyes, long brown hair, and a slender build. Max guessed she was about thirty years old, and he skillfully pumped her for information about Alex.

"How long have you known Alex?" he asked.

Jeanne glanced at him as they neared Alex's office. "Oh…over five years."

Just as they arrived at Alex's office, Max inquired, "Is he a lead designer?"

A confused expression ran over Jeanne's face for a second, and she started to reply when she saw Tom smiling and shaking his head. She immediately understood and smiled back at them. "Uh…yes, for small projects. Alex should be here any minute. Would you like some coffee?"

Max declined, but Tom accepted her offer. "I'll go with you if you don't mind."

He watched them for a moment and then entered Alex's office. He slowly smiled at the Hindenburg memorabilia that virtually covered the walls of the small office. Her computer even used the famous film footage of the Hindenburg's last moments as a screensaver. His attention was drawn to a three-foot-long scale model of the Hindenburg resting atop a file cabinet. Pictures of the crew and its designers were mixed with interior photographs of the most famous dirigible in the world. He also noticed a long shelf on one wall that was lined with various collegiate athletic trophies. He was trying to read the inscription on one of them in the dim office lighting as Tom and Jeanne returned. A few curious cubemates overheard Tom and Jeanne's discussion about Alex and followed them from the coffee station.

Alex had just finished leading a scheduled early morning one-hour design meeting that had lasted two hours, and she was exhausted. She hoped to have some time to rest in her office before a scheduled afternoon meeting. Her e-mail inbox was almost full, and she had missed the notice from her admin for a scheduled meeting with some "investors." She noticed several people standing outside her office and assumed it was an informal hallway meeting. When they saw her, they moved aside to let her in her office…Strange. A salesman was waiting for her and examining one of her collegiate trophies, and her admin was chatting with another salesman.

"Can I help you?" she asked icily.

Max quickly returned the trophy to the shelf and turned to her. Alex was wearing jeans, a red blouse, and a pair of comfortable tennis shoes. She had light blue eyes, and he guessed her to be in her late twenties to about thirty years old. Her honey-blond hair was slightly curled and fell softly around her shoulders. She was slender, about five and a half feet tall, and was carrying a large graphic design tablet. He instinctively took her for an engineering assistant—a very attractive engineering assistant.

"Yes, I'm here to see Alex Schultz. Would you know when he would be available? I understand he's in a meeting."

Alex had assumed he was a salesman who, like most, thought she was a man based on her nickname.

"I'm Alexandra Schultz," she replied.

"No, I mean…" It suddenly dawned on him. "Oh…"

She offered her hand, and he quickly shook it. He hadn't been this embarrassed in quite some time.

"It's okay," she said. "It happens all the time. Now…how can I help you?"

Jeanne and Tom smiled at each other, while Max quickly gathered his thoughts. "I'm Max Brita, and this is my colleague Tom Babineaux. We read your proposal for a lighter-than-air airship built with today's technology. While it's an intriguing idea, what I guess we didn't see in the proposal is a business justification for doing it."

She was stunned. She was certain her proposal would be lost among the thousands of proposals that Brita was certain to receive for each contest. Her mind leapt to the demonstration cases she had put together in the unlikely possibility that one of her proposals would generate interest. Where were they?

Were they in the trunk of her car?

"Before we can talk about that, I first need to show how today's technology can apply to the lighter-than-air concept, then how this technology can provide a new way of looking at the travel and entertainment industry. I have a presentation prepared to do that, which should also answer all your business-related questions."

Max nodded. "Great. Let's get started."

Alex turned to Jeanne, who had been chatting with Tom, and was too fascinated with the events to leave. The other employees who had wandered over to see what was going on heard Max introduce himself and Tom.

"Jeanne, could you find an empty conference room for about a two-hour meeting?"

"Of course, Alex, just give me a few minutes," she replied automatically. She also needed to find something better for Max than the free coffee available at the coffee stations. Jeanne knew who Max was as she had once set up a meeting for Jack Armstrong with Max when Jack's secretary was on vacation.

As Jeanne returned to her desk, Max and Tom sat down in visitor chairs in Alex's office. Max noticed several large 3-D drawings of a lighter-than-air airship that had even more detail than the drawings in her proposal. The 3-D drawings were mixed in with a sizable photo gallery of the Hindenburg.

"You have quite a collection of Hindenburg memorabilia," he commented.

He laughed when she replied, "This is nothing. You should see my apartment."

Alex had instinctively assumed he would be much older. He was wearing a dark expensive suit and appeared to be in his early to mid-thirties, with dark hair and eyes, and, she guessed, about six feet tall. He seemed to be physically fit.

She wondered how he had made so much money so quickly.

His colleague, Tom Babineaux, was probably the same age as Max. He was also about six feet tall, slender, with blond hair and blue eyes, and wearing a dark expensive suit. She had to admit, they were both good-looking.

4

Concept and Application

Tom and Max settled into comfortable chairs in the well-appointed "client" conference room and Max sipped on a cup of gourmet coffee as he watched Alex place several small aluminum suitcases on empty chairs. Tom pulled out a notebook to take notes as she opened one suitcase and handed Max a small swatch of light-gray material.

"I'd like to begin by comparing the materials used to construct the Hindenburg with the modern materials available today. This is the fabric that covered the basic structure of the Hindenburg. Earlier dirigibles used cotton as the base, but the Hindenburg used silk covered with many layers of gelatin."

Max examined the small piece of material carefully, rubbing it between his fingers. It was very light and soft to the touch yet unexpectedly rigid.

Alex handed him another small piece of white fabric. "And this is a new polymer that resulted from the space program."

The fabric was extremely light and almost seemed to glow in the soft white light of the conference room. He briefly wondered what it would look like in bright sunlight. While he examined the polymer, Alex pulled two large folded pieces of material from the small suitcase and handed one of them to him when he looked up. "This is one square meter of the Hindenburg material, or about ten square feet." She then handed him the other. "And this is one square meter of the new polymer. Feel the difference in weight?"

Max held them both in his hands. The polymer seemed much lighter and more flexible. It was so smooth and slippery it was hard to hold on to and slipped out of his hand. He had to grab it quickly with both hands to keep it from falling to the floor. He handed both samples to Tom, who examined them closely.

"Image the difference in weight multiplied by the thousands of square meters needed for the entire skin of a dirigible."

Max had hardly digested this when Alex placed a shiny fabricated piece of metal on the table in front of him. "This is what a section of a strut of the Hindenburg looked like. It's made of duralumin, an alloy of aluminum, copper, and magnesium. Some things today are still made of duralumin."

As he picked it up, Alex laid a smaller, shinier piece on the table. "This design carries the same structural strength as the other, but it's made of a titanium alloy, similar to the type used today in many aircraft frames."

He picked the smaller piece up. Its shape was radically different than the first and much lighter. He immediately had a mental vision of a World War II bomber sitting next to a modern military fighter. While he was inspecting the smaller piece, Alex commented, "Titanium is actually one and a half times as heavy as duralumin, but you need a lot less for the same structural strength."

When he looked up, Alex was waiting with her arms folded. "Okay. I'm convinced you can make a dirigible lighter today, but why would you?"

"For every pound saved in the design of the ship, I can lift one more pound of cargo or, in this case, one more pound of passenger. So for a ship the same size as the Hindenburg, this would mean more than sixty thousand pounds or three hundred more passengers than the fifty to seventy passengers and forty to fifty crewmen the Hindenburg could carry."

He still appeared confused. "But…why do it at all? It couldn't possibly compete with today's jets that cross the oceans in a few hours."

She paced as she replied, "Imagine a young couple. They are considering a cruise around the Caribbean when they see an ad for a new type of travel—aboard a lighter-than-air airship with virtually no limitations as to where it can travel."

She paused as Max and Tom glanced at each other.

"A cruise ship leaves Los Angeles and travels to Alaska to view the glaciers. This ship could make the same trip—but fly *over* the glacier. On the way back, it flies near the coastline—a much better view than driving along the coast."

She could see a spark of interest in their faces as she continued, "Imagine flying *over* the pyramids in Egypt or *over* the Great Wall of China or *over* Machu Picchu or *over* an active volcano in Hawaii or *over* the Rocky Mountains or *over* the rain forests of the Amazon or even *over* African deserts…virtually anywhere in the world. The possibilities are endless." She had to take a deep breath to calm down, but she was certain she had two new converts. Max jumped up.

"Yes! This is a step-change innovation." Then his expression changed. "But…what about the cost? If this vacation could only be taken by a few wealthy people, we would never recover engineering and manufacturing costs."

"I've done some preliminary calculations. I'm pretty sure the cost to construct and operate one would be no more than the cost of a new medium-size cruise ship."

"Medium size?"

"One that would hold from seventy hundred and fifty to one thousand passengers and perhaps a crew of three hundred." Max was pacing the floor, and Tom and Alex didn't dare interrupt his thoughts. He finally stopped and sat back down.

"How big would it be?"

They laughed when she smiled and said, "I happen to have a preliminary design…"

She lifted a projector onto the conference table and plugged her laptop into it. A few seconds later, a three-dimensional image framed a screen that Tom had lowered.

They stared at a massive lighter-than-air airship floating over the Statue of Liberty in New York to enable a comparison of its size. The actual length was a little more than 1,100 feet.

Max's gaze shifted to a cutaway view on the side of the image. The cross section of the ship was actually an ellipse instead of a circle, the width being twice the height.

"Why is the basic shape an ellipse, instead of a circle?"

"Mainly to enhance the passenger decking and to reduce the height of the hangars required for maintenance."

Alex pressed a button on the laptop. "This is a view of the passenger decking. A floor in the bottom of an ellipse would be much wider than in the bottom of a circle, allowing much more floor space. This design would also maximize the number of passenger compartments with windows. The deck runs almost the entire length of the ship."

While they were thinking about that, Alex elaborated on the height issue. "If the ship's structure were round and the same length, it would have to be thirty to forty percent taller and would require a much taller hangar to contain it, wherever it is based. This would make the ground facilities at all hangar bases much more expensive."

Tom wondered how the ship would land. He had seen movies about the Hindenburg. "A cruise ship can dock in almost any coastal port or tender in. Would this ship require special landing facilities? That could be expensive."

"Yes and no. A small mooring facility would be required at any predetermined landing site, but in an emergency, the ship could fire anchors into the ground and winch down anywhere. There would have to be at least one hangar for refurbishing and maintenance—not all that different from a ship that periodically has to go into dry dock."

Max thought that one over for a moment. "Okay. I think you said there were about one hundred passengers and crew on the Hindenburg, and it was gigantic. Wouldn't this ship have to be a lot bigger to lift thirteen hundred passengers and crew and their luggage?"

"Yes, the structure is much lighter, but the volume of lift gas would still have to be multiplied by a factor of ten. The volume of gas in the Hindenburg was about seven million cubic feet, so this ship would have to utilize about seventy million cubic feet."

Tom was shocked. He knew that small quantities of helium were very expensive, but he didn't have a clue on the cost if millions of cubic feet had to be purchased. "Seventy million cubic feet! Isn't that, millions of dollars?"

"Yes, but that's the initial purchase. After that, you are only buying gas to replace what's lost through leaks."

Max wanted to take a step back. "For those that haven't studied this field, could you elaborate a little on the lighter-than-air concept?"

Alex gazed at him for a few seconds while she gathered her thoughts. "Okay, for a lift comparison, think of a typical storage locker that's ten feet long, ten feet high, and ten feet deep. That's one thousand cubic feet. If it's filled with air at sea level, the air in the locker would weigh a little over eighty pounds, or eight-hundredths of a pound per cubic foot. If it's filled with helium, the weight is about eleven pounds, or about seven times lighter. And hydrogen is even lighter at about five and a half pounds, or about sixteen times lighter.

So a fixed volume will want to rise until the outside density is the same as the density inside. It's the same principle as a hot air balloon. The hot air in the balloon is less dense than the colder air outside and wants to rise to an altitude where the densities are the same."

They still seemed to be following her, so she continued, "In the locker example, one thousand cubic feet of helium could lift the difference between air at eighty pounds and helium at eleven pounds or sixty-nine pounds until the densities equalize. Hydrogen could lift even more at seventy-five pounds. So all we need to know is the weight we have to lift to figure the volume of helium or hydrogen we need. The Zeppelin Company actually used sixty-seven pounds per one thousand cubic feet in their helium lift calculations to allow for impurities in the gas and humidity in the air. However, in the thirties, the US had the world's largest supply of helium, and when the Nazis came to power, the US cut off their supply of helium. This forced the Zeppelin Company to use hydrogen as the fill gas. There is a huge trade-off with hydrogen. It's fifty percent lighter than helium, so the same volume will lift more weight, but it's highly flammable, so you have to take every precaution to avoid catching it on fire. Today most people think the Hindenburg went up in flames because it was filled with hydrogen. That's not true, but I wouldn't begin to propose we fill this new vessel with hydrogen. There would just be too many people who would think it's not safe."

She paused to regain her original point. "The Hindenburg was about one hundred and thirty-five feet in diameter and eight hundred feet long. This vessel would have to be at least one hundred and eighty feet high, about four hundred feet wide, and about eleven hundred feet long to provide the needed lift capacity for the passengers and crew and their luggage of course."

Max was staring at the image on the screen. "Is that feasible? A vessel that's more than a football field wide and almost four football fields long?"

"It is, with today's technology like this." She was holding the titanium strut.

"How long would it take to fabricate it?"

"I'm not an expert in that area, but all the materials needed are readily available so I think it would take about a year to build a factory to make the parts and another year for actual fabrication, then another six months for trial runs and certification by the FAA and other authorities."

"How long would it take to design it?"

"That could be done while the factory is being built."

Max walked to the projector screen for a closer view of some of the details. "You said the cost would be similar to a medium cruise ship. What number are you basing that on?"

Without hesitation, she replied, "Most cruise ships that carry one thousand passengers cost about one billion to build."

He turned to her. "Billion?"

She nodded.

He returned to his chair to think about the whole lighter-than-air issue. "Most people come to angel investors to take their entrepreneurial business to the next level whether it's building a small prototype or to expand. They are usually looking for a few million dollars. This is just a concept, isn't it? And…you are looking for a billion dollars?"

She laid a larger suitcase on the table. "I have a small prototype to demonstrate the concept."

"Great, let's see it."

She opened the suitcase and took out a complex maze of small titanium sticks and something that resembled a deflated Mylar balloon. They were soon standing next to her as she quickly assembled a six-foot-long metal structure that resembled a small dirigible with the deflated balloon inside.

She took a small cylinder of helium out of another suitcase and started inflating the Mylar "gas bag" inside the wire frame structure. She hooked a cable to the helium cylinder when the dirigible started floating. The small dirigible continued to rise and lifted the cylinder off the table.

"Lifting the cylinder wouldn't be possible for a prototype of the same size made with Hindenburg-type materials. I would like to have built a larger prototype, but I didn't have the money. A friend has a metal fabrication shop. He made the metal parts for this prototype as a favor."

Max returned to his chair to think about the next step. Was this concept worth investing a significant amount of time and money? Would he be able to convince his usual group of investors to fund a full-blown dirigible? He needed a better demonstration. "I don't know if I could sell the concept without a much larger prototype. Have you estimated the cost of a small dirigible, perhaps one that could carry about a dozen people?"

"Yes, of course." She pulled out a notebook from a suitcase, opened it, and handed it to him. Tom was soon standing behind him to study the drawing. There was an extremely detailed estimate of the cost of materials for a prototype dirigible about two hundred feet long and sixty feet in diameter. There was a hand sketch of the prototype showing a gondola hanging underneath that would hold ten people. The materials were less than two million dollars.

Tom noticed there was no estimate for labor. "What about the labor required?"

"I can't estimate that as no one outside of Germany or Switzerland has any practical experience building a large LTA vessel. The successor to the original Zeppelin Company builds small vessels today for day tours."

Max was still staring at the prototype drawing. "Is your friend capable of making the structural parts for this prototype if we paid him his usual rates?"

Alex's heart sped up a few beats per minute. At least he was interested. "Yes, I'm sure he is."

"If we didn't have the gondola, how much weight could this vessel lift?"

"About thirty-five hundred pounds. Do you mind if I ask why?"

"I think if you lifted something heavy, like a truck or a car, it would impress my investing group more than lifting ten people, even though the full-size vessel would carry people."

Alex made a sketch in the notebook and showed it to him. "We could do both. I could make the gondola removable, and we could lift something and carry people on a test ride."

"That's perfect. How long would it take to build the prototype?"

She thought for a moment. She knew a factory that supplied airframe materials that could be easily modified for this project. "Not too long, less than eight months."

"Okay. I'm willing to fund the prototype on my own. How soon can you start?"

She seemed embarrassed. "Immediately, but I would have to work on this at night and on weekends, which makes the eight-month deadline pretty tight."

"Okay, consider this an overtime assignment. Keep track of the hours you spend supervising the prototype's construction, and I'll pay one and a half times whatever your equivalent hourly rate is here at Armstrong—if you can have the dirigible ready in six months. You can hire as many workers as you need."

That seemed very difficult, adding this to her already busy workload, but she didn't want to tell him no. "That would be great. Thanks."

Max looked at Tom. "If the full-size vessel is a billion dollars, that's well beyond the range of angel investing. Is it even possible if we included the silent partners along with our private capital group?"

Tom hesitated. "We probably would have to go to an even bigger group. Maybe form a consortium, but we need to sell the concept first. No one will fund it if they don't believe it's feasible and profitable."

They were both looking at Alex when Max asked her, "Are you up to this? This is your concept. You will face a lot of skeptics and have to answer some really hard questions."

She had never had an anxiety attack before, but she imagined it was a lot like what she was feeling. She took a deep break and replied firmly, "I can answer any technical question. Y'all would have to answer the investment questions."

Max smiled. "Okay. Let's see if the concept and the prototype will fly."

Tom laughed but Alex didn't. Max held out his hand to seal the deal. She hoped her hand wasn't too sweaty.

Tom was driving on the way back to the airport while Max was studying Tom's notes and summarized the presentation from his perspective and asked him what he thought.

Tom thought for a moment. "I think she's cute too."

Max stared at Tom. Tom rarely spoke about his own relationships or Max's girlfriends or women in general, so this was a total surprise. What had he said that led to Tom's comment?

5

Armstrong Support

Alex felt drained of energy; but as she returned to her office, she found Jack Armstrong, the founder of Armstrong Aeronautics, and two other people she recognized from corporate bio photos as vice presidents of the company waiting in her office.

Jack was a hard-hitting, no-nonsense type of guy and wasted no time. "Alex, what the hell is going on? Why would our largest investor show up without warning, not even say hello to anyone on the management team and come directly to your office?"

Alex swallowed hard. "I can assure you it had nothing to do with the company. I submitted an idea to one of Mr. Brita's Designing the Future contests, and he just showed up to ask some questions."

Armstrong glanced at his vice presidents. "What's the nature of the proposal?"

"As you can see, I have a strong interest in dirigibles, and the Hindenburg in particular."

"That's obvious."

"I had an idea to make a modern lighter-than-air cruise ship out of materials available today and gave him a presentation with some materials I've gathered, hoping someone would take an interest in the idea."

"What was his reaction?"

"He wants to build a prototype first to demonstrate the potential and then present the idea to a group of investors."

"If Brita is interested, I'm interested. Could you give us the same presentation you gave him?"

"Of course, sir."

He looked at his watch. "It's almost noon. We'll clear our calendars and meet you in the client conference room after lunch at 1:00 p.m."

"Yes, I'll be ready."

—⟋⟍—

As soon as Armstrong and his VPs left Alex's office, Jeanne slipped in and closed the door. Alex noticed she was carrying a soft drink can and a paper bag with a local deli's emblem— coincidentally her favorite local restaurant for lunch.

"So how did it go with Mr. Hunk and Mr. Gorgeous?"

Alex just stared for a moment. "What?"

"Max Brita and Tom Babineaux are just about the most eligible bachelors in the world, silly."

"It was a business presentation, Jeanne."

"Sure it was. I brought your favorite from Sorrento's Deli so you don't have to go out for lunch, and you can tell me all about it, and I can tell you what it seems you don't know about them."

Later that day, Armstrong called Max's cell phone and asked if Armstrong Aeronautics could do all the engineering on the new LTA dirigible, if the proposal were funded. He agreed on the condition that Alex would be the lead designer.

Jack quickly agreed. After all, no one else at Armstrong Aeronautics had a clue about designing a dirigible, but they had a strong team of engineers who could take Alex's basic designs and do all the necessary material, structural, and weight calculations. Tom Babineaux was already arranging a presentation to their usual group of investors in Manhattan— home to many private capital investors and venture capitalists.

Armstrong passed the full -scale vessel concept to his internal estimating group for a rough estimate that was probably within 20 percent of the actual cost of the vessel and supporting facilities, a new manufacturing facility to make all the needed parts, and a hangar where the vessel would be assembled and returned for periodic maintenance. When the first estimates for construction of the dirigible, factory, hangar facilities, and all ancillary supporting functions came in from Armstrong Aeronautics,

Max was forced to expand the potential list of investors to cover the huge start-up costs.

The vessel alone was probably more than a $1 billion, and total costs, more than $3 billion once the cost of the factory, hangar, and engineering costs were included. Construction of a fleet of LTA vessels might be required to recover their engineering and manufacturing costs.

6

Prototype Dirigible

After the go-ahead from Max, Alex immediately stopped by Ed's Metal Fabrication shop. The owner had been a friend of her father for many years, and Alex wanted him to be the first to know the exciting news she had obtained funding for a large prototype.

"How big is the prototype?"

She showed him her notebook with the sketch and materials list. He stared at the list with thousands of strut pieces required. "You can't be serious. I can't do that, Alex."

"It's not a favor, Ed. You'll be paid your usual shop rate."

"But…two thousand struts!"

"And four hundred and thirty-five, to be exact. Ed, there is a factory that can deliver about a thousand thirty-foot long titanium angle struts to your shop in two to three months.

You only have to cut them and fabricate the ends so they can be bolted together…in three months."

"But…fabricate more than two thousand pieces in three months!"

"Can't you pay your guys overtime?"

Ed did some quick mental math. "Sure, but that's over thirty a day!"

"Please…"

That was a lot of work, but Ed had known Alex since she was little, and he didn't want to disappoint her. "All right, Alex."

She hugged him and hurried back to her apartment to work on a detailed design for the prototype. Ed Jenkins scratched his head as he watched Alex drive away. He was happy to have the work, but he hoped he hadn't promised more than he could deliver.

Jack Armstrong approved the assembly of the prototype in a large field behind his company's main admin building. Once the first pieces arrived from the metal fabrication shop, he periodically visited the assembly site. A few weeks later, he stopped by Alex's office to ask her if she could still meet Max's deadline. Finding Alex asleep at her desk, Jack decided to help her build the prototype. He stopped by Alex's direct supervisor and asked him to reassign her other work until the prototype was complete but pay her salary from a development account. From his discussions with Max, Jack knew the importance of the prototype in convincing investors to fund the full-size vessel, and he wanted his company to be involved in all aspects of its design and construction.

From that point on, Alex was always at the assembly site, directing the workers. It would be close, but her estimating spreadsheet predicted the prototype would be ready just in time for the demonstration to the potential investors. Some days, after the workers left for the day, she would walk around the partially assembled skeleton of the airship, shake some of the struts, and tweak a few guy wires. She knew the engineering calculations confirmed the vessel would fly, but few people outside Germany had ever attempted to fabricate an LTA vessel this large in decades, and she had some lingering doubts she just couldn't seem to shake.

Max, Tom, a camera crew, and a handful of close friends and investors arrived at Armstrong Aeronautics one week short of six months to view the new prototype. The visitors met Jack and Alex in the visitor's conference room to review the days proposed tests then exited the back of the building. Max noticed that Alex was wearing a dark blue dress and her skin was bronzed from spending many hours in the sun supervising the prototype's construction. Max knew all the technical details of the prototype but couldn't help being a little awestruck when he saw it floating about ten feet in the air. The 60-foot diameter, 210-foot-long prototype held about 500,000 cubic feet of helium. There was no outer cover or anything that absolutely didn't have to be on the vessel to maximize the weight it could lift. Two small engines were integrated into the structure to provide forward motion.

For the first test, the gondola had been removed, and four cables were connected to Jack Armstrong's full-size pickup truck. He volunteered his truck to show his faith in the LTA concept and Alex's calculations. Alex held a remote control with a few buttons and several joysticks. She began the test by remotely adding more helium from several onboard compressed cylinders to the ten gas bags inside until the ship rose and lifted the pickup truck. A small group of contractors who had worked on the construction were gathered for the test and cheered when the wheels of the truck left the ground. The motors sped up, and the camera crew recorded the ship as it moved forward and rose into the sky. At about one thousand feet, Alex turned the ship, and it circled the company's main building. Max congratulated her and asked about giving the investors a ride. The prototype descended much like a plane landing until the wheels on the pickup truck touched the ground. Several contractors unhooked the cables on the pickup truck one at a time and reconnected them to mooring anchors. A larger truck arrived, carrying the gondola on a flatbed, which was quickly attached to the prototype. When the truck left, she winched the prototype down to a few feet, and a contractor hooked a ladder onto the gondola. Alex, Max, Jack, Tom, the visitors, and the camera crew climbed on board. Alex signaled to the contractors to release the mooring cables, and the prototype lifted off and sped forward. She took them on a short ride over the Clear Lake City (home of NASA's Johnson Space Center) and returned to the mooring site outside the Armstrong building.

Inside the gondola, one investor excitedly declared the ride was much better than a hot air balloon, because a dirigible could take them wherever they wanted to go.

At the end of the test, they all gathered in the conference room to review the results of the tests. All the investors said the tests were convincing enough for a meeting to fund the full-scale vessel.

7

Challenge Session

One day before the presentation to the pool of investors, Max and Alex met with cruise industry consultant Joe Boyles to prepare them to face skeptics with tough questions. Joe was an expert on cruise ship economics but was asked to sign a confidentiality agreement and was told to challenge the dealmaker's proposal, which would deal with a lighter-than-air cruise vessel. He knew nothing about that, so he tried to read up on it in advance of the meeting. In effect, Joe would act as a devil's advocate. Joe was a big man at six and a half feet tall and muscle bound from lifting too many weights. He was surprised when he entered a conference room at Max's Manhattan hedge fund office, and Max Brita (whom he recognized from occasional business news reports) was there with a cute woman he assumed was Max's girlfriend. He was getting paid, so what did he care?

After brief introductions, Joe began with the usual challenges like why is this better than conventional cruise ships, would fares be competitive, what is the payout period to cover start-up costs, how many LTA vessels would be required to recover the engineering and manufacturing facilities, and so on. All of which, Max answered. When he shifted from the economics of the proposal to the vessel's engineering, Alex started answering. Max was known for dating models and movie stars, and Joe was skeptical that she knew much about engineering or design, and his prejudice soon showed as he deviated to a more personal attack on Alex.

"How are you even qualified to design an LTA vessel?"

She wasn't bothered at first. "I have been designing small business jets for several years."

"How does that qualify you to design LTA vessels, little lady?"

"I've also been working on designing LTA vessels for ten years."

"How do we know the vessel will even fly?"

"I lead a team of designers. It's a team comprising many engineering disciplines: structural, weight, materials, and so on. The vessel will fly."

"But how are you qualified to lead that team, little lady?"

She was becoming angry at his attitude. "I have a master's degree in engineering."

"But how does that qualify you in LTA vessels, which no one today designs, little lady?"

She stood up and faced him directly. "If you call me little lady one more time, I'll have to put my foot up your ass!"

Max chuckled, and Joe laughed loudly. "I used to be a wrestler in my college days. I don't think that will happen."

Max didn't like the way the meeting was heading and interjected, "You are supposed to challenge the concept, not insult the presenters."

"I'm just questioning her qualifications to lead the design effort that's all." He returned to Alex. "You didn't answer my question, missy."

"I can *explain* it to you, but I can't understand it *for* you."

It took a few seconds to sink in, and Joe frowned and jumped up. "Are you calling me stupid?"

When Joe jumped up, Max instinctively jumped up as well. Max had grown up on the streets of New York, and he would not let this oaf get aggressive.

She was not the least bit intimidated by Joe's size. "You don't seem to be the sharpest knife in the drawer."

"Why, you…"

Joe tried to grab her, but before Max could intervene, Alex dodged him, and in a move so fast Max couldn't even see what she did, Joe was quickly lying face down on the floor, and Alex was sitting on him and holding his right arm behind his back. Joe struggled mightily but couldn't break her hold.

"You didn't ask my qualifications to whip your ass, so I'll tell you. I'm a certified Krav Maga instructor and used to teach women self-defense against Neanderthals like you."

Max was surprised how quickly she put Joe down, but he needed to end the meeting. He was quickly next to her. "Alex, please let him go. I think we are done here."

As soon as she let go and backed up, Joe jumped up and took a swing at her. She easily dodged him and stepped on his foot and punched him in the face. He fell back and landed on a small refreshments table, knocking it down. She looked at Max. "Life's hard. It's even harder when you're stupid."

Joe would not let a small woman make a fool of him. He came at her again, and she dodged him and punched him in the throat. He gagged.

"That will hurt for a while. If you want more, I can give it to you."

That was enough for Max. He opened the door, grabbed Joe who was still gagging, threw him out, and closed the door behind him. "Sorry, Alex. This was supposed to be an intellectual challenge, not a bar fight. By the way, that was a pretty impressive show."

"I've dealt with guys like that all my life. They usually wise up long before that guy. He probably has some wanted posters in his family tree."

Max smiled. He had already alerted security about Joe. "Can I take you to lunch?"

"Sure. Just give me a minute to clean up."

Joe was waiting outside the door and tried to grab her. She dodged him again, pinned his arm behind, and slammed his face into a wall, then tripped him. "I've faced better, dipstick," she said to Joe, who was sitting on the floor and rubbing his face. As she walked off, building security showed up to escort Joe out of the building.

Over lunch, Alex asked Max about his hedge fund business.

"Max, someone told me you manage some big ole hedge fund. What is that?"

He smiled. "There are several ways to invest if you're wealthy. Besides stocks and bonds, there are exchange traded funds or ETFs, which are a pool of stocks you can trade like a stock. All of those are highly regulated by the government—mainly to protect inexperienced investors. Wealthy investors that can afford to lose a lot of money can invest in more risky companies that manage hedge funds, private equity firms, and venture capital firms. The government doesn't regulate those types of investments. Those investors can take big risks, but they want big rewards in return."

"Don't you also have a venture capital company that sponsored the Designing the Future contest?"

"Yes, I do both."

"Why both?"

"Hedge funds invest in companies that offer a promise of a big return, but they have balance sheets and are usually profitable already. We know a lot about them. Angel investors are looking at individuals with big ideas and tiny companies that need some money to expand their business, build a plant, and so on. Managing both gives me a complete view of all types of possible investments. Hedge fund managers also can earn ten to twenty percent of the profits in their investments as a fee, besides the standard management fee of one to two percent. So I use that money to help fund my angel investments."

Alex was trying to absorb all that while he continued eating.

"What role does Tom play in your investments?"

"Tom and I have been together for a long time. He executes the business side of all my venture capital and private money deals. He makes everything work."

After a while, she asked about the consortium. "Why did Tom say you may have to set up a consortium to fund the lighter-than-air airship and factory? Why not use the hedge fund?"

"Hedge fund investors are risk-takers, but they aren't quite ready to invest in the type of investments that angel investors do. Most angel investments turn out to be worthless in a few years. I work with a pool of investors willing to take more risk than hedge fund investors. Anyone in the pool can make a proposal, and individuals or small companies then decide to invest in the idea or pass on it. If the amount needed is very large, we may decide to form a consortium, and they can join it as active or passive investors. Passive investors take no active role in running the company. They leave that to the active investors."

"So you would be an active investor if a consortium is formed?"

"Yes, someone has to manage the business."

"So you would be the boss then?"

"I have a company that actually would provide business services for the consortium investors—sort of like a contractor. Tom is the president of that company. We provide accounting, payroll, human resources, purchasing services, and so on. All the things needed to make a business work."

"But you would be the boss?"

"Technically, yes."

Alex was glad she was working for an established company like Armstrong Aeronautics. The thought of working for a consortium that might only exist for a few years and then disappear if it didn't make money was kind of terrifying.

The Presentation

Max Brita had presented many unusual proposals to his friends and a small group of investors, but there would be some new faces at this morning's meeting. Max and Alex would have to be on the top of their game to pull this one off. Alex was wearing a black business suit, and when he suggested she looked more like a lawyer than an engineer, she blushed. He took a deep breath and opened the conference room door for Alex. Tom Babineaux had made all necessary preparations, and several displays were located around the conference room, covered with white opaque cloths.

The business and technical presentations, along with Alex's small prototype and the video of the test prototype carrying the pickup truck while it circled the Armstrong building and the ride over Clear Lake City, impressed even the most skeptical investors. They knew they were being asked to fund a totally new type of vessel that would enter into one of the most competitive travel and entertainment fields in the world. Many cruise ships would lose money on every voyage if not for liquor, casino, art gallery, tours, and gift shop sales.

Bob Stevens walked out the conference room, preparing an amazing story to tell Brad Wilson, the CEO of one of the largest cruise lines in the world. Brad had heard a rumor that Max was planning a new venture in the travel and entertainment industry, and he hoped to use his considerable resources to beat Max to whatever he was planning. Brad was shocked when he received the full details of Max's proposal. He had the infrastructure in place to build another cruise ship—but no clue about LTA technology or how his company could design, build, and launch such a vessel—*and* beat Max to the punch. He quickly made some phone calls.

8

Post-presentation Dinner

Max entered the Four Seasons Hotel lobby in Manhattan, still angry over the stupid fight he had just had with Jill. He had opted out of an evening with her to introduce an engineer of his latest project to some of his private investors. Through a confidential source, she found out the engineer was actually a young woman and suspected him of working on his next relationship. When confronted with it, he of course denied that the evening was anything but business. Jill angrily stormed out of his apartment, and he was further convinced he would never understand women. He glanced at his watch. Traffic in lower Manhattan had nearly ground to a halt, and he was already a few minutes late.

He walked briskly around the lobby crowded with wealthy tourists and patrons waiting for companions prior to dinner, concert, and theater engagements. He strained to find Alex but couldn't. Frustrated that he forgot to ask for her cell phone number, he headed for a table with a house phone, passing behind an attractive blond in a black shoulderless evening gown, obviously waiting for her escort. He wished briefly he were available for the evening. She might have accepted an invitation. He picked up the phone and dialed the hotel operator who put him through to Alex's room. As he glanced around the lobby while her phone rang, he almost dropped the receiver. The attractive blond waiting for an escort was Alex! Their eyes met, and she smiled at him. *What an idiot I am!*

He tried not to ogle her as he approached. Alex had spent the afternoon getting her hair and nails done. Slim and tanned, she was easily the most beautiful woman in the room. She smiled at his fawning over her.

"I'm sorry I didn't recognize you. I've never seen you like this. You're stunning, Alex."

She had read an article in a magazine that Max rarely complimented women, but she sensed he was sincere this time. "Thanks. Shall we go?" She took his arm, and he led her to his waiting limousine.

The evening was a blur to Alex. Max introduced her to numerous friends who often invested in his lucrative schemes. He had a near -perfect success rate in picking new investment opportunities and had many friends eager to share in his current interests as silent partners. After dinner, they attended a play and visited a night club for a few nightcaps. He escorted her to her room and, in an awkward moment, asked if he could kiss her good night. She surprised him by wrapping her arms around him and kissing him strongly. Just as quickly, she said good night and closed the door behind her. He stared at the door for a moment then headed back to his waiting limo.

He was still shaking his head as he approached the waiting limousine. Roger, his chauffeur, noticed. "Something wrong, Mr. Brita?"

"No, Roger, everything's fine," he replied, but her perfume lingered in his consciousness, and he couldn't help thinking of her all the way back to his penthouse apartment.

9

Designer Apparel

A few weeks later, Max met with Jack Armstrong and his senior management team to inform them a new consortium with over thirty individual investors and companies had been formed to fund the design and construction of the first LTA cruise ship. He also thanked Jack for his help in getting the large prototype built, and the discussion turned to the engineering effort needed for the first ship.

Later that day, he stopped by Alex's office to tell her about the consortium. Her door was open, and he knocked on the doorframe. Alex was surprised but happy to see him, and was wearing a casual blouse, slacks, and comfortable shoes. She rarely met anyone outside the company and felt no need to "dress up" each day. Most of the designers she worked with wore even more casual clothes. She frowned when he closed her door. What was he up to?

"Alex, you may have heard that we did set up a consortium to fund the dirigible, factory, and hangar."

"Yes, Jack called and filled me in with the basics."

"There will be a lot of meetings with potential investors, and you will play a critical role in convincing them the concept is technically feasible. My job is to convince them they can make a lot of money."

She was still wondering why he closed the door. "Okay."

He almost seemed embarrassed to continue. "I need you to look like a million bucks in these meetings. I know you have a few nice outfits, but I want you to feel comfortable meeting and having dinner with a lot of world-class investors and bankers."

She frowned. "What are you trying to say, Max?"

He walked to her, fished a credit card from his suit coat, and handed it to her. "I want you to buy a new wardrobe just for these meetings and dinners. The card has no spending limit, and I don't care how much you spend. Just get whatever you think you need."

Alex was stunned and stared at the Visa Black Card with her name on it. She heard of no-limit credit cards, but had never seen one. She seemed to struggle with the idea, so he offered some advice.

"I once funded a designer, who is pretty successful now. I can ask her to help you with a new wardrobe if you think that would help."

"A designer is probably thinking about fashion shows, not business meetings. You may not even like what she would come up with."

He thought about that. "Would it help if I went with you?"

She was shocked. "Are you serious?"

"Yes, this is important. Isn't there an upscale mall just west of the downtown area?"

She still couldn't believe he would take her shopping. "Yes, but when do you want to do this?"

He looked at his watch. "I was planning to go back to New York this evening. How about now?"

Alex was tongue-tied but managed a weak, "Sure."

True to his word, he asked around where they could find designer business attire. They wound up in a high-end clothing store Alex would never have entered based on the designer outfits on the mannequins in the window. He asked the store manager if she could help Alex with a new wardrobe for a series of investment meetings. In a matter of minutes, she had several ladies eager to help her. He found a comfortable chair and read his e-mail until she was standing in front of him, in an exquisite dark blue business dress with high-heeled pumps and jewelry. He smiled and nodded. *This could be interesting.*

She returned to the fitting room and glanced at the price tag on the dress and gasped as it was over four thousand dollars. She looked at the attendant who was holding another dress for her to try on. "Four thousand?"

"The designer only made a few copies of that dress, honey."

She looked at the tag on the dress the attendant was holding. "Three thousand?"

The attendant shrugged. "He's paying, isn't he?"

"Yes, but…"

"Let him worry about it…"

It really didn't take as long as Alex thought it would as the store had hundreds of dresses and business suits by designers she had never heard of—in her size. Max even convinced her to try on a few designer outfits for nighttime outings and subconsciously wished he could be her date when she was wearing some of those outfits. She realized she needed some different undergarments for the evening wear, and the attendants helped her add that to the bill.

He paid the bill, and the store made arrangements to deliver the new wardrobe of two dozen dresses and five evening outfits to her apartment. She happened to be standing next to him when he signed the bill and had to look twice at the total—over ninety thousand dollars! After the shopping spree, he took her to an upscale restaurant; and with pre-dinner drinks, wine during dinner, and a few after-dinner drinks, Alex was more than a little dizzy when he drove her home. She kissed him even more passionately than the night after their investor presentation.

He thought about her all the way back to the international airport's private terminal where his jet was waiting.

———ɯ———

Jeanne saw Alex leave with Max and left several messages on Alex's home answering machine. Alex played them back and shook her head when Jeanne asked if it were true she and Max went shopping at a high-end store in the Galleria Shopping Center. How could she have even known that? The next day, Alex asked Jeanne about it.

"When I saw you leave with Max, I waited a while and called his secretary in New York. I told her Jack Armstrong wanted to talk to him before he left Houston. She said Max told her he was going clothing shopping at the Galleria. She commented that it was unusual, because Max always seemed to do all his shopping at a few stores in Manhattan."

Alex just shook her head, so Jeanne continued, "So tell me all about it. What did he buy you?"

Alex didn't want to feed a fire, but refusing to tell her might start some worse rumors. "Just some business outfits for meetings with investors to get the LTA business off the ground—so to speak."

Jeanne guessed that wasn't all and laughed. "Come on, Alex, what else did he buy you?"

"A few evening dresses…"

"And?"

"That's it."

"Sure it is."

Alex shrugged, and Jeanne's imagination filled in the rest as she swapped the latest with a few of her work friends.

10

Design Phase

Alex noticed a change in some of her colleagues when she was named lead designer for a major new project being engineered for Max Brita. She had been totally unaware of the rumor mill Jeanne was obviously feeding. Many volunteered to work on her project, while others seemed to go out of their way to avoid her. Ignoring all that, she concentrated on keeping the design and structural departments busy with draft designs of the structure of the new LTA vessel. She somehow survived grueling daylong meetings and was given a large bonus when the final design and the factory were completed in less than a year and vessel construction began. The bonus allowed her to pay off the balance of her student loans and credit cards and to buy a new hybrid car as her old "clunker" was on its last legs.

In an unusual turn of events, with agreement from Max, Armstrong Aerodynamics had immediately formed a new subsidiary to manufacture all the required parts and to assemble the ship with the expectation and hope of building all the consortium's vessels on a "cost-plus" basis. In effect,

Jack Armstrong had become a cost-sharing partner of the new LTA Consortium and had quickly started on the factory to build all the needed vessel components. Normally, the engineering package would be bid to three contractors with suitable manufacturing facilities. Word spread quickly in the technology manufacturing business, and several companies had already contacted Max, eager to bid on the world's first LTA passenger vessel of the twenty-first century.

Near the end of the design phase, Alex, Max, and Jack reviewed the list of potential crew positions and discussed hiring the ship's officers first to bring them on board as soon as possible in the planning phase. In her design role, Alex had met many test pilots and a few corporate pilots for the new business jets Armstrong designed. One came to mind, and at her suggestion, they interviewed Mike Hovenski for the captain's position. No one, of course, had any practical flight experience piloting an enormous LTA vessel, but as an experienced test pilot, Mike should be able to adapt quickly.

Once hired, he provided some suggestions for the other officer roles on the new vessel. He even had some suggestions for the layout of the equipment in the ship's control center.

They started with the crew positions on the Hindenburg, but due to technological advances, many of those functions were obsolete, like riggers, sailmakers, rudder men, and elevator men; and they needed many more crew to serve one thousand passengers. Many meetings with the newly hired ship's officers were required to develop role descriptions for all three hundred crew on the ship. Max even lured a top-ranked chef away from a cruise line to design a new menu for the ship and to head the food staff.

Alex realized her dream was now a reality, and the new vessel would soon be a livelihood for many people. Eventually, role descriptions were developed for all crew positions, and the team identified the minimum number of ground staff needed at each landing site. Jack volunteered his HR department to hire all the remaining crew. Fortunately, they had almost a year while the ship was built to fill all the positions and train everyone. Out of curiosity, Jack Armstrong attended some of the interviews for the ship's officer positions. He was surprised when Alex started chatting in German with Eric Bendorf before his interview for the chief engineering officer position. After the interview, Jack asked her about it.

"I didn't know you knew German."

"My grandfather's family migrated from Germany when he was ten years old and settled in the German community in Schulenburg, Texas. My father became a tool-and-die maker and eventually came to Houston to find work. He hardly ever spoke German, but I spent some time with my grandfather and learned it from him. Coincidentally, Erik Bendorf emigrated from the same small town in Germany as my grandfather did."

"What do you think of Bendorf as a candidate?"

"He has lots of experience, and I recommended him to your hiring manager."

Factory Acceptance Test

A year passed while the new vessel, tentatively named the Magellan, was constructed. Max stayed in frequent contact with Alex and Jack Armstrong but rarely visited. The hedge fund he managed was undergoing a large expansion and required more of his time than he liked. He didn't normally attend factory acceptance tests, but he was eager to see the new dirigible and witness the functional testing required prior to the first commercial flight.

Max, Tom, Alex, and Jack attended an early morning "kickoff meeting" to review the tests that would be required to certify the ship as airworthy and obtain a license to operate as a commercial passenger vessel.

Just before the meeting, Jeanne brought in some coffee and pastries and walked by Alex on her way out, who asked her, "When did you start delivering coffee and pastries to meetings?"

"I do when they include our largest investor." She looked at Max and sighed, then leaned toward Alex and whispered, "No ring yet?"

"What?"

Jeanne laughed. "When he asks, don't say, 'What?' Say yes."

Alex just stared after her with a confused expression.

After the meeting in the admin building, they walked from the rear of the building to an enormous new hangar over twenty stories high and entered through a small door.

Max and Tom stared in awe as they had never seen anything like the massive vessel nearing final assembly.

The design reviews had resulted in some changes to Alex's initial drawings, and the final size turned out to be twelve hundred feet long, a little over two hundred feet high, and four hundred feet wide to provide the overall volume needed of more than seventy million cubic feet of helium. Following the basic design of the Zeppelin airships, elliptical structures connected every fifty feet by horizontal struts formed the basic skeleton of the vessel. Each elliptical structure was made up of dozens of titanium struts and was formed and kept rigid by more than a hundred guy wires. There were two unsupported ring structures (16.67 feet apart) between each structural ring to provide support for the outer covering between the structural rings. Spacing between the elliptical structures in the upper part of the ship formed the volume space needed for the gigantic gas bags that would be filled with helium.

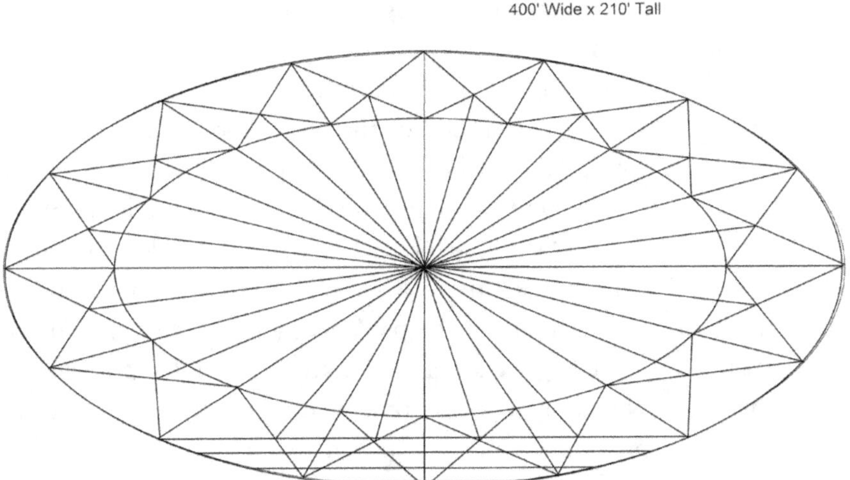

Passenger compartments in the lower portion of the vessel were sealed from the upper portion and well insulated to maintain a comfortable environment regardless of the ship's altitude. The white polymer covering the frame seemed to glow even in the limited light within the hangar.

The crew's quarters were in the lowest level, and each room had only a porthole-sized window, which faced almost completely down. Passenger staterooms were on the next two levels so that, from a distance, there appeared to be only three rows of windows on both sides along the bottom of the vessel. The two lower rows were passenger compartment windows, and the top row provided large panoramic views for the common-area facilities. All the regular windows along the bottom of the vessel were slanted inward from the top and would provide an excellent viewing angle of the ocean or ground at the normal cruising altitude of one thousand to two thousand feet. There were four passenger entry stairs that could be raised or lowered either by push buttons inside near the hatches or remotely from the command center located in the bottom of the nose of the ship.

They entered the ship from the rear-access hatch at the crew's quarter level and had a choice of taking one of the four elevators to the fourth floor or using the large stairwell.

They walked up three flights of stairs and viewed a massive promenade that ran the length of the ship. As they walked along the promenade, there were numerous doors or openings to a sundeck, four restaurants, a huge lounge, a casino, a spa, and many other facilities. A large theater capable of seating five hundred was located in the front of the ship above the command center. The front end of the promenade connected to the command center, where Alex tried to explain the consoles and displays, but the descriptions soon went over Max and Tom's heads. They complimented her on the visual design of the control center hardware and left to tour the rest of the ship. They entered an enclosed cargo lift near the command center and soon were high above the passenger levels. The tour followed the structure down through a dozen levels and seemingly endless stairs. Alex pointed out the compartments that would contain the helium gas bags that would provide the "lift" required to raise the vessel into the sky. Alex then led them through the passenger levels. Ninety percent of the passenger compartments were outside cabins with a large UV-rated window that would give an excellent view of the ground or the ocean when the ship was underway.

Most outside cabins had either two queen-size beds or a king-size bed, a dresser, a large TV, and large bathroom. Each of the inside cabins had a huge two-meter (eighty-inch) OLED TV that alternately displayed images from a dozen cameras under the ship (when it wasn't used as a regular TV). The tour then continued down to the crew's quarters in the bottom of the ship. Each crewman had a small stateroom about ten feet wide and fifteen feet deep that included a bed, a dresser, a small TV, a small closet, and small bathroom in the back of the stateroom. The crew's quarters also contained a buffet next to a dining room and the ship's large laundry room. A much smaller floor was located below the crew's quarters and served as the ship's passenger entry-and-exit area and temporary space for luggage being loaded and unloaded at the start and end of each tour.

At the end of the tour, the team returned to the admin building to review the plan forward to finish. Jack Armstrong committed the construction subsidiary to a test flight in four months. A new embarkation center near the LTA annex would also be ready then as its security system would also have to be approved by several government agencies. Near the end of the meeting, a vice president of the construction company entered with some shocking news. He turned on a TV in the meeting room, and the whole team watched a press conference by Brad Wilson, the CEO of Aurora Cruise Lines, announcing the development of a new type of cruise ship for which they would soon be booking tours. Brad went on to describe a lighter-than-air vessel capable of carrying five hundred passengers virtually anywhere in the world. He even passed out brochures to the press to provide additional technical information for their news stories.

There was a shocked silence in the room that was finally broken by Max. "There must have been a spy in our investment meeting in New York. This can't be a coincidence."

Alex was so furious, she kicked a chair over. "It's impossible to take the Hindenburg design and make a modern passenger ship in less than two years."

"Well, they just did," replied Jack. Max just smiled at Alex's frustration.

She refused to believe Aurora had the capabilities to design and build an LTA vessel in such a short time, even if they spent a fortune to do it. Unknown to Max and Jack, she bought a ticket on the first flight of the new Aurora vessel. She would have to see it to believe it. No one could build a ship in that amount of time without some design or safety shortcuts.

Just a week before a media marketing voyage of the Aurora vessel, representatives from the certifying agencies, along with the key investors of the LTA Consortium, filed on board the Magellan to witness its test flight. This was the final test required for certification, and a lot was riding on it. They couldn't afford any further delays or problems if they had a chance at competing with Aurora, which had already spent an inordinate amount of money advertising its vessel's first commercial flight.

The Magellan was attached to a large motorized transporter that crept out of the hangar with a minimal amount of fanfare.

When the ground crew released all constraints holding the ship to the transporter, the ship rose quickly, and the engines slowly pushed it ahead. The investors found favorite windows on the sundeck and were treated royally with champagne and caviar as the huge ship began a series of maneuvers necessary to convince members of the certifying agencies on board the Magellan of the ship's airworthiness.

At the end of the day, all required tests were completed, and the LTA investors were informed the ship had preliminarily passed. That night Max, Tom, and Alex celebrated with the rest of the investors and completed plans for the first commercial flight.

No one asked any questions when Alex announced she would take the next week off to rest. In reality, she hurried home to finish packing and then headed for the airport to fly to Miami to join the rest of the passengers assembling for the Aurora LTA vessel's first flight. Alex had once been on a cruise with her boyfriend but hadn't enjoyed it much as he spent most of the week seasick, despite various anti-nausea medicines available from the ship's medical facility. She wanted to enjoy this cruise.

11

Aurora LTA

urora didn't need to make any modifications to their cruise embarkation facility. The same security procedures were in place to x-ray all checked luggage and all carry-ons. After the initial screening, Alex joined a group of passengers as they walked out of the terminal toward the waiting LTA vessel. She was chatting with some of the other passengers and didn't look up until she neared the rear passenger ladder. When she glanced at the rear of the vessel, she stopped in her tracks, forcing some of the passengers to walk around her.

She immediately realized how the Aurora Corporation had built an LTA vessel so quickly. They had started with the basic design of the US Navy's Macon–class dirigible. They had merely doubled the length of the vessel to provide enough lift and room for the passenger cabins and crew quarters. This vessel was significantly larger than the Magellan. It was over fifteen hundred feet long and three hundred and fifty feet in diameter. If built entirely of Hindenburg-era materials, the weight alone would be much more than the largest modern airliner. Many gigantic gas bags would be required to lift the enormous craft into the air. All that didn't matter. Without significant design changes, this vessel would be susceptible to the same forces that ultimately destroyed the Macon.

What should she do? Her instinct was to run away, but she didn't want to draw too much attention to herself. She leaned over and pretended to be sick. The other passengers walking to the ship gave her a wide berth, and she turned and walked quickly back to the terminal. When she told the security personnel she was sick, they let her out without a question, and she grabbed a taxi and headed for the airport, trying to decide whether she should warn the appropriate authorities of the danger to the five hundred passengers who were probably leaving even as she neared the airport. She was careful to change her return flight to avoid possible scrutiny from buying a one-way ticket with cash.

She stared at her cell phone while waiting for her flight and started to call Max several times but hung up. How could she explain why she even bought a ticket? How could she explain the huge problem she found? She was so torn she didn't realize how much time had passed until they called her flight. As she hurried on board, she resolved to meet personally with Max and Jack Armstrong and explain the design issue. She just hoped the first flight of the Aurora vessel would be uneventful.

—⚏—

Two days passed before she would meet with Max and Jack in the admin conference room. She first had to answer their questions about why she had booked the cruise.

"I just couldn't believe they could design and build an LTA vessel in two years, when I have spent almost ten years working on possible designs and making preliminary calculations based on the use of modern materials. I just had to see it for myself."

Jack nodded, somewhat relieved. He had heard nothing negative in the six years she worked in the design department and had been impressed with her leadership of the design team working on the Magellan. It was partly due to the rapid progress made early in the design phase and with concurrence from the engineering management team on the commercial viability of the final product that he had committed Armstrong Aeronautics to set up a subsidiary to build and assemble the first of what they hoped would be a fleet of LTA vessels.

Max was more concerned with the design problem. Alex started sketching on a graphics tablet wirelessly connected to a projector, illustrating the problem with the tail design of the Aurora LTA, connecting it back to the US Navy's Akron and Macon dirigibles and the resulting crashes that effectively ended the use of dirigibles as military observation and support vessels.

"The design problem has to do with wind shear. You've heard of airplanes unable to land because of winds blowing at right angles to the runway. That is a type of wind shear."

"In the Macon and Akron design, the tail fins were just attached on the outside of two or three of the rear circular support structures. The Hindenburg's tail fins were part of an integral structure known as a cruciform or cross-like structure and were connected to at least four structural members. This design difference in ability to withstand wind shear in a thunderstorm was huge. The Hindenburg could withstand wind shears of twenty-five thousand pounds on the top fin, while the Macon and Akron could only withstand eighteen thousand pounds on the top fin before the connection joints start to flex the entire frame."

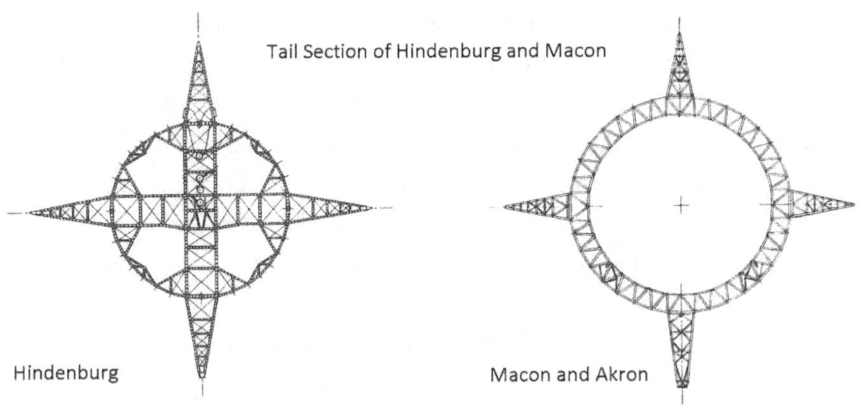

Figure 1

Max and Jack weren't exactly getting it until she finally used a metaphor. "In a storm, wind shear could force the tail of the Macon design to flex so much it would look like the tail of a fish swimming."

That did it. They exchanged worried looks as they now knew of the risk to the passengers. Did they have a legal obligation to report a potentially unsafe vessel to the authorities? Jack quickly phoned Armstrong's legal department and held a teleconference to discuss their options.

Unfortunately, it was too late. One of the lawyers changed the teleconference video feed to a news channel, and they all watched a report that all contact had been lost with the vessel in a thunderstorm and some aircraft had been sent to investigate. Alex felt sick and hurried to the bathroom, while Max and Jack continued the teleconference with the legal department. The news was not only bad for the Aurora Corporation but the LTA industry in general. Much would be made of the safety of these vessels that had nothing to do with the final moments of the Hindenburg. News of the crash would fill news reports for days, and they had planned to start press releases and advertising trips on the Magellan in a few short months.

— ∞ —

The news reports got worse. The Aurora vessel had crashed on a beach of an island in the storm, and six people had died, and scores were injured. Fortunately, US Navy resources were nearby and shuttled the survivors and the injured to hospitals, which prevented additional loss of life. A criminal investigation was kicked off to determine what exactly had happened and if Aurora knew of any design or construction issues it ignored.

It took less than two weeks for the National Transportation Safety Board and FBI to request a meeting at the Armstrong LTA construction facilities. They took over a meeting room and interviewed several employees, starting with Alex.

At least, the company had a lawyer present to prevent Alex from volunteering too much information that could somehow adversely affect Armstrong Aeronautics if not the manufacturing and construction subsidiary.

The lead interviewer began by showing Alex a surveillance photo of her walking out of the terminal with the other passengers. She admitted she was there, and when asked why, she began with the investment meeting in New York and the announcement of the Aurora LTA in less than two years and her belief that it was impossible to design and build a dirigible with modern materials in less than two years without some design or safety shortcuts. She basically gave the same explanation she gave to Max and Jack on the design deficiencies of the Aurora vessel and, when she saw the vessel's tail, she never even boarded the vessel. One interviewer commented that there was no electronic record of her entering her cabin or using any of the ship's facilities in the three days prior to the crash. The three-hour interview finally ended, and she was so mentally and physically exhausted she went home and spent the rest of the day recuperating.

Predictably, news of the Aurora crash filled the news programs for days. Rumors of consortium personnel on the Aurora's ship fueled speculation of possible sabotage.

At a routine press conference, when asked about possible sabotage, an FAA spokesman could not confirm or deny any information obtained from interviews with Armstrong personnel. The possibility of sabotage seemed to escalate until Max felt they held no choice but to hold a press conference to unveil the Magellan, talk about a new Web site where potential customers could learn more, and sign up for trips.

The press conference would, of course, also address the Aurora tragedy and enable them to deny any role in its demise.

News Conference

Max stuck to a predetermined agenda for the conference. Alex, along with two LTA Consortium lawyers, was there for technical issues to limit possible legal issues. The press was skeptical at first that another LTA vessel was being promoted as a commercial passenger vessel, when the first one in almost eighty years had just crashed. Max turned it over to Alex, who described the airworthiness and certification tests performed on the Magellan and the many thousands of engineering man-hours spent in design to confirm the vessel was safe and would perform as advertised.

Some news organizations had done their own investigations into the events that led up to the Aurora crash and one reporter asked point-blank why Alex had bought a ticket and then changed her mind and not boarded.

This time, she was ready and showed excerpts from public documentaries describing the issues with the design of the Macon. She explained that when she saw the tail of the ship, she realized the design had not significantly changed and was too concerned to actually board the vessel. When challenged if she had any responsibility to tell the authorities of the design problem, she said the information just presented had been publicly available for decades and the Aurora vessel must have passed all required airworthiness and certification tests.

There were a few more contentious questions before Max took over, describing the effort required to bring Alex's vision into reality and the huge investment the consortium had made to ensure safety and comfort of the passengers. He then passed out brochures with much more technical information than Aurora had provided. The press conference finally ended on a high note, and Jack congratulated Max and Alex on possibly saving the LTA industry.

Brad Wilson watched the consortium's press conference with his senior management team. Trying to beat Max and the consortium to a whole new area for the cruise industry had been an expensive lesson, and Brad knew his job could be on the line if he didn't fix this. He told his team to come up with a strategy to compensate the families of the victims, the injured, and the remaining passengers. He needed to get Aurora out of the news, even if it meant offering a cash payout or a free cruise to any crash victim who wanted it. Brad didn't agree with the maxim that any publicity is good publicity. He was determined to restore his company's good reputation.

Two weeks after the press conference, Jeanne again delivered gourmet coffee and pastries for a morning meeting. Alex and Jack were waiting for Max, and when Alex looked at her, she pointed to her left-hand ring finger and gave Alex a questioning look. Alex just laughed. Jeanne passed Max on his way into the meeting. Soon, they were reviewing the early reservations, and all were surprised the first trip of the Magellan had sold out quickly despite all the negative news still swirling around the Aurora disaster. In fact, the first five voyages were almost sold out. Now they had to deliver.

12

Preflight Check

One week before the inaugural flight, Alex was making a thorough inspection of the Magellan and scribbling copious notes on her tablet. More than two hundred workers and most of the crew were making last-minute finishing touches to almost every public room in the Magellan. Only the passenger cabins were totally finished. She inspected a few cabins with the housekeeping manager, and all seemed in order. Even the least expensive outside cabins had a magnificent view from the large high-impact and UV-rated window. One huge difference between this ship and a typical cruise liner was the size of the rooms. The smallest inside room—with a king-size bed, a large bathroom with a large shower, and the huge OLED TV—was over three hundred square feet, a size typical of a balcony cabin on a cruise ship. The six largest rooms were truly suites with separate bathrooms, bedrooms, and a sitting room spread over twelve hundred square feet.

Satisfied that the passenger cabins were in order, Alex started down the massive promenade, checking on the progress of the restaurants, lounge, casino, fitness center, and spa. Although many people were working in these areas, she knew the work left was mainly cosmetic. She made a quick inspection of the kitchen area. Alex had been surprised how heavy most of the stainless steel kitchen equipment was. All the equipment brought onto the ship that was required (such as the kitchen, electrical generators, and diesel motors) and the equipment that was essentially entertainment based (such as the fitness equipment, five hundred seats in the theater, etc.), in total, actually weighed more than the ship's basic structure (frame, walls, floors, outer covering, etc.).

Most of the food staff was busy making last-minute adjustments to the food-handling equipment. The food freezer and cooler were already piled high with boxes. The only thing left to bring on board were fresh vegetables, eggs, and other perishables that needed to be delivered at the last moment.

There was a Mexican buffet set up to feed the workers, so Alex took a break to try some enchiladas and tacos. She was pleasantly surprised at the quality of the buffet's seasoning and flavors and finished with a soda from a nearby bar that was already functional.

She resumed her inspection tour at the command center, which was finished except for some labeling. Large TV screens displayed views from dozens of cameras inside and outside the vessel. The command center was similar to the bridge on a modern cruise ship. The pilot steered the ship with a joystick and controlled the speed of the engines with a throttle position lever. Windows above the consoles provided almost three-hundred-degree views to the command staff.

Several dedicated computers were networked together to a massive ultrahigh-definition OLED TV display in the front of the command center that displayed a wire outline image of the Magellan superimposed with the current value of thousands of temperature, gas bag pressure, and guy wire stress sensors. There was a separate display for the dozens of special helium gas detectors located throughout the upper levels of the vessel. Any leak from a gas bag would sound a warning alarm in the command center.

The mechanical equipment room was just below the control center, and Alex ran into the Chief Engineering Officer Erik Bendorf and one of his mechanics making a last-minute tune-up on one of the ship's four huge engines.

She chatted with him in German about his family back in Germany until she saw the mechanic just staring at them. She continued in English. "How are the engines, Erik?"

"Great. They're smooth as silk. We'll be ready a few days early."

"How about the grey water system?"

Erik replied with a thumbs-up sign and returned to the engines. The grey water system was similar to systems on cruise ships, which collected water from the sinks and showers, purified it, and made it available again for showers.

The sanitary system collected waste from the bathrooms and was also similar to systems on cruise ships. Sanitary water was filtered to remove all solids then sent to a multi-step purification system using ozone and UV lights to kill all bacteria. In theory, the water was so clean it could be used for drinking, but in reality, no ship wanted a potentially faulty system to make all the passengers sick, so the purified wastewater was routed to the ballast system. The ballast system used a series of tanks located throughout the ship. Computers pumped ballast water from tank to tank as needed to keep the ship balanced from side to side and front to back. When the waste system provided too much water to the ballast system, a computer would dump the excess water. Ballast could also be dumped manually in an emergency. Most of the time, ballast dumping would be done over the ocean.

Computers monitored the electrical system and many other mechanical systems to provide an early warning whenever measured variables exceeded preset alarm values. Displays for the monitored systems were located throughout the mechanical room.

During a voyage, the Magellan would typically cruise between one thousand and two thousand feet for short trip segments of one thousand miles or less and four to five thousand for longer duration segments and the outside temperature while they were underway would be 55 degrees Fahrenheit (13 degrees Celsius) or lower. The space between the outer skin of the ship and the interior walls near the bottom of the ship was well insulated, and only a small heating system would be required to maintain the temperature of the common areas and the passenger cabins.

Most of the heat required could come from heat exchangers on the exhaust piping of the ship's engines; the rest would be supplied by a forced air electric heating system not all that different from home central heating systems. A central air conditioning system would provide cooling when the ship was moored at a port of call, and the entry doors were open for a length of time. While moored, power would be supplied from the mooring site, and water would be pumped on board as needed to replenish the fresh water system. When the ship was underway, two large diesel generators provided power. Dozens of small electric water heaters provided hot water to all bathrooms and the kitchen area.

Alex left the mechanical room, satisfied that all the ship's mechanical systems would be ready in time. She made a quick inspection of the theater, several lounges that would host bingo and other passenger games, several night clubs, and the Internet cafe. The crew were making last-minute adjustments to equipment in almost every room, and she decided not bother them. She hadn't planned on visiting the upper area as part of her last-minute inspection, but after a quick cargo lift ride, Alex walked along a catwalk in the topmost level of the ship, thinking back to when this was all just a dream on a computer display and a drawing in a proposal she thought would never come to fruition. She ran her hand gently along a strut and tweaked a guy wire to listen to its vibration echo.

Something fell and jerked her back to reality. She looked around quickly but saw nothing. She held a remote control in her hand that enabled her to turn on all the lights within a one-hundred-foot radius. The LED lights were very bright and were only turned on by motion sensors when needed.

Only a few would be on at a time, so a worker wouldn't be dazzled by the intense blue-white lights reflecting off countless polished metal surfaces. Even with the additional light, she couldn't determine what fell or if anyone was within the one-hundred-foot radius of the remote control. Who would be in this area now? The only thing left to do in the upper levels of the Magellan was to fill its huge gas bags with helium, and that wasn't scheduled to begin for a few days. She pulled out a radio and called Mike Hovenski, the ship's captain, who seemed to be everywhere at once ordering, cajoling, and yelling when necessary to get the crew to finish all final inspections.

"Yes, Alex?"

"Mike, should anyone be working near the gas bags?" Mike glanced at his clipboard's daily task list. "No one should be up there."

"Okay. I thought I heard someone, but I could be wrong."

As she put the radio back into a holster on her belt, something hit her on the back of the head. She tumbled forward to the edge of the catwalk and passed out.

Something tugged for Mike's attention at the back of his mind. What was it? He wondered if Alex had found someone who shouldn't be there and called her on his radio. When she didn't answer, he ran to the cargo lift near the control center and pressed the button for the top floor.

Mike exited the lift to total darkness. Why were the light motion sensors not working? He took a small LED inspection flashlight out of his pocket and flashed it around.

Walking as fast as he could along the catwalk, he flashed the light left and right along smaller walkways that branched off to the edge of the vessel and almost stumbled on Alex, who was unconscious and hanging partway off the catwalk. He quickly lifted her to the walk and tried to wake her. His hand felt wet, and he realized she was bleeding. He managed to get his radio out and call for help. Luckily, the ship's doctor was completing the equipment in the medical center and heard his call. He ran to the cargo lift. Other workers arrived, and together, they carried her to the lift and rushed her into the medical center. Mike called Jack's office and left a message describing what he had found. He had a cell phone and called Max. Max was in Houston when he got the call and raced through the afternoon traffic to the hangar.

Mike pulled out his radio and called one of his command staff to check the lights on the electrical system display. They quickly found the problem and reinitialized a breaker that must have been turned off manually. With the lights on, he saw blood on the catwalk where Alex had fallen. It didn't take him long to find a large turnbuckle used to adjust the tension on a guy wire hanging near the catwalk. The guy wire must have broken, and the turnbuckle swung down and hit her. At least, that's what it appeared.

Max rushed into the medical center to check on Alex. The doctor in charge stopped him. "She's asleep. She probably has a concussion, but we won't know until tomorrow."

"Why don't you move her to a hospital?"

"This medical center has a fully functional emergency room. We took an x-ray and a CT scan, and there is no internal bleeding. She had a laceration on the back of her head, and we sewed that up." He put his hand on Max's shoulder. "All her vital signs are normal. She'll be fine. She just needs to rest. I'll let you know if anything changes."

Max nodded, and as he left the medical center, he ran into Mike Hovenski, who was coming to check on Alex.

"How is she?"

"She took a pretty hard blow to the head, but there is no internal bleeding. The doctor thinks she will be okay by morning. She's resting now."

"That's a relief."

"What happened up there?"

"Preliminary indication is a guy wire broke, and the turnbuckle swung across the catwalk she was on. Possibly, she was just in the wrong place at the wrong time, but we will investigate until we're sure."

Max nodded. "Keep me informed."

"Of course."

Max reluctantly left the medical center area and wandered around the ship. There seemed to be a lot left to do with only a week to go before the first commercial voyage. He found the Mexican buffet and stopped for a quick meal.

The next morning, Max stopped by the ship's medical center to check on Alex. She was asleep, and Max took her hand and leaned over and kissed her forehead. As he left to talk to the ship's physician, Alex woke up. She had just dreamed that Max had kissed her. It was unusual, because she rarely dreamed.

When Max returned to his office, Mike called that he had some disturbing news and needed to meet. It was a little out of the norm for Mike to ask to meet Max privately, and Max noticed that Mike seemed upset when he entered his office.

"It seems someone cut the guy wire attached to the turnbuckle. There's no way it was a mechanical failure. In fact, we found many guy wires with partial cuts. It looks like sabotage, Max."

Max stared at him for a second, then picked up his phone and called the head of security for the LTA Assembly Company. He demanded the entire site, including the hangar, be locked down until they found the person or people responsible. He also called the Houston police to help in the investigation. An intense security search started with everyone working in the hangar at the time. Fortunately, everyone had to badge in and out of the hangar, so they knew who was there. It would take longer to figure out who had left their designated assignment and was trying to make small cuts in the guy wires that could cause them to fail, probably once the ship was underway.

Every possible worker was pressed into the investigation of the guy wires, and it still took two days to check every guy wire on the vessel and replace those with partial cuts. During the repairs, a wire cutter was found and fingerprints lifted from the handle. They would find the culprit.

The next day, an electrical helper didn't show up for work, and the police went to his apartment with a search warrant. Unfortunately, he was gone, and a national arrest warrant was issued along with a reward from the consortium for his capture.

Alex was ordered by her doctors to take it easy for a few days and tried to direct activities from a sofa in her office.

Three days before the first voyage, the culprit, Jorge Cazalas, was arrested in Miami and quickly extradited back to Houston for questioning.

Two days later, Detective Trey Watkins entered an interrogation room in the main Houston police station, and Cazalas jumped to his feet, declaring he didn't mean to hurt anyone. Watkins motioned him to sit back down and asked him why he was trying to sabotage the new vessel. Cazalas replied he was just paid to make small cuts in some of the guy wires, not hurt anyone. Watkins reminded him he could be responsible if the ship crashed because of his action and hundreds could be killed or injured. Cazalas just stared. He hadn't thought of that. Watkins then asked him who had paid him to make the cuts, and he gave him the name of the president of the design firm the Aurora Corporation had hired to design their LTA ship. Apparently, he was now on the run from the NTSB and FBI for his role in the Aurora debacle, and he wanted revenge for being identified as the source of the ship's design problem.

13

The First Voyage

The first rays of the sun peeked over the horizon and fell onto the gleaming white hull of the Magellan. They weren't even noticed by the workers and drivers of dozens of trucks scurrying around the huge vessel, making just-in-time deliveries to the LTA Consortium's first flight. Alex was at the center of the organized chaos—directing, yelling, signing invoices, and generally maintaining a constant flow of last-minute goods into the ship. At 9:00 a.m., the last of the delivery vans pulled away, and Alex took a break in the massive ship's main lounge. As she sipped on a margarita, she reflected on how crowded the lounge would soon become with staff eager to help vacationers start the cruise with a libation.

All the crew was busy with last-minute preparations as passengers would arrive in a few hours, and boarding would begin at noon. She walked to an open gangway and watched the ground crew roll out a red carpet from the embarkation center to the ship. The heat and humidity were rising quickly, and she pressed a button to close the access ladder and hatch. The press would also arrive soon, and she needed to shower and change clothes. She was still unhappy with the requirement (mainly from Max) that the officers wear a white naval-type uniform. The crew had been given dark blue uniforms that had been specially designed for the Magellan with an LTA Consortium logo. She showered and put on the uniform and stared at herself in the mirror, sighed, and went off to greet the press and passengers.

From a monitor in the control cabin, ship's Captain Mike Hovenski watched the last of the reporters and passengers file up the rear access ladder. Another monitor showed the mobile luggage conveyor belt, similar to the ones used to load luggage on airplanes, backing away from the forward hatch. He picked up a radio and called the aft-loading hatch.

Tom Andrews, second mate of the Magellan, confirmed the rear loading hatch was empty and the luggage conveyor was heading back to the terminal. A display from the security station's computer confirmed all passengers and crew were onboard. Mike pressed several buttons to close all the stairs and hatches and glanced at the half dozen command staff waiting on him to confirm everything was ready.

"We're ready to go!"

He opened a window in the control center and, in keeping with dirigible tradition, yelled to the ground crew.

"Up ship!"

The ground crew released all the mooring cables, and Mike pressed a button. Ten computer-driven wenches slowly wound the mooring cables in, and the ship lifted gently into the air. At one hundred feet, electromagnets in the ten remaining emergency cable hooks released, and the hooks slid out of their mooring rings and were quickly reeled in.

The Magellan was finally free of all restraints and slowly rose into the sky. A cheer erupted from the passengers and crew alike as their weeklong odyssey was about to begin. A brief vibration signaled the start of the ship's four engines, and the Magellan slowly turned and followed the Houston Ship Channel toward the Gulf of Mexico. Alex was in a daze as passengers and the press crowded around to congratulate her. Millions had seen her on TV at the consortium's press conference, and largely due to her detailed explanations and assurances, thousands had signed up for the first five trips offered on the Web site.

The inaugural flight of the Magellan had begun on time at 5:00 p.m. on a beautiful cloudless day. A warm gentle breeze blew in from the gulf. Many passengers quickly found a favorite chair or seat near the numerous windows that lined both sides of the ship's common area deck. The deck windows were slanted inward and were louvered. Passengers quickly opened them to feel a warm breeze that quickly cooled as the ship neared its cruising altitude. Others wandered off to explore the massive ship's restaurants, lounges, casino, fitness center, spa, Internet café, theater, nightclubs, and the numerous bars, of course.

In the early evening, TV displays all over the Magellan advertised a passenger orientation session in the theater, and it filled quickly. The entertainment staff went over the onboard activities for the week and passed out a list of tours and activities available at the ports of call for those who hadn't already signed up for them on the Web site. Alex answered questions about the Magellan, its size, fully loaded weight (over four million pounds), cubic feet of helium (seventy three million), the initial cost to fill with helium (almost six million dollars), how fast it could go (over one hundred mph), how high (over ten thousand feet), it's structure made up of titanium struts and numerous guy wires, and so on. Several passengers signed up for a special guided tour of the non-passenger area of the ship.

On the first night of the cruise, all the common area facilities were full, as the passengers were too excited to remain in their staterooms. The casino was especially crowded. The early- and late-seating performances for the two live shows by the onboard theatrical group were completely full. Only the moon and stars were visible as the Magellan cruised slowly over the gulf at two thousand feet, but the huge main lounge was still full of groups of passengers excitingly discussing the next days' activities. There was also a long list of onboard activities to choose from. A Texas Hold'em poker tournament with significant cash prizes filled up quickly.

Alex had touch screen terminals installed in all the common areas to enable passengers to find almost anything about the cruise. Out of curiosity, she walked around the common areas after midnight to see what people were doing. Even though Wi-Fi was available in every stateroom, the Internet café was still full as were the nightclubs. There was also a large crowd still in the casino, but many common areas were almost empty.

She hoped it was due to the early arrival the next morning and passengers had retired to their staterooms to rest.

After a leisurely trip of eight hundred and thirty miles, the ship arrived at 8:00 a.m. to its first port of call, on the island of Cozumel, Mexico. The four members of the waiting ground crew had been trained in Houston but had never seen the dirigible while it was under construction. They were awestruck by its size when it suddenly appeared out of the clouds and slowly descended to the mooring station. Cables were lowered, and the waiting ground crew quickly hooked them into mooring rings. The computer-controlled wenches gently lowered the ship to the ground, and the four gangway and access stairs were lowered. Power cables, a fuel supply line, and a large freshwater hose were lowered, and the ground crew connected the cables to a local power source, the fuel line to a diesel pump and storage tank, and the hose to a pump and freshwater storage tank.

Passengers could leave on any stairs, but security on the three forward stairs was limited to scanning their badges as they exited. Signs at these exits reminded the passengers that reentry was only allowed on the rear stairs. Passengers could exit via an elevator in the rear or by stairwells to one of the three forward exit stairs. The rear entry had a much larger stairwell and four elevators to accommodate many passengers leaving or returning and two security lines with scanners for their parcels on reentry. A large tent was set up near the rear access stairs, with tour staff to assist any passenger with questions or problems with tours and to hand out bottles of water. A mariachi band serenaded the exiting passengers, as the staff directed them to a caravan of buses waiting to take them on snorkeling tours, to fishing boats, and other local activities. Some passengers even took the ferry to the mainland to shop at the city next to the ferry terminal, Playa del Carmen.

Alex watched as 95 percent of the passengers disembarked for the myriad of tours. She made some notes on how to speed up the entry-and-exit process then held a short staff meeting to review their current status. So far, everything was working as planned. Max even called her on her cell phone to ask how things were going at the ship's first port of call. He seemed pleased with the results so far and asked her to call him if she needed any LTA resources. She walked around the ship to see what the fifty passengers who hadn't left on tours were doing.

Some were in the Internet café, and some were in the library. The entertainment staff had provided decks of cards and some board games on request. An ad hoc bridge tournament was underway in the main lounge. Alex wondered why people would take a cruise and spend time doing things they could do at home or anywhere.

The cost of tours could not be a limitation as the ship had landed near San Miguel, the only real town on the island, and the main square,

Plaza Del Sol, was only a five minute walk. The plaza was surrounded by shops and restaurants and attracted tourists from the many cruise ships that docked nearby.

Alex had befriended the ship's pilot, Camila Rodriguez who was born in Cozumel and offered to show her around the island. They left with other crew members once a security station was established outside the ship.

The Backpack

All crew and passengers returned prior to a 6:00 p.m. deadline, and the Magellan lifted off for its next destination, Puerto Vallarta, twelve hundred miles across northern Mexico to the Pacific Coast. Since there wasn't much to see at night, the ship climbed to four thousand feet, and the speed was increased to eighty-five miles per hour to allow an early morning arrival. At 8:00 p.m., Alex met thirty passengers who had signed up for the tour of the non-passenger area of the ship. They were warned there were a lot of stairs on the tour, but no one backed out. She had thoroughly trained the ship's second mate, Tom Andrews, to lead the tour as she would probably not be available to lead tours after this voyage.

On this tour, she would still be available to answer questions the second mate couldn't answer, and she wanted to follow the passengers to corral any strays and ensure everyone kept together. Motion sensors turned lights on and off, so there was adequate lighting everywhere in the tour. If, however, someone wandered off and fell or somehow became injured, their condition could worsen if they were not found for a while; the crew would not normally be present in the upper area of the ship.

The tour started in the control center, with a handful of passengers allowed in at a time until all had been through it, having been given a warning to not touch anything, of course. On exiting the control center, the small groups entered the enclosed cargo lift, which took them to the top level of the ship. The interior of the non-passenger area of the Magellan had a clean and bright appearance. Titanium struts gleamed in the bluish-white glow of numerous LED lights. Even the titanium walkways and stairs had a polished look, and passengers commented on the complexity of the strut and guy wire system that kept the frame from flexing.

Alex smiled at some of the questions and only once had to answer something the second mate couldn't answer. As she was bringing up the rear of the tour, she passed a monitoring station, which was basically a small computer desk and terminal with several monitors showing the status of nearby temperature, pressure, and guy wire stress sensors that were located in ship's structure.

Something dark near the station caught her eye. It was a dark green backpack leaning against the station's desk. That wasn't right. There was no reason for anyone to bring a backpack to this station. There was no serviceable equipment and nothing that required tools or anything that had to be carried. Tool stations were located throughout the structure, and all required an access code to open. So no one needed to carry tools or anything around the structure.

She left the tour and started to pick up the backpack, but at the last moment, instinct grabbed her hand, warning her against it, and she backed up and quickly rejoined the tour.

She pulled out her cell phone and was surprised that they were in range of a cell tower and let the tour proceed while she called Max. She excitedly described the backpack and asked him to contact the police at the next port of call. Max tried to calm her down and assured her he would take care of it. Max contacted a friend at the Mexican consulate in Houston and relayed the events unfolding on the Magellan and asked him to contact the police in Puerto Vallarta. His contact assured them he would, and they would find a way to enter the ship without drawing too much attention to the problem.

Mike Hovenski hung up from an urgent call from Max and consulted with his first officer and navigator. They decided to travel across northern Mexico at full speed of 110 mph during the night to arrive several hours early in Puerto Vallarta on the Pacific Coast. Mike obtained permission to deviate from their scheduled path from the Directorate General of Civil Aviation of Mexico in Mexico City and passed the word along to the navigator. Passengers were expecting an 8:00 a.m. arrival, and hopefully, only a few would be up and about at 5:00 a.m. When the ship arrived at a little past five, the ground crew was waiting for them. Mooring lines were lowered and hooked into the mooring rings, and the Magellan slowly descended to the ground. The rear access ladder was immediately lowered.

A contingent of police and bomb disposal experts entered quietly and was quickly escorted to the backpack. After some internal discussion, they opened the backpack with manipulators attached to long poles. When nothing happened, a bomb disposal expert shined his flashlight into the bag and signaled to the others. They carefully removed a small package of plastic explosives and studied it. The timer was showing all zeros, so basically the bomb had failed to activate. After further study, they found the problem and completely disabled it. They carried it to a disposal truck and drove away before 6:00 a.m. virtually undetected, even by early risers.

The explosives experts met with Alex and Mike and said the bomb maker had made some amateur mistakes and, based on their estimations of the size of the explosives and where the bomb was placed, concluded the small bomb was intended to damage the Magellan but not hurt the passengers as it was more than a hundred feet away from the passenger levels.

Even if the bomb had gone off, it could not have seriously hurt anyone. Alex had added a multilayered explosion-proof and fireproof barrier between the passenger compartment and the rest of the ship to protect the passengers should a catastrophic failure occur somewhere in the upper levels of the ship. Few outside the Armstrong LTA Manufacturing Company would have known this.

In a videoconference with Alex, Max and Jack concluded the bomb was small enough to cause enough damage to put the final nail in the LTA industry but not hurt anyone. Who would benefit from that? Aurora's name kept coming up. At the end of the videoconference, Max complimented Alex on her stylish uniform, and she blushed. Max turned everything over to the FBI and the Houston police as the bomb had originated in Houston.

After the attempted bombing, security on the Magellan was tightened even further. Experienced cruise passengers did not question the security as they were well aware of similar procedures on cruise ships throughout the world. Alex made copious notes during the voyage and questioned numerous passengers about their impressions, looking for ways to improve the LTA experience. She had a long wish list for the next vessel. The limiting factor in every desired enhancement was always its weight.

The Magellan was the first cruise vessel to pass over Mexico on the way to Puerto Vallarta. This time almost 100 percent of the passengers and as many of the crew who could leave left for tours. After the scheduled stop in Puerto Vallarta, the voyage proceeded north along the Pacific

Coast for a daylong stop in San Francisco. Mooring facilities at the former Presidio near the Golden Gate Bridge enabled the Magellan to land and again disgorge almost 100 percent of the passengers for bus tours of the city, especially Fisherman's Wharf and Alcatraz Island. The next day, the tour proceeded along the coast to Seattle, and after another daylong stop, the voyage continued along the coastal region of Alaska for a flight over the Mendenhall Glacier and a daylong stop in the cruise-friendly city of Ketchikan, Alaska. Whenever the Magellan passed over a cruise ship, it would blow its horn, and the Magellan would respond in kind. The tour then provided magnificent views as they flew over the Rockies and made a brief stop at the Banff Resort in Western Canada. The last part of the tour over the middle of the US included a brief stop in Saint Louis before finally returning to Houston. Nautical miles covered in seven days also set a record.

The first cruise of the Magellan ended without any reported problems or issues and was hailed in firsthand reports in the press as a fabulous alternative to conventional cruises. The next tour would be completely different, with many new points of interest in New York, Montreal, Calgary, the Hubbard Glacier in Alaska and Ketchikan, Los Angeles, Phoenix, and finally back to Houston. The rest of the planned voyages filled up quickly. Alex turned over her role as operations manager to the first officer and happily returned to Armstrong LTA Manufacturing to work on the next vessel. She had a long list of ideas to make the next one even better.

14

The Next Big Thing

The conference room in the admin building of Armstrong LTA Manufacturing was becoming a familiar haunt for Max. He visited whenever he could and wanted to keep on top of developments for the next LTA vessel. Just before his next review, his cell phone rang with an urgent call from Tom Babineaux.

"Yes, Tom?"

"Max, we have a big helium problem. I had to beg, borrow, and promise a lot to get the seventy-three million cubic feet needed to fill the Magellan. The US government just announced an increase in price to eighty-four dollars per one thousand cubic feet, but they are also planning to limit large purchases to ensure there is enough supply for all the current users. There are a lot of medical devices that use helium, and those manufacturers will be high on the list when there isn't enough to go around."

"Why is there a shortage?"

"The US is by far the largest supplier of helium in the world. In 1916, the US Government set up a huge storage facility in a cave near Amarillo, Texas, to ensure there would be enough for the future. That storage is now down to ten to twelve billion cubic feet, and they are only authorizing release of two billion cubic feet per year. So that reserve will only last a few more years, and worldwide demand has been growing for many years."

"What are our options?"

"Most helium comes from natural gas. One natural gas field that borders Texas and Kansas has the richest concentration at one point nine percent helium, but there just aren't enough extraction plants to keep up with the demand."

"So what do we do?"

"I would recommend we either form a joint venture with a natural gas producer in that area, or buy a small production company. We could then build our own extraction plant, process the natural gas, and then resell it once the helium has been extracted. Natural gas is currently selling for four dollars to six dollars per one thousand cubic feet, but if we extract the nineteen cubic feet of helium out of each one thousand cubic feet of natural gas, it's worth one dollar and sixty-five cents. A plant can process millions of cubic feet per day of natural gas, and we could have enough helium for the next LTA vessel in less than a year."

"It sounds like we should be in the helium extraction business. Can you look into the cost of an extraction plant and the feasibility of partnering with someone or buying them outright? We don't have a lot of time to figure this out before the next vessel is done."

"I've already made a few calls, but I'll put a team together to figure this out."

Max had just ended his call with Tom when several design assistants arrived to review Alex's early designs of the next, larger vessel that would hold fifteen hundred passengers. They had just started the review when Alex rushed in and tugged on his sleeve. Max smiled. He didn't even realize how he was now paying even more attention to her appearance. Alex had just come from a press conference on the Magellan's first voyage and was wearing a dark red designer dress and carrying a small black duffel bag. She looked agitated, and Max was careful. He didn't want her to whip his ass as she described it to the cruise consultant, Joe.

"You look nice. How was the press conference?"

"Thanks. It went fine. Max, did you just buy my employment contract from Armstrong Aeronautics?"

Max hesitated then asked the design assistants to wait outside. "Yes, there won't be time for you to design any more business jets for Jack. The consortium will need to build several ships to recover engineering costs and the factory. Each one will probably be different as we learn from prior designs. Is that a problem?"

"And how many full-time employees does the consortium have—not counting your contract employees?"

He wondered where she was going with this. "Right now, with you, it's five."

She was afraid of that. "So…a company with only five employees?"

"Technically, yes. But if you count the contract employees, there are over four hundred, mostly the crew on the Magellan, which in time will become permanent consortium employees."

She ignored his comment about the future. "So…I work for you now?"

"You work for the consortium."

"But you are the active partner. No one else takes an active role in making it a success but you."

"Yes, but that doesn't mean I would manage you. I don't think I could do that even if I wanted to."

"But you are still my boss."

"Technically, but you know there is a difference between functionally reporting to someone versus administratively reporting."

"Yes, but you are still my boss."

Frustrated, she wouldn't give up on it, he finally had to agree. "Yes."

"Okay. I just wanted to get that cleared up and show you something new."

Max breathed a huge sigh of relief. "What it is?"

"Close your eyes and hold out your hand."

"The last time I did that, I was six, and a friend put a frog in it."

Alex was visibly irritated again, and Max reluctantly closed his eyes and held out his hand. She put something in it.

"How heavy is that?"

Max shrugged. There was something in his hand, but it seemed to have no perceptible weight. "I don't know. Is it a feather?"

"Open your eyes."

Max was holding a large black lump of material about the size of a softball that was literally lighter than a feather.

"What is it?"

"It's called graphene. It's pretty amazing stuff that's been around for years but only in small quantities in R&D labs. Our development lab has found a way to manufacture it in large quantities. It's stronger than steel, can be formed into rigid structures, and with the right chemical addition, it can conduct electricity better than copper."

"Okay. Can you be more specific on how we can use it?"

"Some forms of graphene are fifty times lighter than titanium. If the frame of the next vessel is made the most common type of graphene, the ship's basic structure would be about fifty percent lighter. Think of the additional weight we could carry. In fact, once we bolt the graphene strut pieces together, we can add a graphene seal over the bolts. The structure would then be, in effect, one gigantic graphene skeleton, immensely hard yet still flexible. In fact, in the unlikely event the ship crashed, it would probably bounce back up. Graphene is pretty amazing stuff."

Max squeezed the graphene chunk. It was surprisingly hard, yet he could barely feel its weight in his hand.

"How long will it take to make enough of it?"

"We need some funding for the machines to make it in large quantities, first."

"How expensive are the machines?"

"Tom guessed about seven to eight hundred million for the factory and machines. The cost of the basic material is negligible."

Max coughed. "That could take a while." He was already working on a new round of financing, but it wasn't a done deal at all. They needed a new angle to help sell the LTA concept to new investors. Maybe this was it.

The Magellan completed its first month of voyages to rave reviews almost to the day when the new round of financing was completed, and Alex was appointed as project manager to design and build the new factory with several graphene manufacturing machines.

15

Investigation

Fingerprints on the backpack and the bomb led the FBI to Miami and several suspects who had quickly abandoned their apartments when they realized no news on the Magellan meant the bomb had failed. It didn't take the FBI long to connect them to the Aurora Cruise Line. They unceremoniously hauled Brad Wilson through a crowd of photographers and reporters into their headquarters in New York for interrogation. Max was in New York, and the investigators let him know that Brad Wilson wanted to meet with him. He was not inclined to do that, but he was curious.

Several investigators met Max and briefed him on Wilson's statement. Brad was seated in a stark interrogation room and looked up when Max entered. He motioned to Max to sit in a chair.

"I just wanted to let you know that my security department began an investigation when some disturbing internal communications were uncovered. After the crash of our LTA vessel and when the initial reports indicated your designer could be implicated, a few low-level managers took it upon themselves to retaliate by ruining your reputation by placing a low-level bomb on board. It was small and intended just to do some minor damage but not hurt anyone. I guess they figured if we were now out of the LTA business, you should be too."

Somehow Max wasn't surprised and didn't respond, so Brad continued, "When I found out about it, I was furious and ordered the security department to turn everything over to the FBI. I didn't want anyone to think this was a terrorist event, and to be truthful, I was greatly relieved that the bomb failed. This would come back to me and damage my company even more than yours. So I want you to know that while I'm a fierce competitor and look for every business angle, I won't do anything illegal to benefit the company. The reason I wanted to meet you today was more than just to let you know this, as you would find it out eventually."

Brad stood up and walked around the table and handed him a report. "I believe if you can't beat someone, you should join them. I first thought about asking to join the LTA Consortium, and I know you probably need to build a few more vessels and could use some additional funding. I also guessed you would oppose this based on our history, so I undertook a due diligence investigation of the assets of the consortium. I also know you are building a new factory for some reason, and I normally wouldn't show that report to anyone, but I wanted you to know that the Aurora Company would like to buy the consortium's assets and any related patents for the value stated plus twenty percent to convince your investors this is good for them. You can then take that profit and do the next big thing—whatever that factory will produce."

He returned to his seat while Max skimmed the report. So far, there wasn't anything out of the ordinary. The last page was surprising as the valuation also included intangibles, such as the value of having the only LTA vessels and future revenues. Adding 20 percent to that would value the deal at slightly over five billion dollars. He looked up at Brad.

"Is this a hard number?"

"Absolutely."

"I think the consortium could agree to that." Brad walked over to him and offered his hand. "No hard feelings?"

He stood up and shook it. "No hard feelings."

"And…the Next Big Thing?"

Max smiled. "I'll let you know."

He started to leave but stopped and turned around. "Did your guys have anything to do with partially cutting some guy wires so they would fail when the vessel was in flight?"

Brad shook his head. "I haven't heard anything about that." Max started to open the door. "Max?"

"Yes?"

"Just out of curiosity, where did you find your designer?'

"She entered one of my Designing the Future contests."

"I wish I had thought of that. You sure were lucky to find her."

Max nodded and thought about Brad's final comment all the way back to the consortium's headquarters in Manhattan.

He gave the due diligence report to Tom and asked him to follow up on it and to verify the value of the assets in the report. Tom said he would start on it immediately. Max's biggest problem was figuring out how to tell Alex he could be selling everything she had wanted to do for many years. How would she take it? The deal would take some time, so he had some time to figure out a way to tell her.

16

Job Offer

Alex was surprised when Brad Wilson phoned and asked her if he could meet her. It didn't seem wise with the bomb investigation still underway, but she agreed. The next day, Brad knocked and entered her office. She guessed Brad was in his mid-forties, slender, with dark brown hair and green eyes. He was wearing a dark expensive suit, and a few streaks of gray hair made her think he could be a politician running for office. Why would he come to see her?

For his part, Brad thought she was even more attractive in person than in the TV press conference. At Max's insistence, Alex had met with some investors in the morning and was wearing a dark green designer dress with a matching green-and-white scarf. *Nice*...He looked around the office, which was covered with side-by-side wire frame drawings of the Hindenburg and the Magellan to allow comparisons. Some of the 3-D renderings of the Magellan were amazing.

"I've heard a lot about you, Alex."

Alex instinctively brushed off compliments. "Don't believe everything you hear."

They shook hands and sat down. "I want this to be a friendly meeting. Max and I have settled our differences, and I was curious how he was able to put together an investment team and a vessel capable of entering into the cruise industry so quickly until I saw your responses at the press conference. That's when I decided I needed to meet you."

She was curious. "What exactly was the nature of your differences with Max?"

"We go back a few years. Max funded a company that specializes in buying up patents and then suing companies that don't pay them royalties. I thought it odd for an angel investor like Max to be involved in something like that, but eventually that company bought some patents related to equipment used primarily in the cruise industry. They came to us, demanding royalties and threatening to sue us if we didn't pay them. My lawyers argued these patents were too broad to enforce, so we went to court. We won, but it wound up costing us more in legal expenses than the fees they wanted. I tried to contact Max to reach an agreement before the case went to trial, but he was never available to talk or meet me. I figured all he had done was give them enough money to buy a boatload of patents they could use to extort money from companies."

She was staring at him with a blank expression, and Brad couldn't tell if she had lost interest or just wasn't interested. She sat back in her chair. "Okay. So there must be some other reason for your visit."

"I would ask you to dinner to talk about some things, but someone told me you probably wouldn't agree to meet me like that."

She frowned. Who would have told him that? She decided to change the conversation from herself. "Why do men always think they have to take a woman to dinner to ask her something? If there is something you want to ask me then ask!"

Brad laughed. He had been warned she would be direct. "Would you consider coming to work for me?"

Her response was immediate. "Thanks, but no."

"Don't you even want to hear about the job?"

"I have a job I like, so no."

"What if I offered you three times your salary here?"

She tried not to show her surprise but couldn't help it.

"Tempting, but no."

"What if I said five times what you make here?"

That was a lot of money, but she really didn't want to leave the consortium. There was so much left to do. She had a nice apartment, a new hybrid car, and no debt; but that was a lot of money. She managed a weak reply that almost sounded like a question to herself. "I have enough money."

"Everyone wants more money…Aren't you even interested?"

She decided to humor him. "Okay, what job?"

"I would offer you a job as principal designer, but I know you have that here. So…how about chief technology officer?"

"That's probably a management position."

"It is, but you would direct the engineering and design departments and incorporate the latest technology into the company. Even you would be surprised at the new technology we look at every year in the cruise industry."

"I have that role now, without the title or the responsibility to hire and fire, do goals and performance discussions, promotions, salary discussions, and so on—all of which I avoid as much as possible."

He was running out of arguments. "Won't you even think it over?"

"You probably have three or four people tripping over each other for that job."

That was true, and Brad had to smile. "So you won't consider it?"

"Sorry, but no."

"How about dinner to talk about some other LTA issues?"

She ignored the dinner part of the question. "After that crash, I doubt you're even still interested in LTA." She paused. "But I do have a question for you."

"Sure."

"How did you find a company that said they could build an LTA vessel in less than two years? Few people outside Germany have any practical knowledge of LTA."

"This was so new to me, I trusted a small design and construction firm in Miami when they claimed they had the knowledge and capability, for the right price of course."

She laughed until it was obvious Brad was waiting with another question.

"So what about dinner?"

He sure was persistent, and she was incredulous. "Are you asking me out?"

"Yes, actually."

She tried to let him down gently. "I'm sure there are many women that would love to have that invitation, but no."

"Is there someone special?"

"That's a pretty personal question."

"Is it Max?"

She couldn't hide her surprise. "What! Why would you say that?"

"Just an impression I had from seeing the two of you together at the press conference."

"No. My guy is an old friend from my college days." Brad stood up. "Okay, thanks for your time. I just have one more question."

"Yes?"

"Where did your extreme interest in the Hindenburg and the LTA concept come from?"

Funny, even Max had never asked her that. "My grandfather was a member of the ground crew at the Lakehurst Naval Air Station the night the Hindenburg crashed. He saved several passengers and was recognized by the navy. His brother was lost on the Akron when it crashed four years earlier."

"Quite a family history in dirigibles. Okay, I hope we can see each other again professionally."

Brad was almost out the door. *What the hell….*"Wait. I'll go to dinner if there are no business discussions."

He grinned as that was exactly what *he* wanted. "Tonight?"

She nodded.

"When and where can I pick you up?"

"Here at 7:00 p.m."

"I'll meet you in the visitor's lobby. See you, Alex." He walked off, whistling, to meet Jack Armstrong.

She sat there for a while. Why did Brad think she was involved with Max?

—m—

Brad took her to one of the most exclusive restaurants in Houston. Since she had met Max, she had some pretty nice dinners with investors, but they always required reservations. She knew Brad must have pulled some strings to get a reservation at this restaurant on the same day. He turned out to be a complete gentleman, asking about her interests without being too personal. He had learned that lesson earlier in the day. They actually had a dedicated server who unobtrusively waited near their table in case they needed anything.

Alex didn't notice when Tom Babineaux and a small group of potential investors entered the restaurant and were led to a table. Tom happened to see Alex and Brad and confided to one of the investors that she was the consortium's lead designer and largely responsible for convincing Max to invest in LTA technology.

Meanwhile, Brad tried several times to compliment her, but it always seemed to backfire on him. "You are the prettiest engineer I have ever met, Alex."

She stared at him for a few seconds. "I'm not sure that's even a compliment."

He thought about that then laughed.

After dinner, Brad took her to her apartment, and despite his many attempted compliments to her during the evening, he could only get a polite kiss good night.

"That's okay, Alex. You'll come around to my charms. I'm a patient man."

As she closed the door, she replied, "Don't count your chickens before they hatch!"

Brad laughed loudly and headed for his limo.

The next day, Max was having lunch with some potential investors when Tom called to fill him in on his investment meeting. He mentioned he had seen Alex during his team dinner. That quickly got Max's attention.

"Who was her dinner companion?"

"I've seen him somewhere, but I can't recall. I don't think he's an investor."

That further piqued his interest. Was that her sometimes boyfriend—taking her to an expensive restaurant? Didn't he lead adventure tours?

Then Tom remembered. "Oh, that was Brad Wilson. I saw him at the press conference when Aurora announced their first LTA vessel."

"What!"

"I know. Maybe she's working on her own deal." Tom looked at his watch. "I have to go, Max. Call me later on the outcome of your meeting."

Max excused himself and went to the washroom. He splashed water on his face and stared at himself in the mirror.

Was he jealous? What did he really feel about her? He needed to sort this out soon. And what the hell was she doing talking to Brad Wilson? Would the consortium even have a future without her?

He needed to get to know her better.

17

The New Contest

Alex was so absorbed in her CAD program she didn't hear Max knock on her open door or see him enter. He suddenly was standing next to her, and she jumped.

"Please don't sneak up on me like that Max."

"Sorry, I knocked on the door…"

She turned her chair toward him. "What's up?"

"I have another Designing the Future contest wrapping up, and there are even more entries in this contest than the one you took part in. I was wondering if you would help review the remaining entries from a technology feasibility point of view."

That seemed interesting. "How much time would this take? I'm pretty busy now."

"Oh, not more than a day or two."

"One or two days!"

"Yes. No more than that."

"I don't think I can take that much time away from our tight design schedule."

"We can review the proposals here, so you won't have to travel. And we could take breaks for you to keep your project going."

That seemed doable, and she was curious to see what people were proposing to an angel investor. "Okay. When do you want to start?"

"How about tomorrow?"

There was a note on her office door when Alex arrived the next morning. Max was waiting in a nearby conference room. She was surprised he was there so early. There was a huge pile of folders on the conference table, and Max was flipping through one.

"We have to go through all of them?"

Max looked up and noticed she was wearing a dark gray designer dress. "I do. I'll make the initial screening pass for business potential and only give them to you when I need some technical help, like these." He pointed to a small pile next to the huge pile. There were two chairs in the room, and she sat down next to Max and reviewed the ones that passed the business test. She soon finished those and, out of curiosity, picked a few off the top of Max's pile.

At noon, a local restaurant delivered a hot lunch, and they chatted while eating.

"You look pretty fit, Alex. What do you do to keep in shape?"

"Not much. I took part in a lot of sports in high school and college, but now I just watch what I eat and try to run or walk a few miles three times a week. I also practice to keep my Krav Maga skills current."

"Do you do anything for fun?"

"Not really. I have some pretty long days here." She turned to him. "Why are you asking these questions?"

"Oh, I just want to make sure you have an appropriate work-life balance."

Alex was skeptical of that answer but returned the favor. "So what do you do for fun in your free time?"

"I race cars."

She was sure he was joking. "What kind of cars, bumper cars?"

"No, Le Mans LM1 Prototype. I raced stock cars in college and got away from it for a while. One of my early angel investments was funding a new Formula One team. They started winning and were bought out by a large European bank. I made a lot of money on that deal. Later, I funded a new Le Mans team. I joined that team a few years ago but can't find time to race more than three or four times a year."

She realized her jaw had dropped. She never would have guessed that. "Are you serious?"

He showed her a picture on his cell phone. "Yes, here is the team." In the picture, Max was standing with two other race car drivers in front of a Le Mans–type racing car. They all were wearing race team uniforms.

"We came in second in Le Mans last year. Have you ever been to a Le Mans race?"

She shook her head, still too stunned to answer.

"Would you like to be my guest at my next Le Mans race?"

"Oh yes! My father used to race stock cars, so I sort of grew up at the racecourse."

"Great. I'm sure you'll like Le Mans."

After that shocking revelation, it was difficult, but she returned to reviewing the contest entries. She found one that had some promise and left it out of the reject pile. She quickly became absorbed in the proposals until her cell phone chimed. It was Brad Wilson reminding her of their date that night. Max was furious but kept a calm outward appearance.

"I thought you had a boyfriend."

"We seem to be drifting apart. I was thinking about calling him and going to see him in a few weeks to try to reconnect."

She looked at her watch, then exclaimed, "Oh no!"

"What's wrong?"

"My sister is at my apartment, and Brad will probably arrive before I do."

"You have a sister?"

"I have an older brother, two younger identical sisters, and an identical twin, who's staying with me for a few days. Yes, there are five of us…"

"So what's the problem?"

"You don't know my twin. She's kind of jealous of me. I don't know what she'll tell Brad."

She hurried out of the conference room, and Max made some discreet phone calls. He noticed the proposal she had set aside and opened it. It was a proposal for a personal flyer that could be put on much like a backpack. Several fans lifted the backpack, and a joystick enabled the passenger to control the direction of flight. Max knew of several similar concepts, and nothing seemed to justify additional review.

The limitations on similar systems were always passenger weight and distance that could be traveled before the battery pack had to be recharged, which basically ruled it out as a viable commuter transport system. *Why had she singled this one out?* Max stuffed it into his briefcase and left to meet Jack Armstrong to discuss her idea for a new LTA vessel made from graphene. He needed a hard estimate for the factory that Alex was designing to fabricate large quantities of graphene. Several investors seemed interested in joining the consortium, and the cost of the factory and the graphene machines could be the justification needed for expanding the investor pool in case the deal with Aurora fell through. Then there was the helium extraction plant to fund…

Ashley Schultz

Brad did arrive first, and when Ashley Schultz answered the door, he held out some flowers. He was a little surprised that Alex was still wearing casual clothes and tennis shoes. "Hi, Alex. We need to leave soon. Will you be ready?" *Funny, she seemed to be wearing more makeup than normal.* He did notice her tight black sweater and jeans though.

Alex had forgotten to tell her about her date with Brad, but she knew who he was, from the TV press conferences and the numerous news stories on the crash of the Aurora LTA. She didn't know that Alex even knew him, and yet, here he was. She smiled, took the flowers from him, and kissed him passionately. "I'll be right back." She ran into the guest bedroom to change clothes.

Brad was surprised at her greeting. He had barely managed a polite kiss at the end of their first date and the two dates they had since then. Like many men, he wouldn't have noticed a new blouse or new jewelry or even a new hairstyle, but he did notice her change in attitude toward him. Something was different, and was that a new perfume? He was still trying to figure it out when Ashley returned a few minutes later, wearing her "little black dress," which certainly looked great on her. Brad quickly opened the door for her, and they left on the fourth date, or so he thought.

Alex ran into her apartment. "Ash! Where are you? Ashley!" It took only a minute to find her black sweater and jeans on the bed in the guest bedroom, and Alex knew she had probably pretended to be her when Brad showed up. She was angry and kicked the bed frame so hard the whole bed fell to the floor.

By the time they were seated in the restaurant, Brad knew something wasn't right. Ashley had snuggled next to him in the limo and pumped him about his personal life, even asking if he had someone special. Alex had avoided those discussions at all costs.

After the waiter took their order, he studied her while she looked around the restaurant. "I'm not the most observant person, but I know something's going on. Either you had a huge change in attitude, or you are not Alex."

She stared at him for a minute and then laughed.

"I'm her twin sister, Ashley."

Brad smiled. Such a huge change in attitude would have been too good to believe. He held out his hand. "Nice to meet you, Ashley."

She shook it. "Thanks. Sometimes Alex and I play jokes on each other. I didn't know you were coming, so she is probably pissed at me right now." She laughed again.

It didn't bother him. "So tell me about yourself."

"I own a fitness studio in San Diego. Alex and I get together a few times a year to catch up. She's helping me develop some new equipment for my studio." She paused. "Sorry, I didn't mean to be aggressive on the ride over here. I was just curious why Alex was seeing you."

"I've been trying to get her to come to work for me in some technical role, but she's rejected every offer I've made."

"Interesting."

"She also keeps reminding me she has a boyfriend."

"That jerk! I don't know why she even calls him a boyfriend. They have nothing in common."

"I'm certainly not an expert, but sometimes people say they are in a relationship as an excuse to avoid the truth and to fend off people who may be interested."

Ashley was surprised at Brad's insight. He probably was right about Alex. She decided to change the conversation.

"You seem in pretty good shape. Do you exercise often?"

"Two or three times a week, whenever I can."

"If you ever make it out to San Diego, stop by my studio. I'll get your heart pumping."

Brad laughed. "Unfortunately, we don't have a cruise terminal in San Diego, but I go to Los Angeles from time to time. I'll call you the next time I'm out. I'd like to see your studio." Brad poured some wine for them and studied her.

"Alex said she grew up in Houston. How did you wind up in San Diego?"

"I was working on a degree in graphics design when I met a guy at the University of Houston, who was a kinesiology major. He was always talking about starting a fitness studio. We started dating, and in our senior year, a friend told him about a small studio for sale in San Diego, and he convinced me to join him once we finished our degrees. I had some money saved, and we went fifty-fifty on it. That worked for a few years until, one day, he just decided he didn't want to own a fitness studio anymore, and wanted out. I bought his half for a dollar, and he split. I haven't heard from him since, but I still kind of miss him. He was a nice guy, just had a problem with commitments."

The appetizers arrived, and when Ashley started eating, Brad noticed she wasn't wearing any rings. "No time for a new guy?"

"Most of the guys I meet at my fitness center are more interested in how they look, than me. I would love to find the right guy—just haven't met him."

Brad sat, thinking. In her own way, Ashley was almost as intriguing as Alex. He would never have met her if it weren't for Alex. Alex was a paradox for Brad. She was attractive, but aloof. He knew she was extremely bright, and that intrigued him. Brad had a lot of short-term relationships that usually ended when the physical attraction alone wasn't enough to take it to the next level. He had been hoping to get past Alex's apparent aversion to PDA and see if they could develop a relationship. So far, it hadn't worked. He looked at Ashley and realized the same physical attraction was there, and she was the opposite of Alex in many ways. Her perfume also seemed to have had an effect. *What was going on? Why was everything about her so attractive?* She smiled and laughed a lot and seemed fun to be around. He wondered what it would be like to get to know her better. After dinner, they left for a nightclub, and on the way there in his limo, a friendly kiss turned into a mutual groping exercise until she asked him if they could just skip the nightclub and have some drinks in his hotel.

Alex grew tired of waiting up for Ashley and fell asleep. She woke up when she heard her telling Brad good night and closing the door. She confronted her.

"It's 4:00 a.m. Where in the hell have you been…with Brad?"

"We just had a lot of fun. Don't worry. I didn't ruin your reputation. Brad's a smart guy. It didn't take him long to know I'm not you."

"But where have you been until now?"

"I don't kiss and tell," she said as she closed the door to the guest bedroom.

Alex kicked her bed and fell on it, exhausted.

A few days later, Brad called Alex at her office to apologize that their date didn't happen.

"Ashley told me the basics," she said.

"I was going to ask for another date, but I got to thinking." Uh oh, she could guess what was coming next. "I just don't have the time or energy to climb over that wall you've built around relationships. Ashley and I got along really well, and she invited me to visit her in California, and I agreed. So I just wanted to tell you I hope everything works out with the consortium."

He said good-bye, and when he hung up, Alex sat there thinking about his comments. What did he mean about a wall around her relationships?

18

Reconnecting

Alex finally connected with her on-again-off-again boyfriend for a brief vacation. They hadn't communicated much lately, and she wanted to see if there was anything left in their relationship.

Bill Allen was extremely "green." He lived in a remote mountain cabin and only connected with people in the nearest town when he needed to buy groceries. He ran an Internet blog on environmental issues and managed to find a few small companies that built home-based solar power systems or small wind turbines for homes and ranches as sponsors. He supplemented his income by leading tours for Outbound Adventures, which specialized in small group tours of remote locations.

Alex had a hard time finding his cabin. She had been there once but couldn't remember how to get there and wouldn't have been able to find it without the GPS in her rental four-wheeler. She almost didn't recognize him at first as his hair was much longer, and he now sported an enormous beard.

The first few days seemed to go well, but she sensed that something was bothering Bill. When confronted with it, he finally accused her of being a part of an aviation business whose airplanes polluted the atmosphere. He didn't even know of her work on lighter-than-air vessels. This was the last straw, and she ended the conversation by calling him a hypocrite. What had he done to make the world better? Only a handful of people even knew he existed. At least she was helping people find alternative ways to relax from their busy work lives. She almost ran to her rental to get away from him.

Brad Wilson's jet landed at the private aviation terminal at the San Diego airport, and he was pleased to find Ashley waiting for him just outside the security barrier. She kissed him, and he hugged her. He couldn't help notice how shapely she was in a tight fitness uniform with a logo for her club. Ashley certainly didn't mind PDAs and kissed him several times on the way to her car in the parking lot. They even did some "catching up" in the car before they left the lot. Brad was amazed when they pulled into the fitness center parking lot. Brad assumed she would have a small studio in a strip shopping center. Her fitness studio was a massive standalone building with an indoor pool and basketball court.

"This is your studio?"

Ashley laughed at his surprised look. "Yes. I found a niche training center concept and was able to franchise it a few years ago. I take all the money from that to improve this center."

Brad was impressed at the bright, clean, and modern look of the center. It was packed with clients; many of them knew her and called to her as they walked around.

"Who does your marketing? You have some interesting graphics and displays."

"I do all that. Remember, I had a graphics design degree before I got into fitness training. I have a business manager who handles the day-to-day business, but I set the direction and supervise all changes to the center."

True to her word, Ashley provided Brad workout clothing, and at the end of program she selected for him, he was relaxing some aching muscles in a hot tub. He didn't know she put a "Closed for Cleaning" sign on the door to the hot tub area just after he entered and was wondering why no one else was in the hot tub when Ashley entered wearing a tight red bikini. He couldn't help staring at her.

"How are you doing?"

"Great. Just trying to ease some aching muscles."

"I think I can help with that." She slipped into the hot tub and motioned him to turn around then started massaging his neck and shoulders. He was thoroughly enjoying the massage when he saw her bikini top float by him in the hot tub. As soon as he turned to her, she put her arms around him and kissed him. When she let go, he laughed when her bikini bottom floated by.

She put her arms around his neck. "I told you I would get your heart pumping."

In the evening, Brad took her to a nice restaurant. He had been thinking hard about how he could be around her more without coming on too strong. When they had ordered, he gave it a try.

"Ashley?"

"Yes?"

"Would you come to work for me?"

She laughed. "I have my own business here, Brad."

"You have a business manager who handles the day-to-day business."

"Yes, but there are always things to do to keep ahead of the competition."

Funny, the more he talked to her about business, the surer he was her graphic design talent could help his company. He was convinced all cruise lines could do a better job using graphic displays, printed or electronic, to inform or direct people around their ships.

"You have some interesting marketing ideas that could help me."

She shook her head. "You have a marketing director, and I'm sure he or she is doing a good job."

Damn. He knew he needed a different angle. "How about a consulting role? We use many consultants for new ideas."

She thought about that. "Okay if I could still be here most of the year."

That was a start. "How about going on a cruise to get some ideas on how you can help?"

"Great! I haven't been on a cruise in years." He was smiling at her, and she suddenly realized there could be a second meaning to that invitation. "Did you mean with you?"

"Yes, or by yourself if you prefer." He was hoping she would go with him. A week with her could settle some of his inner concerns, either way.

She thought for a moment, *Why not?* "Okay. Where do you want to go?"

"How about a cruise around Hawaii? We should make a lot more money on those than we are. Maybe you could come up with some ideas?"

"Okay, when?"

"How soon can you go? We have regular tours."

"What about you? Don't you have to check your schedule or something?"

"I can change my schedule to fit yours. All the management team knows we need to improve the cost structure of our Hawaii trips."

"Let me check a few things, and I'll let you know tomorrow." She saw him check his watch. "When do you have to leave?"

"In about three hours."

She put her hand on his, and he laughed when she said,

"You'd better eat quickly. I have some plans for you before you leave."

19

Graphene Airship

The Armstrong LTA subsidiary built a small office building near the Armstrong admin building basically to provide additional offices and engineering facilities. The new graphene factory was now producing significant quantities of fabricated graphene, and the design of the next LTA vessel based on a graphene structure was almost completed. Although the new vessel would look similar to the Magellan, it would be a little larger in size but much stronger than the Magellan. It would be capable of carrying over fifteen hundred passengers and a crew of four hundred. The design team created a new passenger level for the additional passengers and enlarged the crew's quarters. The new level allowed the staterooms to be even larger. There were now four rows of windows visible on each side of the vessel along the bottom.

Most of the added crew would be devoted to entertaining the passengers. There would be so many activities on board; no one could attend them all.

During the design phase, Alex had a one-hundredth scale model made for testing. The model was twelve feet long, four feet wide, and two feet tall. One test was videoed in which the model was tossed off the top of the Magellan's hangar and fell two hundred and forty feet to the ground. The prototype bounced a few times, and upon detailed inspection, no damage could be found. Max found that hard to believe, even after he watched the video several times. Alex was cautious not to use the word *indestructible*, but if the vessel were to crash somehow, only instrumentation in the control center and anything not bolted down inside would be harmed, not the vessel itself. Almost all the material on the ship was nonflammable, except for bedding material, so it would be extremely unlikely the vessel would be harmed by fire if, for example, someone were to go to sleep while smoking (even though smoking in a stateroom would not be allowed).

Max asked Alex to investigate ways to reduce the ground crew at mooring sites. So far, the crews were only needed for a few hours each week when the Magellan landed on its tours. Alex developed an enclosed cargo lift that would hold four crewmen and would be lowered to the ground via cables. The crewmen would connect the ship's mooring lines and the fuel, power, and waterlines to the mooring site. In effect, the airship crew would take over the mooring duties. The existing ground crews would be re-trained for other jobs in the consortium.

Tom found a helium extraction plant near the helium-rich natural gas field that needed funds to upgrade its facilities and negotiated a deal to buy it from the owner. Max agreed to buy and upgrade the plant so that when it was done, the LTA Consortium could supply all the helium it needed for its cruise vessels. Tom also entered into a joint venture with a small natural gas producer in the area to supply the helium-rich gas the extraction plant needed. Max brought on a few new investors to cover the cost of the extraction plant.

Fabricated graphene weighed 90 percent less than an equivalent strength piece made from titanium, which made the overall vessel structure weigh 40 percent less and require much less helium for lifting. Over 60 percent of the basic ship's structure was now made of graphene. This enabled many new desirable features to be added. Alex figured out a way to have several waterslides on board. The slides started on the fourth level and ended on the first level. A small escalator made of graphene returned the sliding passengers to the starting point. A swimming pool was still out of the question due to the weight of water, but a slide required very little water that could be recirculated. A stronger frame also allowed the designers to incorporate a large atrium in the middle of the ship that extended from the sundeck high into the ship's structure, which added an interesting visual effect as it was over one hundred feet high and five hundred feet long. An open atrium allowed a rock climbing wall to be installed, yet another desired feature. The only thing separating conventional cruise ships from this new vessel was a swimming pool. She was even working on that.

Hawaiian Cruise

The Aurora Cruise Line operated several cruise ships to Hawaii from California. Ashley chose the fifteen-day round-trip from Los Angeles voyage as it only required a two-hour drive from her home near San Diego to the cruise terminal. She entered the Aurora Dawn cruise ship alone as she wanted to be free to look at all aspects of the cruise ship without anyone noticing her, which would not be the case if Brad were around. Almost everyone knew who he was. After unpacking in her stateroom, she headed for the nearest bar. The ship wouldn't be leaving for a few hours. Alex had given her an electronic tablet for her birthday, and she started making notes. She had plenty of time to do her research as Brad could not join her until the ship docked at Hilo, its first port of call in Hawaii. He had overnighted a special "VIP" card that provided premier access to specialty restaurants and unlimited refreshments. He wanted her to look at everything without having to worry about reservations or costs.

By the time the ship docked four days later, she had a long list of items to discuss with him. All the crew seemed eager to meet him when he boarded. Brad didn't make many cruises, and many of the crew had never seen him. When he saw Ashley, he kissed her, and the crew left them alone.

It didn't take long before they were in her stateroom, not discussing business.

Over dinner, Ashley tried to discuss some of her findings with Brad, but he seemed to be distracted and not paying attention, just staring at her. She wondered if he were already bored with her. She finally snapped her fingers in front of his face.

"Brad!"

He jerked back into reality. "Sorry. I was just wondering what it would be like to be with you all the time."

A shocked expression ran over Ashley's face. She didn't expect that answer, and it showed. "What!"

"As soon as I saw you, I wished I could have changed some things in San Diego and convinced you we need to be together."

Ashley was too confused to answer, and Brad smiled at her. "Come back to London with me, and let's try to make a relationship work."

It was difficult to find a reason to say no. "I have a business in San Diego."

"I'll buy it from you if that's a stumbling block."

She hadn't expected this and was too tongue-tied to answer. She had hoped to have a lot of fun on the cruise and do a little business. What did she really feel about him? Was she ready for a relationship? Did she really want to live in London?

Brad saw the confusion and anxiety on her face. "This is an offer, Ashley, not a sentence. We can have a lot of fun while we figure out if it's best for both of us."

In an instant, all of her anxiety seemed to fade away. What would it hurt to see if they had a lot in common other than the nighttime fun?

"I don't know, but let's take some time and figure out what we want."

"Sure."

While they tried to figure it out, Brad and Ashley didn't even leave the ship at its designated stops in Honolulu, Kauai, and Maui. On the last night of the cruise in the Hawaiian Islands, Ashley agreed to give a relationship a try. They celebrated that night, and Ashley discussed her plan to return to San Diego so she could meet with her business manager and plan for her to be gone for an indefinite period.

Brad left before the ship left Hawaii and thought about her all the way back to his corporate headquarters in London. The cruise had answered all his questions.

Ashley worked on some new signage and graphics for the Aurora Dawn on the four-day voyage back to Los Angeles. She e-mailed them to Brad when she returned to her fitness studio and started packing. A few days later, Brad had his jet waiting for her, and from the top of the ladder, she looked around wondering if she would ever come back. She also looked forward to being with Brad.

When the jet arrived in London, a limo driver met her, collected her luggage, and drove her to Brad's home near Hambleden, just west of London. Ashley was shocked as it resembled a medieval castle surrounded by a large forest.

The head of the house staff led her to her room, and Ashley was sure she was in the wrong house. Surely, Brad wasn't that wealthy…Although the exterior of the house looked very old, the interior had obviously been redone with modern lighting and plumbing. It was almost like being in a former castle that had been converted to a hotel. She noticed a section of the house in the back blocked off, and she wondered if it had not been refurbished yet.

She spent the rest of the afternoon wandering around the grounds. Ashley loved horses, and Brad had a stable of six horses. There was an exercise yard next to the stable, and Ashley walked several horses around the exercise yard. She then finished her tour of the house and tried to meet the rest of the staff. By her count, there were at least a dozen staff including the groundskeepers, maintenance staff, and the driver. She felt a little uncomfortable at first as the staff acted like she wasn't there. It would take some time, but she would come to understand they rarely interacted with Brad's guests.

The head of the staff vaguely knew that Ashley was there as Brad's guest, but little else.

Brad finally arrived, and they hugged and kissed. Dinner was served in a large dining room with a massive table that could seat two dozen people. Brad sat on one end and smiled when Ashley sat down next to him instead of the other end of the table. It seemed to surprise the food preparation staff as well when they served dinner.

"I know CEOs of companies make a lot of money, but I don't think very many live in castles. Did you inherit a bunch of money?"

"No. My parents were middle class. When I finished my business degree, I immediately joined Aurora as a first line manager in the finance area. I worked on a lot of projects, including the construction of port terminals. I lived pretty frugally and saved a lot of money from my salary and occasional bonuses."

Ashley winced when he said he lived frugally. She wondered what else she didn't know about him as he continued.

"Every time the markets went down, I bought all the stock I could. Travel and entertainment stocks always drop a lot more on average than the markets do. I think investors overreact and sell airline and cruise companies at the first signs of economic problems. Anyway, during each sell-off, I accumulated a lot of stock in the company, and each time the economy recovered, the travel and entertainment stocks usually returned to their former levels. The results can be quite dramatic when you do this five times as I have in about twenty years."

Ashley continued to eat while he explained his accumulation of wealth. "Okay, so you have a lot of stock. How did you buy a castle?"

"I bought it as a 'ruin' as it had been abandoned for fifty or sixty years. It was originally built by an earl about five hundred years ago, but over the ages, the last of his family died or moved away, until it was totally abandoned. I think none of the remaining family members could afford the taxes. Fortunately, the castle's roof was still largely intact, and the interior of the house wasn't in too bad a shape. I think the mayor of Hambleden near here practically salivated at the prospect for new taxes and helped me find all the craftsmen I needed for the repairs. I didn't restore the area in the back that's blocked off as that was a barracks and armory for soldiers back in the earl's days, and I didn't see the need to spend money to fix it up. So I had the roof repaired, put in modern plumbing and electrical systems, along with heating and cooling systems, had the walls repaired, and restored some of the wall decorations. You may have noticed the fox hunt paintings and the large painting of the house when it was first built."

She nodded. "Yes, and the circular display of swords and the suit of armor in the living room." She thought for a moment. "How about the staff?"

"I brought them on near the end of construction. Some of them had been with me for a long time, and when I sold my house in London, they came to live here with me."

"I did a self-guided tour when I arrived, and it looks like there are only nine or ten bedrooms. Where does the staff sleep?"

"The basement was just used for storage, so I completely redid it and converted it into a kitchen, a dining room, and fifteen bedrooms for the staff."

"The staff sleeps in the basement?" Ashley had a shocked expression, and Brad laughed.

"It sounds terrible when you say it that way, but their apartments are completely modern. Each bedroom has its own bathroom and is quite comfortable. And yes, they are heated and cooled with modern systems, just like the house. They told me their arrangements here are better than the flats they had in London. They all appreciate the extra time they save by not commuting to work each day. Some of the staff are also married couples."

Ashley thought about that as they ate dinner. "We seem to be in the middle of nowhere. Doesn't it get kind of lonely living out here?"

Brad shrugged. "I guess you get used to things like that. We have satellite TV and Internet, so we aren't cut off from the world. I didn't bother to run a new phone line as the cost would be horrendous, and everyone seems to have a cell phone these days."

"Okay, so what do you do for fun?"

Brad seemed to not understand the question. "Fun?"

She frowned. "You do take time to relax and have fun now and then, don't you?"

"I read a lot..." He thought for a moment. "There is a swimming pool in the greenhouse. If you want to use that, we can have it re-plastered and install new pool equipment."

Ashley just shook her head. "What do you do on the weekends?" He just stared at her until she asked, "How far is London?"

20

Personal Histories

During the yearlong design phase of the new vessel, Max stopped by whenever he was in Houston on hedge fund or LTA Consortium business. He usually convinced Alex to have dinner with him so she could update him on the ship's progress. To an outsider, they looked like a couple. It took some time, but Alex slowly came to trust him. They even shared personal data when they were alone, something Alex almost never did even with several girlfriends she still kept in contact with from college.

She asked about Jill, and Max admitted their relationship was on the rocks. Max had met Jill Thornton, an international model, at a charity auction benefiting lung cancer research.

They both had relatives that had succumbed to lung cancer. They hit it off and soon started a relationship. Jill's mother was from Jamaica, and her father was English. They met while he was on holiday and returned to London where Jill grew up. Unfortunately, Jill traveled all over the world on fashion shoots, and Max traveled often on hedge fund business. Although they both called Manhattan home, they were rarely there. The added effort by Max to form the LTA Consortium made matters worse.

Alex found a trashy Web site that someone had devoted to Max, showing all his "conquests." There was a Mexican actress, a South Korean TV personality, a Brazilian model; and it went on and on in a rogue's gallery–type format. It was not flattering. Alex asked him about dating so many models and actresses, and he didn't deny it. He just said it was hard for him to meet women who were not in business or investing, and it seemed to Max that most successful business women were married. He often met models or actresses at business or charity events. Alex really didn't want to know more.

Max asked her about her boyfriend. She met Bill Allen in college, and they dated often, but he was averse to commitments, and Alex was always working several part-time jobs or on designs for possible LTA vessels. After college, he moved to Colorado to lead tours for Outbound, and their communication became almost nonexistent. She didn't mention her latest visit.

She had searched the Internet about Max and found a lot about his Designing the Future contests and some of the ideas that had been funded from them, but she couldn't figure out how he made so much money. He confided that he had a wealthy uncle who had married several times and died when Max was just out of college. During the reading of the will, the current wife and the ex-wives were fighting over his estate, especially the half dozen homes he had around the world.

None of the other relatives really noticed, or cared, that Max inherited seven patents for technical innovations his uncle had made in the telecommunications business. His uncle hadn't really pursued possible royalties by several companies using the technology, but Max hired a patent attorney and took the companies to court and won many millions of dollars. That provided the seed money he needed for his angel investing business, which he soon multiplied many times over.

Max finally asked her about her interest in dirigibles, and she related the story she had told Brad about her grandfather and the Hindenburg and his brother's loss on the USS Akron in 1934. She also said that while she was in college she had tried to build a large prototype with her friend who owned a machine shop. It was just large enough to carry her, and she controlled the rudder and ailerons with ropes from a small gondola on the bottom and had incorporated a lawn mower's engine to propel the prototype. She had his full attention as she described her first flight and the thrill she had as she flew around in the countryside just outside Houston. He asked what happened to the prototype, and she sheepishly admitted that she had been unharmed when it had crashed. She later found a tear in one of the gas bags, which she never figured out how it could have happened. Her interest in structural engineering was a natural progression, and after college, she landed the job at Armstrong, initially as a team designer. She finished a master's degree in structural engineering at night, and her master's thesis had described the engineering required for a cruise-size LTA vessel. The master's degree enabled her to be promoted to senior designer and take the design lead on several small corporate jets for Armstrong while she continued to work on the design of an LTA cruise vessel at night.

He told her he knew she had studied the crash of the Hindenburg for years and asked if she had an opinion on what happened.

"Every person who has studied the crash has an opinion."

"I know, but what do you think happened?"

"First, I don't think it was sabotage. That would have been a huge black eye for the Nazi government, and they were determined to rule that out and pretty much did. There still is no proof it was sabotage."

"So what happened?"

"The day of the crash, there was a huge weather front with constantly shifting winds over New England that gave the captain and his officers severe problems when the ship arrived in New Jersey. My grandfather even noticed the changing wind directions and the severe course changes the ship was making as it neared the mooring tower. I agree with one theory that the severe course changes stressed and broke one of the guy wires, and it slashed a gas bag. That was the beginning of the end."

"I thought the Hindenburg had many gas bags."

"Yes, but whenever the ship descended, the officers vented hydrogen. Normally, the vent valves are connected to a vent tube, so the vented hydrogen goes up the tube and vents on top of the ship. Even in a highly charged atmosphere from thunderstorms, this small amount of hydrogen wouldn't be a problem, but a slashed bag would vent a massive quantity of gas at the top of the ship. My grandfather and other members of the ground crew saw a blue glow on the top near the tail of the ship before it caught on fire. Some thought that could be Saint Elmo's fire, but it could have been a discharge of static electricity that built up on the skin of the ship and discharged to a piece of structural metal while all that hydrogen was venting from the broken bag."

Max was staring at her but not from her telling her version of the crash. He was actually wondering how he could develop a relationship with her. She wondered why he was staring at her, but continued. "Hydrogen burns with a clear flame, and you can't normally see it, but the Zeppelin Company's hydrogen-making process left impurities, and when it burned, it actually made a blue flame. The huge quantity of hydrogen from the broken gas bag caught fire and ignited the skin of the ship. Ironically, the gelatin coating on the ship's outer cover is a distant cousin of modern solid-state rocket fuel. Once it caught on fire, the whole outer covering burned away in less than a minute. That's what you are seeing in the famous footage of the crash. Everyone who was there said the burning material made the fire yellow and red. Clearly, it was not the hydrogen burning. As each gas bag caught on fire and failed, the hydrogen just rose rapidly into the atmosphere. Since the gas bags in the back broke first, the rear of the ship hit the ground first, and as the rest of the bags broke, the ship settled to the ground."

Max realized she had finished. "That couldn't happen on the Magellan?"

"No, unlike hydrogen, helium can't burn, and all the outer covering is nonflammable. All the interior walls and the decking are also nonflammable. There just isn't enough material that can burn to harm the vessel."

He asked about other possibilities for catastrophic failures, and she convinced him the design team could not come up with a combination of system or design failures that would cause the ship to crash.

He thought about that for a while and then asked, "What about sabotage?"

"There is always that possibility, but how can you design against humans creatively trying to circumvent engineered systems?"

He couldn't answer that and hoped he wouldn't have to worry about that.

Slowly, she trusted him enough to go with him to movies or the theater after dinner, even if she didn't call it a date. At least, she kissed him good night each time, and from his point of view, the kisses seemed to get longer each time.

One night, they went to an upscale continental restaurant, and the waiter asked some clarifying questions about their order in a heavy German accent. Alex answered in German, which surprised the waiter and Max. He asked her about it, and she related the story of her grandfather's immigration to Texas and learning German from him. Max surprised her by describing his father's family immigration from Brazil to New York at an early age. Like most first-generation children of immigrants, Max really didn't learn to speak Portuguese very well.

During dinner, he remembered the contest proposal she had left aside for further review. For some reason, he was still carrying it around in his briefcase and thought of it. He pulled it out of his briefcase and laid it on the table near her.

"I've been carrying this around for a while. Why did you separate this when we were reviewing the proposals for the contest?"

She picked it up and flipped through it. "I know this isn't anything new, but I was wondering if this could be commercially viable if it were made with graphene."

He thought about that. A personal flyer that weighed almost nothing might make it viable for commuting. "What about the battery? You once said with the right chemical addition, graphene can conduct electricity. Could you make a battery from graphene that would allow the flyer to be used by commuters?"

She was surprised that he remembered that comment. "Yes, I'm sure it's possible." She took out an electronic tablet from her purse and started sketching on it. After a few minutes, she showed the sketch to him. "It wouldn't look like a regular battery. It would actually be a part of the backpack. Since it's made of graphene, it could be a lot bigger—and more powerful." She stared at the sketch for a moment. "A lot more powerful."

He nibbled on a breadstick while he studied the drawing.

"Why don't you make one?"

She laughed. "In my spare time?"

"Make a detailed sketch, and I'll get a prototype made."

"Are you serious?"

"The LTA Consortium is always looking for new ventures for LTA technology, especially when it doesn't cost a billion dollars."

She winced at that comment. "Ouch."

She had laid the tablet down, and he put his hand on hers. "That was a compliment. You are obviously an excellent saleswoman."

She felt a hot flash when he put his hand on hers. She hoped it was static electricity and not a hormonal response to his touch. Later, when she kissed him good night, she felt the hot flash again. She quickly closed the door to her apartment and realized she was actually panting. What was going on?

21

A New Type of Graphene

Two months before the round-the-world voyage of the Columbus, Max was in his new office in the admin building's LTA annex when Alex barged in, wearing white fire-retardant clothing streaked with what appeared to be black soot. Before he could say hello, she dropped an aluminum suitcase on his desk.

"What now?"

"Look at this." She opened the suitcase and took a brick out and quickly closed the suitcase.

"A brick?"

He stared in amazement as the suitcase floated slowly off the desk. He grabbed it while it was still reachable. When he opened the suitcase, she warned him, "Be careful."

Five softball-sized balls of what appeared to be graphene flew out of the case and bounced along the ceiling a few times until they came to a rest near the room's lighting fixture.

Another was actually floating in the air near his face. Alex grabbed it. "This one must have a defective seal…"

"What the hell is going on?"

"We just found a way to impregnate graphene with hydrogen then seal it. We can even create a cavity in a block of it, fill it with hydrogen then seal it. The impregnated material is basically lighter than air all by itself."

He shook his head, trying to understand the potential for the new material. "So a vessel made of this material…"

"No, think bigger, much bigger. Do you remember the sky city in the *Star Wars: The Empire Strikes Back* movie?"

"A floating city—made of this stuff?"

"It's surprisingly cheap to add hydrogen and then seal it after we make the graphene structure."

While he was thinking on that, she handed him a folder.

"What's this?"

"The design for a personal flyer made from graphene. If we use the new hydrogen-filled version, the backpack would almost float all by itself. I did some further calculations. It could carry your weight for about twenty miles before it needed to be recharged. It should only take a few hours to recharge the graphene battery."

"That almost sounds commercially viable. What about the cost?"

"That, of course, depends on how many are made. If that's a few thousand, the cost would probably be out the range for most commuters. If we made a million, the cost would probably be the same as a motor scooter."

He shook his head. "Another billion dollar deal, Alex?"

She shrugged. "You asked."

"Could you make just two, one for you and one for me?"

She took the folder from him, opened it, and stared at her sketch and her estimated bill of materials. "That's probably more than a hundred thousand dollars each."

"So?"

She made a face at him. "Why only two?"

"I thought we'd try it some weekend, just to prove it works."

She gave him such a skeptical look. He laughed. "Why wouldn't it work?"

"I know you will make all needed lift and weight calculations, but sometimes, there are practical aspects that have to be proven, like the prototype airship you made in college."

"Are you willing to risk your life on my calculations?"

"You would risk your life as well, and I know you wouldn't try it unless you were sure."

"Good point. I'll ask my guys to start on it this afternoon." She started to leave but stopped and looked back. "Are you up for a race?"

"Always."

She laughed as she closed the door behind her.

Max was struggling to keep ahead of Alex's new hardware and designs. He had already communicated privately with Brad Wilson, asking him to revise Aurora's bid for the consortium's assets to take into account the new graphene factory and patents of the consortium. This could make the assets and patents even more valuable, but he thought the impregnated graphene may be something the LTA Consortium would license but not sell to the Aurora cruise line. He hoped to find other applications for it outside the cruise industry.

World Tour

Construction of the new graphene airship was completed in a year. During that time, a special "mooring team" traveled to each prospective landing site to purchase twenty acres; arrange refueling facilities, freshwater, and power connections; and construct mooring rings needed for landing. After a few months of trial runs and certification testing, the LTA Consortium announced an even newer type of LTA ship, known as "Columbus." The main news was Columbus's first voyage, which would be a round-the-world tour that approximated the same route as the Graf Zeppelin in its round-the-world tour in 1929. This tour would begin at the LTA Company's mooring site in Jersey City, New Jersey, near New York City (instead of Lakehurst, New Jersey), then proceed across the Atlantic to Iceland, then to Europe, with stops in London, Paris, Berlin, and Vienna. It would then continue across Russia, with a stop in Moscow, across China, with a stop in Beijing, before continuing on to Tokyo. The next segment would involve stops in Hawaii, Los Angeles, and St. Louis before a return to New York. Estimated duration was ninety days. In reality, the same tour could be made in much less than half that time as the Columbus could travel more than 2,600 miles per day at full speed. A much slower pace allowed for many more stops and more time on board for passengers to spend money.

Like other cruise lines' round-the-world tours, passengers could sign up for the whole tour or parts of it. Consortium marketing personnel researched round-the-world tours by other cruise lines and priced the Columbus's tour competitively. Max convinced Alex to reprise her role as operations manager for the round-the-world tour. She really didn't want to be away from the design studio for that long, so he arranged a special office for her on the new vessel with an equivalent computer system and a satellite communication link back to the design department. This would allow her to continue work on the next vessel part-time while observing the operation of the new graphene vessel.

During the construction of the Columbus, Max had to inform Brad and Aurora's board of directors that several members of the LTA Consortium did not want to sell and had even offered to increase their funding to build several more vessels. The proposed deal underwent numerous revisions and still was not completed when the Columbus was introduced at a press conference and eager passengers signed up online for the world tour.

Alex insisted Mike Hovenski captain the new vessel, and the consortium, which was really Max, agreed. Except for Max, the investors preferred to remain silent partners.

The design team had learned quite a lot from the Magellan, and she wanted passengers on the Columbus to have an unforgettable experience.

Two weeks prior to the world tour, Alex was in her office making final preparations for the world tour when, out of the blue, Bill Allen called her. He tried to apologize for the way their last meeting turned out. She was noncommittal about what happened, so he told her he had met someone on one of his Outbound tours and hit it off really well. He said he was sorry, but he just needed be free to see if this new friendship could turn into something more. She wished him well and hung up. Funny, she wasn't upset or angry at all. It seemed she was finally over him.

Graphene Flyer

The next day, Jack Armstrong helped Alex and Max put on their prototype "graphene flyer backpacks." She went through a quick review of the control box for Max, then stood back some. She forgot to mention to him the speed control was not linear, and when he pressed it all the way down, he rocketed up to several thousand feet before he could throttle back. Jack and Alex laughed as it was almost like watching a hero in a cartoon fly away. She carefully started the fans on her flyer and slowly pressed the speed control until she lifted off the ground. At about one hundred feet, she looked up and couldn't even see Max. Where was he? She almost dropped her control box when he "buzzed" by her and yelled, "What are you waiting for?" She pressed the speed control and was moving almost as fast as he was until she looked down and became dizzy. Letting go of the speed control, she swallowed hard as she was at least one thousand feet off the ground. She didn't know she suffered from vertigo until now as she had always been inside something when she was in the air, but now when she looked down, all she could see was the earth below. The power indicator on her control box showed that she had hardly used any power, but she carefully swung around and started back toward the Columbus's hangar.

Max was having a great time flying all around. The power indicator showed he had less than five minutes of power left, so he decided against finding out the hard way what would happen if he ran out of power, so he headed back to the hangar. He finally landed just outside the hangar, where Jack Armstrong was watching him. "You really have faith in her calculations."

He smiled. "I have faith in her."

"Can I try that?"

"It only has a few minutes of power left."

Jack pointed, and Max saw Alex slowly returning to the hangar. When she landed, Jack helped her take the backpack off, and she helped him put it on. They both watched as Jack zipped into the sky.

"You didn't tell him the throttle is nonlinear?"

She grinned. "Oops."

Later that day, Max held a videoconference with several of his close friends who were also investors in the LTA Consortium. He described the graphene flyer and moved his computer so they could see the prototype. After a brief discussion, they all agreed the consortium would build one hundred flyers and demonstrate them to potential distributors. He surprised Alex the next day with the keys to a luxury sports convertible. She invited him to a tour of the countryside, with the top down naturally, and, at the end of the day, kissed him like she did on their night out after the investor presentation. This time, she didn't run off and hugged him as well.

22

Dana Schultz

The next day, Alex was returning to her office and, from a distance, saw Max standing outside her office then walking in. That seemed strange. Max had stopped by to see how Alex liked her new office in the annex. The lights were out, and at first, he thought she wasn't in, but then he saw her typing on the computer lit only by the glow of the monitor.

She called out to him. "Hi, Max."

"What are you working on in the dark?"

"Come and see."

He walked over to her desk to look when she suddenly jumped up and kissed him passionately. It was totally out of character, but he thought, *What the hell…* and kissed her back.

Alex entered and turned on the lights and stopped in her tracks. Dana had her arms around Max and was kissing him!

She couldn't tell if he was kissing her back or not.

"Dana! Max!"

Max stepped back and had to look twice. It was almost as if he had stepped back in time to the day he first met Alex.

There were some differences between Alex and her younger sister, but you sure couldn't tell them apart in the dark.

Dana was smiling as she had successfully ambushed Max. She was tired of hearing Alex talk about him…Max this and Max that. She wanted to meet him and invited Alex to go to lunch with her, hoping he would be there.

Alex had mentioned her younger sister a few times. She had bounced around from charity to charity until she found a home running a center for battered women in Houston. Dana knew that Alex met a lot of investors and hoped to make some contacts that could lead to some large donations for her shelter. Expressing emotions and feelings came naturally to Dana, even more than Ashley and the exact opposite of Alex. Her hair was similar to Alex's, but she was a lot "curvier" and dressed so it showed in a low-cut dark green dress that seemed to cling to her.

"This isn't what it appears to be." That was lame but the best Max could come up with at the moment.

Dana laughed. "I was just having some fun, Alex."

Alex was furious, but she maintained a calm appearance.

He tried to change the subject. "Could I take you both to lunch?"

During lunch, Dana talked to Max, while Alex was still fuming over her kissing him like that.

"You've been to a lot of charity fundraisers?"

"Yes…many."

"Could you tell me what worked and what didn't work for the sponsors. I have a big fundraiser coming up and need some advice."

He had never thought of that. He had attended many fundraisers. Some were memorable and successful; many others were not. He sat thinking for a moment then gave her a list of what he considered appropriate and effective themes and overall event planning. Funny, no one had ever asked him that question.

Alex cooled off when it seemed Dana had just come to meet Max and get some pointers for her upcoming event. She was still pissed about the kiss, though.

Max remembered Alex's comment about an older brother. He asked them about him, and they both seemed reluctant to talk about him.

"We don't talk much about him," replied Alex. Dana nodded in agreement.

"Why not?"

Dana and Alex sort of stared at each other for a moment until Dana answered. "He works for NASA and spends most of his time at some government lab in California on some top secret, hush-hush stuff. We hardly ever see him anymore, and when we do, he won't talk about anything he does. It's kind of weird being around him."

"I'd still like to meet him."

Alex shrugged. "You might, someday."

Max remembered that Dana was a twin. "How about your twin sister?"

Dana laughed. "She's a lot like you, always involved in business deals and stuff. She stops by the shelter now and then, and we go to lunch, but I haven't seen her in months."

Alex agreed. "She moves around a lot on the West Coast. I think she's in Seattle now."

"What's her name?"

"Lindsey Schultz."

Alex saw a shocked look on Max. "What's wrong?"

"I know her!"

Alex was the most surprised. "You know her?"

"She's an angel investor. We've both tried to fund the same start -ups a few times. I've actually never met her, but I know a lot about her business activities."

"She's not rich. How can she be an angel investor?"

"She probably manages speculative investment money for one or more wealthy individuals."

Alex wondered what Max was thinking as he was shaking his head. She would ask him later. She also wondered why it bothered her to see someone else kissing Max. Was she jealous?

After lunch, Max left them in Alex's office to attend an afternoon meeting with Jack Armstrong and his management team. Dana immediately pumped Alex for more information about Max.

"So are you doing it with Max?"

"What! No, we're just friends."

"What are you waiting for? He's cute and rich and a pretty good kisser."

Alex frowned. "He has a girlfriend!"

"Why not give him a choice?"

"Dana!"

"You always were too slow in the relationship department. Are you still seeing Bill Allen?"

"He called me a few days ago to say he met someone on one of his tours and said he wanted to be free to see how it worked out. So I guess that's over."

"Good riddance. Did you tell Max?"

"Why would I tell Max?"

"You are the only one that can't see how much he likes you."

"He has a girlfriend."

"He wouldn't spend so much time with you if that were true." Dana smiled slyly. "A Max in my hands would be worth more than a host of Bills in the bush."

Alex just shook her head. Eventually, she returned to her work, and Dana left to find Max. Surely, he was around somewhere. She wanted to know more about him and pick his brain some more.

Dana found Max waiting on a sofa in a lounge, reading his e-mail. She sat down next to him and smiled. Max suspected she was up to something, but smiled back. "Hi."

"Don't worry, Max. I'm not here to ask for a donation or any favor or anything."

She laughed at the skepticism on his face.

"Did you know there are over two million nonprofits and charities in the US alone and over seven million in the world?"

Max had never thought about it. "No, I guess not."

"Competition for charitable money is tough. I need to set my shelter apart from all the other charities operating in Houston."

She went on to describe her shelter and indirectly ask Max if he could help somehow, not necessarily with money. He listened and offered some helpful suggestions. Dana asked him to stop by if he was ever in the North Houston area. The international airport was there and the private terminal where he flew in and out. He said he would stop by when he had the time. He stood up when she started to leave, and she surprised him again by kissing him strongly, then running off. Max watched her leave and shook his head. *Just like Alex.*

Women's Shelter

A few weeks later, Max returned to Houston for a meeting with Jack Armstrong. Dana had e-mailed him several times to remind him to visit if he was ever in town. He entered the shelter's address in the rental car's GPS. It was a short drive from the international airport, and he was a little surprised when he saw the shelter. He had expected it to be a converted house, but it looked like a school building.

He entered, and a receptionist led him to Dana's office. It appeared Dana was on her computer when he entered.

Lindsey Schultz was in town on business and had stopped by to go to lunch with Dana. She had been waiting for Dana to return from an errand and was checking her e-mail on Dana's computer when Max knocked on the open doorframe. She immediately knew who he was from business Web sites. Dana had mentioned Max several times and hoped he would visit.

"Max, great to see you!" Lindsey jumped up and kissed him. He had to remind himself she was not Alex. Lindsey was wearing a dark skirt and white blouse. Her hair was similar to Dana's…She even wore the same perfume. Lindsey knew that Dana was even more outgoing than Ashley, and she had described Max as a "great-looking guy who's rich and a good kisser." She wanted to check out the last part of Dana's description.

"I don't have a lot of time, but I wanted to stop by and see how you, and your shelter, are doing."

She motioned him to sit down in a chair by the desk and pretended to be Dana. "You may have guessed this was an old elementary school."

"I was thinking it looks a lot like a school."

"The school district built a new, bigger one near here and planned to demo this one, but I scraped enough money together to buy it from them. They almost gave it to me." She laughed. "This was the principal's office."

Max looked around. The walls were lined with dusty empty shelves, and the walls held marks where pictures had hung. The more he looked, the more it became obvious Dana was running the shelter on a shoestring budget.

"So would you like some coffee?"

"Water would be fine."

"Come with me, and I'll show you around."

He followed her to the receptionist's desk. She opened a cooler near it and handed him a bottle of water.

"Okay, let me show you the place." Just as they were about to start a tour, Dana returned from her errand. She couldn't believe Lindsey and Max were chatting. Weren't they business competitors? "Hi, Max. I'm glad you could make it."

Dana walked over to Max, put her arms around him, and kissed him strongly. Lindsey just laughed.

"It looks like you've already met my twin, Lindsey."

Max couldn't believe his eyes. Identical twins Dana and Lindsey seemed to differ only in their clothes. Dana was wearing an outfit similar to Alex the day he met her.

Lindsey looked at her watch. "I was just about to give Max the nickel tour. Why don't you lead the tour? I need to run to a business meeting, but I'll be back around an hour and a half."

Dana started the tour of the former school building, and he followed her past several former classrooms that had been converted to sleeping quarters and the former library, which was now a play area. There were several women and children in the kitchen. The shelter wasn't full, but there were a lot of women and children there. Some women just stared at him, while others seemed afraid and moved away from him.

They all noticed he was wearing a dark expensive suit. Some wondered if he were a lawyer.

Three women walked up to him. Two were carrying small children, and one asked, "Are you Max?"

He wondered how they knew his name. "Yes?"

"We heard someone named Max would come to help us, and you don't look like an angry former spouse or boyfriend."

He swallowed. "I may be able to help some."

They unloaded their desperate situations on him until Dana cut them off and pulled on his sleeve. "Max understands, ladies, but he needs to leave soon." Dana whispered to him, "Don't worry, Max. They're okay here."

Less than a third of the former school appeared to be occupied. The rest was closed off, probably from lack of money. Many of the lights were out, and he noticed an Out of Order sign on most of the water fountains in the hallways.

They returned to Dana's office after the tour, and she closed the door.

Before he could sit down, Dana hugged him. "It's nice to have someone to talk to who doesn't want to unload on me." He hugged her briefly reminding himself that Dana was not Alex, even though she looked like her, smelled like her, and sounded like her. He let go and sat down when Dana sat down on the edge of her desk in front of him.

"I didn't see any security personnel. Don't you have problems with former husbands and boyfriends dropping by?"

"It's a big problem, but I don't have the money for full-time security people. There are some Houston police officers that volunteer on the weekends. That's when most of the problems occur."

He sat thinking for a while, trying not to stare at Dana. She sure looked like Alex.

"I could make a donation, but that would only solve your problem for a while. A long-term fix is really needed."

"I'm open to whatever you can do."

Several things came to mind. "I know a firm that specializes in raising money for various causes. I can hire them for a year to help you establish a Web site and set up an annual fundraiser. There is a security firm that owes me a favor. I'll ask them to beef up the security here. There are some others who owe me a favor. I'll see if they can help too."

Dana jumped up, ran around to the back of his chair, and put her arms around him. She kissed his cheek and whispered in his ear, "Thanks so much, Max. You're a lifesaver."

He closed his eyes. Dana's voice in his ear and her perfume were getting to him. When she let go, he stood up to leave. Dana put her arms around him again and kissed him passionately, then hugged him.

He fought off some pretty basic urges. "Thanks for showing me around. I'll be back in touch with you."

She was still hugging him when she whispered, "Are you sure you don't have about thirty minutes to spare? You can pretend I'm Alex. It's okay."

He laughed, but not too loudly. Damn, she knew his weakness. When he was back in his car, he realized he smelled like Dana…and Alex. In the rearview mirror, he saw her lipstick imprint on his cheek and collar. He certainly couldn't go to Armstrong Aeronautics like that. He needed to find a clothing store with a bathroom. Luckily, he still had his overnight bag in the trunk of the car.

A week later, Max was in Houston again and stopped by to see Alex. She surprised him by kissing him as soon as he walked into her office.

"Dana called and said you stopped by the shelter and offered to help. Thanks so much, Max. I wish I could help her, somehow."

He wondered what else Dana said about his visit, but Alex didn't pursue it, so he let it pass. "How are the preparations coming along for the world tour?"

"Great, we're actually ahead of schedule in many areas. Did you know we're almost sold out?"

"I heard that might happen. That's really good news."

"Max, I know you're pretty busy, but can you try to make it for at least a part of the tour?"

"I don't know."

"Please, Max…"

He smiled. "Okay, if I can, I will. I haven't been on a cruise in some time."

She hugged him and he held her.

Graphene Vests

Dana mentioned Alex's and Max's help in fixing up the shelter to one of the police officers who volunteered on the weekends. He read several stories about Max and Alex's graphene innovations and wondered if the LTA Consortium could develop a better bulletproof vest with graphene. There was a lot of competition for the army's protective-vest business, but competition among vendors for police applications was not that strong, and demand could be high if the right product could be developed.

Dana contacted Alex about the possible application, and Alex said she would think about a solution. Machines in the consortium's factory could vary the properties of graphene a lot, and Alex put together a demonstration vest comprising several layers of graphene with different densities, about twice as thick as a normal bulletproof vest. The graphene was so light she could add a thin metal plate to the vest, and it was still lighter than a regular vest. A thin metal plate would protect the user from being stabbed in a knife attack.

She contacted Dana and, eventually, the police officer who asked for it. He arranged a test at a police practice range and fired several types of handguns and rifles at the vest. He was the most surprised of all the observers when the vest captured the bullets intact, rather than capture and deform the bullets as most bulletproof vests did. The outermost layer stopped most of the force of the bullets, and each successive layer damped the velocity until the bullet was totally captured. Alex arranged the next test of the vest on a dummy.

Several pressure sensors were added to the back of the vest to measure the force the wearer would experience when a bullet impacted. They tested the vest with a range of weapons from a Saturday night special to a .44 Magnum. The impact of the force experienced by the user was much less than a regular bulletproof vest and better than Alex expected, and she provided a dozen vests to the police department for further testing. A few days later, the vests protected several officers engaged in a gunfight with a group of bank robbers. After the incident, the officers gathered around to inspect the vests and were amazed as more than a half a dozen bullets were captured. The officers said the impact of some of the bullets felt like being hit with errant golf balls (one officer said he had been hit with a golf ball on a course once). Larger bullets captured felt like getting hit with baseballs. All the officers were amazed the bullet impacts left no bruises. A SWAT team leader asked Alex if the consortium could supply a complete outfit of a vest with pants and a helmet. She soon had those available, and the consortium donated a dozen outfits to the SWAT team in the department in exchange for feedback on their effectiveness in a real situation. It didn't take long to get confirmation that the new graphene outfits were effective and, when used by police in non-SWAT situations, could save lives.

The Houston Police Department contacted other police departments to inform them of the newly available bullet-capturing graphene outfits.

23

Anniversary

Ashley was waiting for Brad to come home so they could celebrate their first anniversary as a couple. A lot had changed in that year. The staff now interacted often with her, especially when Brad was at work. She was still working to improve the graphics on board Aurora's ships, and Brad insisted she take at least one cruise a month to become familiar with Aurora's fleet of ships. She was actually enjoying that part of the job. Fortunately, she could do her graphic designs from a small office she set up in one of the old "drawing" rooms in the house. She thought it was a little ironic that she was "drawing" graphic designs on her computer in the drawing room, something that had probably not happened in a century or more.

Ashley was very outgoing and liked to chat with the housekeeping staff that comprised six full-time employees. She rarely saw the driver as he was always shuttling Brad around to meetings or the groundskeepers or the maintenance staff. The housekeeping staff soon realized Ashley's new and important position in Brad's life and wanted to get to know her better. With Brad's okay, she refinished the swimming pool and installed new pool equipment. Her fitness center manager shipped a few exercise machines to her, and she set up an exercise room in a room at the back of the house. She encouraged the house staff to use the pool and the fitness equipment whenever they had some free time. When she found a weighing scale, she gasped with horror as she had gained five kilograms (eleven pounds). She hit the swimming pool and fitness machines hard to exercise those pounds away.

When Brad arrived, he changed clothes quickly, and they left for dinner in a nice restaurant in London, followed by a theatrical play. Brad's life had changed for the better, at least that's what he told his closest friends and business associates. Ashley kept him in shape, and they went to the theater and nightclubs on the weekends. He finally introduced her to his closest friends and held a dinner party that filled up the huge dining table. Ashley had a great time, and the wine and hard liquor flowed freely. After the party, Ashley and Brad celebrated with an "all-nighter."

Business Deal

Max was in his annex office two weeks before the Columbus's world tour for a meeting with Jack Armstrong and to review the ship's final preparations for the tour. He had to fly to London the next day on hedge fund business for a few weeks, and then he would try to join the tour as he had promised Alex.

"Hi, Max." Lindsey was smiling at him from his open office door. He wondered what she wanted. She was wearing a dark blue business suit and carrying a laptop bag and purse, something he had never seen Dana do.

"Hi, Lindsey! Come in."

She walked over to him, and he turned his chair to her but didn't get up. He didn't want her to kiss him again just to see if she could.

"I'm in town on some venture capital business and wanted to talk to you about joining forces on a deal."

He was immediately skeptical and motioned her to sit. "Why now? You always tried to beat me to the punch on deals before."

"I saw how you formed a consortium for this LTA technology that Alex is always talking about and have a possible deal that probably is too big for my investors. I thought we might go in together on it." She opened her laptop bag and handed him a folder.

Max skimmed the proposal and tried not to show he was interested. This was right up his alley in the materials technology area. Several technology geeks had claimed to have invented a new type of lightbulb that was ten times more efficient than an LED bulb. If the technology could be scaled up, they would be going up against some of the largest companies in the world that were currently scaling up to mass produce LED lights in a sufficient quantity to drive the price down where most people would be willing to try them.

They wanted to take their garage-shop invention to the next level and needed capital for a factory to manufacture their new bulb in large quantities. It seemed strange that Lindsey would want to go together on this as the inventors were only asking for ten million dollars. Lindsey had beaten Max to the punch on deals larger than that for her investors. The true cost of going head-to-head with the large conglomerates like Phillips and GE would be enormous. Maybe that's what she was talking about. Whatever the reason, Max was interested.

When he looked up, she confirmed what he was thinking. "These guys have no clue about the cost of a factory to make millions of their bulbs. I've had some discussion with some manufacturers in some very general terms, and they were thinking it could be up to a billion dollars. That's why I'm here."

Max wondered how she knew he was in Houston, but Lindsey probably had some inside sources in the consortium. "Have you seen this new bulb?"

"No. I was hoping you would go with me to visit them. You know more about scaling up from benchtop inventions than I do."

"I wish I could, but I have to leave for London tomorrow on hedge fund business."

"That's okay. These guys are in Houston. Would you have time this afternoon?"

That was short notice, but he had already made a quick tour of the new ship and was almost done with his review of a status report that Mike Hovenski had e-mailed him. He wondered if these guys had something really new. "Okay. Give me their address, and let me know when they are available."

"We can go there anytime. There's no point us both driving, so I'll drive."

Something didn't seem quite right. She was being too nice. "Okay."

Lindsey had a new hybrid convertible and had the top down as she drove to the potential business venture. It was strange for Max watching Lindsey driving as he could easily picture Alex in that role. She laughed and joked with him as they drove a relatively short distance to an industrial area just east of Clear Lake City.

Max laughed when they drove into the parking lot of what used to be a maintenance facility for the local power company. These guys probably paid next to nothing to rent this facility.

There was a small office in the front that used to be a facility where customers of the power company could come in and pay their bills. A receptionist led them to a shop area where Lindsey and Max met the two inventors. After suitable introductions and a brief description of how the new bulb worked, they demonstrated it against equivalent-wattage LED and compact fluorescent bulbs. Their power meters clearly showed the new bulb using much less energy for the same light output.

Max was impressed. He had a vague idea on the cost of a factory to manufacture a few thousand bulbs a month, but would probably need help to determine the cost of a factory that could produce millions in a year, assuming it was cost competitive and could be scaled up quickly and it didn't involve some exotic or hard-to-obtain materials.

They thanked the inventors, and Max told them they would get back to them with some ideas for funding.

It was early evening when they left the former maintenance facility, and Lindsey asked Max if he had time for dinner to talk over a path forward. He was really thinking about the new lightbulb and agreed.

Lindsey drove him to an upscale Mexican restaurant, and when they were seated, she ordered margaritas for them. Max was still thinking about the invention when the drinks arrived. When he saw the drinks, he started to decline, but Lindsey was already holding her drink glass up for a toast to the new venture, so he joined in. He wasn't a big fan of margaritas, like Alex, but this one was better than he remembered and a lot stronger. She ordered more for them.

Lindsey seemed to enjoy the evening and, at the end of the dinner, said she was a little drunk and asked Max to drive her back to her hotel. He should have known better. Max normally prided himself on being able to hold his liquor (usually whiskey sours), but he was feeling a little drunk himself. When he said good night, she kissed him strongly and whispered in his ear that he could stay if he wanted.

Maybe it was the liquor and the fact that Lindsey looked like Alex and smelled like her and he really wished she were Alex that he stayed—for a while at least. When the margaritas wore off, Max realized where he was, dressed quickly, and left her sleeping. He had the front desk call a taxi for him. He had a horrendous headache that kept him from sleeping on the way back to his hotel. How had all of this happened? What would happen if Lindsey told Alex? What would he say? He needed a better excuse than he was drunk. She wouldn't even believe that.

24

Columbus World Tour

One week prior to the start of the tour, Alex was making a last-minute inspection of the Columbus. This vessel was slightly longer at thirteen hundred feet but taller and wider to accommodate the additional passengers. Even though the total enclosed volume was over ninety-four million cubic feet, the Columbus required only forty-two million cubic feet of helium due to the additional lifting capacity provided by the graphene structure. Tom reminded Max and Alex in an e-mail that the consortium had saved over $3 million by having their own helium source for the Columbus.

The larger overall size allowed the design team to add many more amenities for the passengers: more specialty restaurants, more gift shops, a dedicated art gallery for art auctions, the waterslide, the rock climbing wall, a larger Internet café, video arcade, movie theater, etc. Only the swimming pool was not feasible…yet. Water in a typical cruise-ship pool twenty feet wide, thirty feet long, and four feet deep weighed 150,000 pounds, a lot to lift with helium, unless it could be used for other purposes as well (showers, flushing toilets, ballast, etc.).

The interior of the Columbus seemed even brighter than the Magellan. All the windows could be larger due to the added structural strength. Large colorful graphics and directional signs guided the passengers through the common areas. Everything seemed bigger. Alex had installed even more informational touch screen monitors around the ship than on the Magellan to help passengers find anything they needed.

If she hadn't been so involved in the design she thought she could get lost in the huge vessel without the colorful graphics. Virtually all the crew and hundreds of workers were making final preparations for the first voyage. Although technically she was a member of the crew and would have had a small room assigned to her in the crew's quarters, Max had insisted she take a midlevel stateroom. These staterooms were not all that different from a four-star hotel.

After wandering around for a while, she returned to her "office" on the crew level. It was small, but it had everything she needed to continue her design work. She was surprised to find an e-mail from Max. He was in London on some hedge fund business and confirmed he would join the tour there.

There was another e-mail from Lindsey that just had a happy face. She wondered what that meant.

The Columbus's inaugural round-the-world tour began on a beautiful fall day in New England. Following the usual chaos of last-minute deliveries, Alex rested in the main lounge and enjoyed a margarita, while the four hundred member crew scrambled to make everything ready for the fifteen hundred passengers who would arrive shortly.

Each passenger was provided an electronic card key that could be scanned from a distance, which sped up the boarding and off-loading of passengers. All carry-ons were scanned at the new embarkation terminal, so the passengers just walked up the entry stairs and entered the ship. The colorful graphics and myriad of TV screens made it easy to find their staterooms. All passengers were on board early, so the Columbus actually left slightly ahead of schedule from the LTA Company's mooring site in Jersey City, New Jersey. The huge vessel circled Manhattan Island in New York to give the passengers some unique and unforgettable views, then headed out to sea for Iceland.

Crossing the Atlantic on every cruise ship requires a lot of onboard activities for passengers to while away the hours (and days). On the first evening over the Atlantic, virtually every passenger was engaged in some activity. The Internet café was always crowded for some reason, as was the casino. The theatrical productions were also completely full. A Texas Hold'em poker tournament had seemed popular on the Magellan, and it proved even more popular with twice as many players competing on the Columbus as there was a lot more time to while away on a three-month world cruise than a weeklong tour. In-theater movies were shown each night in several small lounges via a satellite link. There was a teen nightclub, but once Alex set up a video game server and held a twelve-hour tournament in the Internet café, there weren't many guys in the teen nightclub.

The air temperature at four thousand feet over the Atlantic in the fall was cooler than normal at 34 degrees Fahrenheit (1 degree Celsius), but the interior temperature of the passenger area of the ship was maintained at a comfortable 75 degrees Fahrenheit (24 degrees Celsius). A few passengers in the main lounge liked fresh air and opened the louvered windows briefly, then closed them when a cold icy mist blew in. Alex took the cargo lift to the upper levels of the Columbus for a quick visual inspection. With the added lift capability of graphene, Alex had added a thin layer of insulation to the ship's outer covering, but it was still too cool for her liking in the upper part of the ship, and she hurried back to the warm passenger area.

The Columbus set a slow easy pace of about 50 miles per hour at four thousand feet for the 2,609-mile flight to Iceland, which was not exactly a major cruise-ship destination. However, many tours had been prearranged with companies in Reykjavík, and when the ship arrived early in the morning two days later, almost 100 percent of the passengers and most of the crew disembarked.

Alex had never been to Iceland, so she put on a sweater and the heaviest coat she had and joined Mike Hovenski for a day tour to visit some old Viking ruins and a Viking reenactment by a local acting group, a tour of the countryside and a visit to a hot springs spa and finally dinner and show in a tavern in Reykjavik. Mike laughed whenever Alex took "selfies" of them to e-mail to Dana, Lindsey, and Ashley.

Life on board any world cruise allows passengers to take it as easy as they wish or to take part in many onboard activities.

The Aurora Corporation had given Alex a long list of favorite games and pastimes on their cruise ships. She wasn't a fan of some of them, but as she wandered around the ship in her free time, she noticed the more experienced cruisers seemed to take part in everything offered, while the younger passengers seemed to just hang out together in small groups. She hoped that would change, and they could get more people involved in fun activities like scavenger hunts and trivia games—activities with cash rewards or vouchers for drinks at the bars.

Two leisurely days and 1,174 miles later, the Columbus landed in the early morning just outside London. Word passed through the crew that Max Brita would board in London, and when he came on board, he was immediately surrounded by members of the crew eager to meet him and shake his hand. All the other investors in the consortium were silent partners who took no active role in its day-to-day business, and the orientation for all new employees identified Max as the lead investor and active partner responsible for the business. Most of the crew understood that their captain, Mike Hovenski, reported to Max. Some business-savvy employees even knew that Max was an angel investor and managed a large hedge fund from several business Web sites. Once the crush to meet him subsided some, Max spotted Alex waiting; and, like old friends who hadn't seen each other in a while, they hugged and kissed. She gave him a short tour that ended in her office.

"Everything here seems really bright and colorful. Were those graphics your idea?"

"Actually, Ashley designed them, and a graphics company in Houston made them and put them up."

"Is she still seeing Brad Wilson?"

"Yes, she's in London with him, and working as a consultant for his cruise line."

"Well, the graphics sure look great."

Max complimented her again on her uniform and went off to make some phone calls to potential investors eager for his first impressions of the Columbus. Alex wondered why Max had a "thing" for women in uniform.

Alex and Max passed on guided tours of London the first night and instead met Ashley and Brad for dinner and a theatrical play. When they returned to the ship, she kissed Max good night and ran off to work on her design program. Max never knew what to expect from her after an evening out together.

On the second day, Max acted as tour guide and showed Alex some of his favorite places in London. After lunch at a pub, they returned to the ship.

At the end of the second day in London, all passengers had returned to the ship as required, and the Columbus left London precisely on time at 6:00 p.m. for Paris. Max and Alex changed to evening clothes and met for dinner in a specialty restaurant, then attended the late-seating show in the theater.

Afterward, they shared a few drinks in the main lounge. They dragged some chairs near a window and watched the lights of the French countryside pass by below as the Columbus cruised leisurely at two thousand feet for the 211 miles to Paris. As they neared the City of Lights and the Eiffel Tower, they both stood up to get a better view. They were standing very close, and as they cruised over the romantic city below, it seemed natural to kiss.

Once the ship was moored, Max picked up a bottle of wine, and Alex picked up some wine glasses, and they joined a late-night tour of the city. In a little while, the tour bus stopped on a bridge, and the guide described it as one of the most famous and romantic bridges in Paris, the Pont Alexandre III Bridge over the Seine River in front of the Invalides Museum. They left the tour, and something about Paris seemed to have an effect as they stood on the bridge, watched the lights and boats on the river, and kissed several times. They were in no hurry to go anywhere or do anything except enjoy the city.

Alex savored their time together as there was no discussion of business, only some small talk. They had almost finished the bottle, and Max poured the last bit into her glass. Alex was feeling a little dizzy, and he held her for a while. When she asked to go back, he hailed a cab, and they returned to the Columbus. Once through security, he asked her if she would join him in the lounge for one last drink. She surprised him by putting her arms around him and kissing him again like she did on their night out after the investor presentation. She whispered in his ear, and they almost ran to her stateroom.

Alex woke up with a huge hangover. She opened her eyes to her familiar stateroom, but something was different. Why was she sleeping without any clothes? When she glanced over and saw Max asleep, she rubbed her eyes in disbelief. She couldn't remember anything that happened and slipped out of bed and tiptoed to the bathroom. Max was still asleep, so she quickly put on her underwear and uniform and closed the door behind her as quietly as she could. What would she say to him when they met later in the day? Since she couldn't remember what happened, she practiced several lines in front of a mirror in the hallway by the elevator until she had an answer that seemed credible. Maybe it would be easier if she just told him the truth. She needed some coffee and something for a throbbing headache. She exited the elevator on the fourth floor and headed for the breakfast buffet.

Max woke up, and Alex was gone. He dressed quickly and went looking for her on the fourth floor but couldn't find her. He found himself near the breakfast buffet, and his nose reminded him he hadn't eaten in a while. After a quick bite, he resumed his hunt for Alex. He even tried the control center without luck. As he was leaving, he ran into Mike Hovenski.

"Have you seen Alex?"

"She was here earlier, but I haven't seen her in a while. You might try the mechanical room. She spends a lot of time there."

Max laughed, thanked Mike, and headed for the mechanical room. Alex was in an earnest discussion in German with the ship's chief engineering officer, Erik Bendorf. Max waited until she was done. She sure looked appealing to Max in her white uniform. When she saw him, she smiled.

"Good morning."

She didn't say anything about last night, so he waited until they were alone. "Is something wrong with the ship's systems?"

"I thought I felt an unusual vibration just before we moored last night. I just asked Erik to check all the engines while we're moored."

They walked to the main lounge for coffee and sat down by one of the huge windows. The early morning sun lit the city just two miles away.

It was awkward, but Max had to know. "About last night…"

Alex smiled. "Yes?" She wished she could remember what happened.

"It was great for me…each time."

Each time? "Me too." At least she hoped it was. "But, Max?"

"Yes?"

"I sometimes do impulsive things when I've been drinking…things I sometimes don't even remember the next day, so don't jump to too many conclusions. Let's just see what happens."

Max was happy for that much. "Of course." Now some things were finally making sense. Just before she fell asleep, he had whispered in her ear he loved her. She had whispered back she loved him too. Now if he could only get her to say that when she hadn't been drinking…He also filed away her comment about doing impulsive things after a few drinks. Maybe he could use that excuse if Lindsey ever mentioned his night with her to Alex.

The passengers returned from their day tours to the ship on time, and it left Paris precisely on time at 10:00 p.m. for a leisurely overnight 544-mile trip to Berlin. Max tried not to interfere in Alex's design work or her role as the ship's operations manager. He found her in her office absorbed in her CAD program, designing the next LTA vessel and decided not to bother her. Max wasn't a big gambler, except on entrepreneurial start-ups, but he stopped by the casino and played poker until he yawned so hard it almost hurt his jaw muscles. He headed for his stateroom.

When he woke up, he took a slow tour of the ship before the Columbus arrived in Berlin at 10:00 a.m. Surprisingly, there were several people already in the reading library, which had all the classics and the current bestsellers in hard back books. There were also dozens of electronic terminals where many thousands of e-books were available. Max couldn't understand why the large Internet café was so crowded as Wi-Fi was available in all the passenger staterooms. Maybe it was the free coffee and pastries, one of the included amenities on the ship.

Like many cruise ships, the Columbus had many boutique shops. Vendors also sat up tables on the promenade and displayed various goods that changed on a daily basis. Just like every other cruise ship, there was a gallery where photos of the guests on tours were displayed. Max saw pictures of Alex and Mike at the Viking reenactment in Iceland and laughed as they hammed it up for the camera. There were freelance videographers and photographers on board who traveled with guests on their tours, taking video and pictures they hoped the guests would buy later. The videographer had already started a complete tour video by incorporating stills of each planned mooring site and adding actual tour videos as the trip continued.

The casino was already crowded, but Max passed it by until he came to a small lounge near the front of the ship. Max watched bingo games for a few minutes then continued on. He wasn't a fan of bingo. His tour continued to the front of the promenade deck where he saw a line of adults and children laughing and talking excitedly while waiting for the waterslides. There were actually five slides, and the line moved quickly. Everyone seemed to have a great time, and if Max had a bathing suit, he might have joined the line. In a little while, he found the spa, and the staff convinced him to try a massage. He thoroughly enjoyed that and, after a quick shower, found the theater where a full-dress rehearsal was underway to prepare for the night's performance.

He continued his tour until he found Alex taking notes and talking to a group of passengers. She was consistent. She saw him and waved. After a few minutes, she joined him for brunch. The ship finally arrived in Berlin around ten in the morning. Max and Alex joined in a day tour that included a late lunch and an early evening show at a cabaret. When they returned and passed through security, Alex kissed Max and headed back to her office, ending any thoughts he had they might repeat the first night in Paris activities.

He was heading for his stateroom when he passed a bar and saw Mike Hovenski nurturing a cocktail and stopped to say hello. The conversation eventually turned to Alex, and Mike mentioned they had been on a few day tours together and he had even asked her to dinner a few times but she always seemed too busy. Mike heard that Alex still had a boyfriend from college and assumed that was the reason she didn't seem interested. Max wondered if that were true still. Then it came to him.

"You live in Houston?"

"Yes?"

"I know someone you really need to meet."

Mike frowned. How would a wealthy investor like Max Brita know someone he should meet?

Max looked in his cell phone contact list and wrote Dana's phone number down on a napkin, but not her name, and handed it to Mike.

Mike stared at the number. "Whose number is this?"

"You wouldn't believe it if I told you. Just call her when you get back to Houston. Tell her Max sent you to help. She'll know what that means."

That seemed strange, and Mike was skeptical, but he stuffed the napkin in a pocket of his uniform.

25

Saboteur

Early in the afternoon of the next day, most of the passengers had not returned from their day tours, and the ship was nearly empty. Alex was in her office when the chief engineering officer rushed in. She looked up, surprised at his worried look.

"What's wrong, Erik?"

"You won't believe this, but someone put maple syrup or something like that in the generator tanks and started one. That generator is messed up and needs a major overhaul. We found the problem in time to keep the bad fuel out of the other generator, but…"

She finished his sentence. "We can't run everything on one generator."

"While we're moored, we're okay as we have a power feed from the city, but we can't get underway at half power. While we could run all essential services, much of the ship would be dark."

"How long will it take to overhaul the generator?"

"We probably have all the parts, but it's a huge machine…Probably two days."

"So we're pretty much stuck here for two days."

Erik nodded.

As the operations manager, she was responsible for the fix. "Get started on it immediately. We'll look in Berlin for any parts we don't have, or airfreight it from somewhere in Europe if we can't find it here."

"Yes, Alex. I'll keep you informed."

He almost ran back to the mechanical room. Alex sat thinking for a minute. *Sabotage?* She called the head of security on her radio as she headed for the security office. She saw Max in the security office. Apparently, word moved fast among the staff. Max was already discussing the problem with the head of security. "Who has access to the mechanical room?"

The head of security consulted a computer screen. "Most of the staff does. Current security policies don't provide clear guidelines on access by the staff. The good news is everyone has to badge in and out, so we know who's been there since we left Paris."

Records showed fewer than a dozen people had been in the room, most of them mechanics. The non-mechanical technicians also had some reason to be there, but they would be interviewed.

When the passengers returned from their day trips, they were given a handout explaining the delay in leaving Berlin, with a promise the ship could make up the time and arrive nearly on time in Vienna. There would even be free drinks at the bars and in the lounges to make up for a delay that could be as long as two days.

The generator was overhauled in less than one day, and the trip resumed. Alex purchased several dozen locks in Berlin, and now every cabinet and every drawer that could be locked in the mechanical room was locked with a case-hardened steel lock to keep everyone out of the ship's systems that hadn't been authorized. Erik held the keys to the locks.

Some passengers immediately noticed the increase in speed from the normal leisurely rate. The investigation continued with no results. No one had any reason to want to sabotage the generators. All appeared to be happy working on the Columbus. Alex had a tight design window to finish the next vessel and was very busy and rarely available. She didn't even notice Max leave at the final European stop at Vienna until the ship was underway, and she went looking for him. A security guard checked on a computer and informed her Max had left.

She went back to her office and sat thinking. Did she just miss an opportunity to get to really know him—beyond their night together? She sat thinking about the romantic interlude on the bridge in Paris, and if she could have, she would have kicked herself. She even recalled Brad Wilson's comment that she seemed to have built a wall around herself to avoid relationships. Funny, someone she had only seen a few times had picked up on that. It was amazing that Max still seemed interested after three years of fending him off. What should she do? She thought of Tom

Babineaux, one of Max's closest friends and business associates. If anyone knew Max, it was Tom. She looked at her watch. It was a little after nine in the morning in New York. She picked up her cell phone and called him.

"Hi, Alex. How was Vienna?" Tom seemed to always know where the Magellan and the Columbus were.

"I've had a few issues here and missed the Vienna tours. I heard the passengers raving about it, though."

"So what's going on? Why did Max leave the tour?"

"I hate to say it, but we've had a few mechanical problems, and I didn't have much time for him."

"That's too bad. He really likes you." It was strange hearing Tom say that.

"I messed up, Tom. Something always seems to be in the way for me, and I was wondering if you could answer a question or two about Max."

"Sure."

"What about Jill…Thornton?"

"They broke up a few months ago. I thought you knew."

That was a shock to Alex. She wished she had known that in Paris.

"No, I didn't know."

"Confidentially, I think you are the reason."

Alex unconsciously jumped to her feet. "What!"

"Max rarely talks about it, but I just have the impression Jill knew Max wishes he were with you, and couldn't take it anymore." Alex stared off into the distance until Tom asked,

"Are you still there?"

"Yes, sorry. You've given me a lot to think about, and I really appreciate it."

"Okay. Good luck on the rest of the tour."

Tom disconnected, and Alex sat down in her chair to think. She decided to call Max. After a few tries, she finally got through to him in London. She apologized for being so busy and not making time for him when she had asked him to join the tour. She asked if he could rejoin the tour in Hawaii or Los Angeles, and Max said he would let her know. When the call ended, she was so emotionally stressed. She turned off her computer and headed for her stateroom.

On the way, she glanced at a tour map on a monitor and noticed the route had changed slightly. If it were not corrected, they would miss their next stop in Moscow by hundreds of miles. They were actually headed for the Arctic Circle, North of Moscow. How was that possible? She hurried to the control center and found Mike recording the day's activity log on a workstation. She tugged on his sleeve.

He glanced at her. "What's up?"

"Why are we so off course?"

He stared at her for a few seconds. "What? We aren't off course!"

"The GPS system says we are."

In the control center, the Columbus had a state-of-the-art Samsung SUR40 graphics table that used Microsoft's PixelSense to display its navigational charts. In reality, it was an extremely sophisticated touch screen navigational computer. The current path of the Columbus was displayed, and it showed they were on course. Alex took out her cell phone and compared its GPS position to the ship's position on the graphics table. The difference was slightly over fifty miles. She showed it to Mike.

"What the hell?"

"Who has access to the navigation system?"

"Only a few people on this ship would have the knowledge or access to change course parameters. No one could mess with it from here. There's always a handful of command staff in here."

"Is there a remote engineering station?"

Mike thought for a moment. "There are many computers in the IT room. One of them may be able to access this system over the network. I'm not sure. Only Sam Bronson would know for sure." Sam was the team lead for the IT group.

Alex pocketed her cell phone. "Let's go find him!"

They found Sam at a workstation in the IT room, a small room near the front of the crew's-quarter's level packed with computer servers on racks and a half dozen workstations. This was the "nerve station" for more than a thousand computers and workstations located all over the Columbus. Sam was surprised they even knew where the small IT room was. He forgot Alex designed the ship.

"Hi, Mike…Alex. What's going on?"

They sat on workstation chairs, and Alex asked if it were possible access the navigation system built into the Samsung SUR40 graphics table from the IT room.

Sam frowned. "It's possible, but hardly anyone knows much about that system. It's a preconfigured software package from Microsoft and Global Navigation Systems. Why are you asking?"

Alex showed him her cell phone's GPS map. "This position is fifty miles off from the position currently on the nav table."

Sam was as shocked as Mike had been. "That's impossible."

"I can assure you it is. The independent GPS system that's displayed on the tour monitors all over the ship agrees with this map."

Sam shook his head. "It's just not possible." He brought up his team member profiles on his workstation and studied it. "Only two people have any programming experience with the nav system."

Mike stood up. "We need to talk to them—now!"

Sam understood immediately. "Yes, sir! One's on the late shift and is probably asleep, but the other is near here in the engineering room. This way."

He led them down a narrow corridor and swiped a cardkey to open the access door to the engineering room, a small room packed with computers, printers, and monitors. Jules DeVry was typing on an engineering workstation and glanced up as they entered. He tried to act as though nothing was wrong, but his wide-eyed expression gave him away. There was only one reason his team lead, the ship's captain, and operations manager would come looking for him.

Sam stood on one side and Mike on the other as Alex showed him her cell phone's GPS map. "You better have a good explanation for messing with the nav computer."

Jules just stared at them. There was no way out of the room, and in the unlikely event he could get past Alex somehow, the ship was high over Russian airspace and hundreds of miles from the nearest town. He knew there were parachutes on board, but he didn't even know where they were. He looked down and merely said, "Money."

They waited. "I owe a lot of money for family medical bills and a software business that failed. I was desperate."

Mike was not sympathetic. "We all have problems, but we don't endanger other people to solve them. Fix it!"

Alex was equally unimpressed. "We are currently on a course for the Arctic Circle. This ship should be able to withstand cold, but not cold and one-hundred-plus-mile-per-hour winds. You are endangering everyone, even yourself."

Sam sat down next to him. "You aren't leaving this room until the system is fully functional again."

Jules noticed two security guards waiting by the door and put his head in his hands.

Alex had one last question for Jules. "Who paid you to do this?"

The name Jules gave them seemed familiar to Alex. After a moment, she shook her head as she remembered. "That's the president of the engineering firm that designed the Aurora's LTA ship that crashed. The FBI and the NTSB have been looking for that guy for some time."

One hour later, Alex and Mike compared the course position on the nav computer with Alex's cell phone GPS map. They were exactly the same.

Alex was studying the current course outlined on the nav computer as Mike entered the day's events into the ship's log. "What do we do with Jules?"

Alex didn't hesitate. "Turn him over to the authorities in Maui."

26

Moscow to Beijing

The next day, the Columbus made a grand entry over Moscow, and a crowd had formed at its mooring site to see the enormous vessel. When the passengers got off for prearranged tours, some of them were interviewed by reporters from radio and TV stations. Alex joined a city tour and especially enjoyed an escorted tour of the Kremlin. At the end of the tour, she returned to her office and found an e-mail from Max. He would be rejoining the tour in Los Angeles. She resolved to make his time on the Columbus worthwhile.

After leaving Moscow, Alex was conducting an informal survey among the passengers, looking for ideas for possible enhancements when an elderly couple and what appeared to be their adult children got her attention. The father appeared to have had a few drinks.

"Commodore, could we ask about the tour?"

His wife patted his arm. "Don't mind him, honey. He's had a few."

The daughter held a tour brochure and showed it to Alex.

"Ms. Schultz, it looks like there is a long flight from Moscow to Beijing."

"Yes, it's almost four thousand miles."

"When we look at the tour map on the monitors, it seems we are always traveling about fifty miles per hour, and it could take almost four days. The countryside is interesting, but we were wondering if we could go a little faster. That would give us more time in Beijing."

The son had another idea. "Better yet, if we go faster, would it be possible to add some new stops on the tour?"

"New stops could be a problem. We wouldn't have a mooring facility to refuel. Going faster and making longer tour stops wouldn't be a problem, except that we would have a lot of pre-arranged tours to reschedule, and we would have to find more."

The family looked disappointed. "Okay, let me talk this over with the captain and the navigator. We might be able to do something like that."

They all thanked her, and as they walked off, Alex called Mike on her radio, asking for a meeting in the control center.

Since the navigation system and graphics table was really a sophisticated touch screen computer, it could also be used to calculate the distances and times involved if they needed to deviate from the planned route. Alex, Mike, and his first and second officers gathered around the charts displayed on the table to discuss tour alternatives.

Mike was noncommittal. "I don't mind going faster and even adding a few stops in China as long as we don't impact the Tokyo stop. We have some overnight tours scheduled there. What exactly do you want to do?"

Alex touched a Route Alterations icon and entered *110mph* for the ship's speed. That brought the ship's icon to Beijing two days sooner.

"If we go full speed, we could be in Beijing two and one-half days earlier, and we could look at adding a few new stops."

She brought up a map of China, and they studied possible new landing sites.

"I've always wanted to see the Terra-cotta warriors. How about Xi'an? We could probably do that in less than a day since we would ask to land nearby."

Mike nodded. "Okay. How about Hong Kong or Shanghai? Tours of either would be fantastic."

She studied the map. "Why not both? Let's see if it's possible." She dragged the ship's icon from Beijing to Xi'an, China, and tapped the screen and then repeated that for Hong Kong and Shanghai and then Tokyo. She entered the requested duration at each new stop as twelve hours, and the route was recalculated. It appeared they could almost make Tokyo on time, only a few hours late. She called Erik on her radio.

"Erik, can the engines handle running at full speed for five to six days? We are thinking of adding some new stops in China and would need to go full speed between the stops to make it to Tokyo on time."

"No problem. We can cruise at one hundred and ten mph indefinitely on these engines, and they still would have additional capacity."

"We'll let you know about the new stops. In the meantime, we want to go full speed until we get approval for the new stops—just in case they are approved."

"Okay."

They all felt a slight vibration as the ship's engines sped up.

Mike's cell phone was patched through to a satellite phone in the communications center, and he called the LTA Consortium's focal point in New York for landing rights and asked if she could obtain landing rights for the three new stops. She said she had a contact at the China National Tourism Administration and promised to have an answer the next day as China was usually very accommodating to tourism requests.

Alex was on her satellite-linked cell phone to the "mooring team" who had secured landing rights and built minimal mooring facilities at their planned routes. She discussed the need to find a power source, diesel, and freshwater supplies for their new stops. They said they had an agent in China and should be able to handle that with no problem.

Mike reminded Alex about the anchors. "We have enough cannon charges to fire the anchors twice. That won't be enough for all the new sites."

"I'm sure we can find what we need in Beijing. I'll start an Internet search for what we need ASAP."

The Columbus could make an emergency landing by firing anchor bolts into the ground, not all that different from a ship's anchor, and letting the landing computer pull them down. That wasn't an elegant a solution as a regular mooring site, but doable.

The next day, landing rights had been secured to add Xi'an, China, (to see the Terra- cotta Warriors) and Hong Kong and Shanghai, China, (for their unique history) prior to the planned stop in Tokyo. When it was announced, passengers were delighted and excitedly informed their friends and families of the new tour stops. By cruising at 110 mph, the Columbus covered the 3,872 miles to Beijing in one and a half days. The consortium had already received permission for the Columbus to fly over the Great Wall, and it seemed almost every passenger and crew member that could was looking out a window at one of the modern wonders of the world.

Entertainment staff on the ship rescheduled the tours in Beijing for the early arrival and planned tours for the new landing sites. The portions of the tour from Tokyo to Los Angeles and Los Angeles to New York were not affected. Alex easily found new anchor cannon charges in Beijing (fireworks were invented in China more than 2,700 years ago).

Columbus's new stops were added to the LTA Consortium's Web site to show the flexibility of the LTA vessels to land virtually anywhere in the world (with local permissions). The stops in all the new Asian cities went flawlessly and virtually 100 percent of the passengers left the ship for prearranged tours. Mike and Alex especially enjoyed tours of the Terracotta Warriors and Shanghai. They enjoyed Hong Kong but wished they had more time to visit as there was so much to see.

Unknown to the passengers, between two of the new stops, Erik found a leak in a fuel line that was spraying diesel in the mechanical room. A hydrocarbon leak detector had sounded an alarm, and luckily, the leak was caught before the diesel contacted a hot surface on one of the generator's exhaust manifolds. Erik asked for a private meeting with Mike and Alex.

"This was no accident. Someone deliberately loosened the fuel line connections. If the hydrocarbon alarm had not worked, diesel fumes could have caught on fire on the engine. That would put an end to this trip."

Alex and Mike were shocked and just stared at Erik until Alex called Paul Stevens, the head of security, on her radio and explained what happened.

"Can you put a guard on the mechanical room 24 -7?" Paul thought for a moment. "I really don't have enough security personnel for that and maintain normal security while we're moored, but I could bring some additional guys on board at Tokyo to handle it."

Mike nodded, and Alex replied, "Let's do that. We can't afford any more sabotage attempts like this."

That seemed a reasonable plan, and Paul immediately made flight arrangement for an additional four security guards. Availability in the crew quarters was also an issue, but they would find room for them somewhere.

Halfway between Shanghai and Tokyo, Erik made another disturbing discovery. He found a lock on the grey water system cabinet filed most of the way through. Someone was trying to access the grey water system, which collected water from the sinks and showers of the bathrooms, purified it, and made it available again to the showers. Why would someone try to access that system? Erik examined the other cabinets and found a small communication wiring cabinet lock that had been filed through, with some grimy fingerprints near the cabinet latch. Inside, he found a small vial with a brown liquid in it and took it to the medical center. They weren't exactly set up to do that sort of analysis, but maybe they could still help in identifying the brown gooey material.

The medical center identified the brown gooey material as low-level botulism. When asked what would happen if the material had been added the grey water return system, the physician in charge said it would appear as if everyone on the ship had come down with a bad stomach virus. However, if the sick were not treated immediately, it was possible a few elderly persons or persons with damaged immune systems could die.

Erik, Mike, and Alex held an emergency meeting with Paul Stevens and his security team in the command center to discuss the ongoing security problem. All these attempts at sabotage were the work of someone with access to the mechanical room and enough knowledge of ship systems to damage them without immediately endangering himself.

Paul had purchased several push button locks in Beijing and added a lock on each mechanical room door so that a badge had to be scanned and the correct code entered on the push button lock to enter the room. Only mechanics could now enter on their own. Others would have to have an escort.

At midpoint on the tour, Alex was looking forward to Los Angeles, where Max would re-board. She had thought a lot about it and wanted to see if Max was as interested as Tom had suggested. She was determined to change her attitude toward possible relationships.

27

Seattle

Max returned to Manhattan from his hedge fund business and found a certified mail package from Lindsey. He dreaded opening it, but it was about the possible joint venture with the lightbulb entrepreneurs. Lindsey had taken some preliminary information from Max and Tom Babineaux and, in a spreadsheet, determined the cost of a full-scale factory to manufacture the bulbs at $900 million. In an accompanying note, she asked Max about forming a consortium to fund the factory and $100 million for advertising and to fund meetings with several large hardware chains and retail businesses to sell them. She wanted him to set up an investor meeting with a pool of potential investors whom Lindsey would invite to the meeting. He wondered why she needed him at all if she were inviting all the attendees. His usual investors couldn't be invited to the meeting anyway as they were too heavily invested in the LTA Consortium to take on a new risky venture. He wondered if Tom wanted in on this deal.

Tom Babineaux supervised the "nuts and bolts" of Max's deals. Max's contract services company often filed paperwork with government agencies, applied for permits, even rented office space when it was required. Tom had often invested a lot of his own money when he understood the deal, and he thought it had a reasonable chance of success. Although he had accumulated a lot of money, he wasn't independently wealthy yet, but he was on his way. In a few years, he hoped to either be retired or the head of his own investment company. Max asked Lindsey if Tom could attend so he could work on the business side of the consortium, and she agreed.

Max was also worried about losing control again with Lindsey and ruining whatever chance he had with Alex. It was bound to come up in Lindsey's and Alex's routine e-mails and phone calls. All the Schultz women seemed to be pretty close. He knew little about Robert yet as no one seemed to want to talk about him. He called Lindsey to discuss the meeting she wanted to set up in Seattle and sent her an e-mail with some comments and suggestions for the investor presentation.

One week later, Max and Tom met Lindsey at a hotel's bar in Seattle to prepare for the meeting, and even when Max and Lindsey were alone, Lindsey didn't say a word about their night in Houston. She was all business. Max had a prior hedge fund commitment for dinner, and Tom asked Lindsey if they could talk more about the consortium at dinner, and she agreed.

Lindsey ordered margaritas for them, and Tom admitted it was his favorite drink. That started Lindsey wondering what else they had in common. Max had provided a résumé of Tom's experience, putting his deals together in case any of Lindsey's investors had concerns. Before they left for dinner, he left for the restroom, and she checked his Facebook page and marital status. She wondered why a good-looking guy like Tom wasn't married. She would try to find out without being too obvious.

During dinner, she discovered the reason he was still single was the same as hers. He happened to ask why she was still single first.

"Most of the guys I meet in my business are young geeks or older investors or businessmen. Most of the businessmen are married or were married and not interested in marrying again. At least that's what they say. It's hard to meet someone my age that's still single."

That sounded oddly familiar to Tom. He had even heard Max say similar things a few times.

"What about online dating sites?"

"I've tried a few, but the guy who shows up is never anything like his profile. Most of them just want a one-night stand or a physical relationship."

She finished her drink. "What about you, Tom?"

"My story is very similar. You'd think it would be easy to meet women in Manhattan, but I don't like the bar scene, and the few businesswomen I meet aren't pretty and smart like you."

That shocked Lindsey. What did he say?

He saw her expression and laughed. "Yes, I think you're beautiful, Lindsey."

She tried to calm down and sat for a moment, then put her hand on his. "Don't go anywhere. I'll be right back." She went to the bathroom and reapplied her nighttime makeup to calm down. She hadn't been this excited about someone in a long time. He was cute, and as one of Max's close investor buddies, he was probably loaded. And, he thought she was beautiful! She would have to be careful not to scare him off. Lindsey had done that a few times when she met a guy and immediately thought or hoped he was the right one and then got too aggressive and scared him off. She didn't want that to happen with Tom. She returned to the table, and Tom was gone! *What the hell?* She wondered if he had left, but he was returning from the restroom and walked up behind her and kissed her on the cheek. She jumped and turned around, saw him, and kissed him in the restaurant, not caring what anyone else thought. When the check came, Tom paid it, and they hurried to her apartment to take it to the next level— whatever that turned out to be.

When they all met the next day with the investors, Lindsey and Max took turns presenting the case for taking the new bulb concept to mass production and competing against the major LED and CF bulb manufacturers. Tom presented some ideas on how the consortium would function and what was expected of passive and active investors.

Max was heavily invested in the LTA Consortium and could only participate in this venture as a minor investor. When asked about his role in the consortium, he said Lindsey and he would both be active partners. Lindsey, Max, and Tom's detailed presentation and Max's participation as an active partner convinced enough investors to join, that Lindsey called the entrepreneurs after the presentation to tell them the good news.

After the meeting, Max hurried to the airport to head for Hawaii. He wanted to surprise Alex and join the tour early. Tom and Lindsey went to lunch to talk about setting up the consortium and starting on the factory. Eventually, the discussion deviated to their night together, and they both agreed it had been fun, and they should get together again. Tom wanted to set up another trip to Seattle to be with her and work on the consortium. They compared calendars, and a few weeks later, Tom was heading for Seattle for a week of business mixed with pleasure.

28

Midway on the World Tour

In the original world tour in 1929, the Graf Zeppelin stopped in Tokyo for six days for minor repairs, restocking and refueling. In this world tour, the consortium scheduled a two-day stopover to allow the passengers to make overnight excursions in Japan and multiple day tours of Tokyo. All passengers returned on time at the end of the second day, and the ship left precisely as planned. Twenty-four hours after the Columbus left Tokyo for Hawaii, Alex was in her office absorbed in her 3-D design program when she noticed something had changed. Were the engines not running? She looked at a GPS clock on the wall in her office—9:00 p.m. local time. She hurried to the mechanical room and found Erik with an exasperated look.

"What's wrong, Erik?"

"You are not going to believe this. Someone swapped the water ballast lines and the diesel fuel lines and manually dumped most of our fuel into the ocean. We only have enough for another few hours, so I've cut the engines back to give us some time."

Alex stared at Erik in disbelief. "How is that even possible?"

"I wouldn't have thought it possible because normally it wouldn't be. Someone actually found two fuel lines in the spare parts inventory and hooked them into the fuel and ballast lines. That gave them the added length to do it. We've fixed it, but that still doesn't solve the fuel problem."

"What about returning to Tokyo?"

"That's probably not possible as it's more than twelve hundred miles now."

The nearest possible landing site was considerably off course. "Can we make it to Guam?"

"I'm not sure. I think our only chance is to run on one generator and transfer the other generator's diesel to the engine's tanks. Even then, I'm not sure."

"How could this happen? What about the new security guards we brought on in Tokyo?"

"I don't know. Maybe they weren't on station yet."

Alex knew she would have to figure out a way to tell the passengers the problem. She told Erik she would let him know what the command staff decided. Mike Hovenski and his officers met Alex in the command center and discussed possibilities. Guam was about eight hundred miles to the south of their current course. Making it to Hawaii was not even remotely possible—as it was almost three thousand miles.

"What about a refueling from a surface vessel?" asked Alex. "The navy has refueling vessels…"

Mike shrugged. "It's never been done, but I know, everything we do seems to fit into that category. Who would I even call to ask?"

"Let me check." Alex had her tablet out and searched the Internet for a phone number at the US naval base on Guam.

Technicians patched her cell phone into a satellite phone in the ship's communication center, and a few minutes later, she was talking to one of the base's officers. She described the problem and asked if they had a way to refuel the Columbus. He said there was a vessel available if they could deviate from their current course. He gave them the coordinates, and Mike entered them into the chart table's GPS system. They were still almost five hundred miles from the refueling vessel. Alex called Erik and asked if they could make it that far if they ran on one generator and flew at a fuel optimum height and speed. After some calculations, he replied that it appeared they could just make it. Alex asked Erik to make the fuel transfers and made an announcement over the public address that an onboard generator had prematurely failed and they needed to run on one until the other one was fixed. This would require they turn off all nonessential lighting and equipment. She asked everyone to return to their staterooms for the night so they wouldn't be stumbling about in the dark.

Nine hours later, as the sun was just rising over the horizon, the Columbus slowly descended through the clouds from its fuel optimum cruise height until it was about two hundred feet above the ocean. According to their navigation charts, they were still about fifty miles from the refueling vessel that was cruising at max speed to meet them. Erik called Alex via radio to tell her they had less than thirty minutes of fuel left in the generators and even less than that in the engine's tanks. When all power was lost, the ship would start to float almost like a hot air balloon wherever the wind took them.

It was a little foggy, but fortunately, there were no storms in the area. Just before the last of the diesel ran out, they spotted the refueling ship in the distance. It was a race to see if they could make it before the fuel ran out. The last engine conked out as they neared the tanker, and they could feel the wind pushing them in the wrong direction. Mike knew he had one chance and maneuvered one of the anchor cannons with a joystick. Alex held her breath as Mike fired the emergency anchor, and the landing bolt flew over the ship and splashed into the sea. Sailors on the tanker quickly gathered in the line and secured it. Mike had to connect the control center's battery backup system to operate the anchor's winch to pull them the remaining distance to the tanker. The sailors on the tanker were taking pictures of the Columbus; they had never seen anything that big in the air. By carefully deflating a few gas bags and slowly drawing the line in, Mike could bring the Columbus almost to the deck of the tanker. Once overhead, they dropped a fuel line. They pumped enough diesel to the generator to get it started before the battery backup system and the pump on the fuel line ran out of power. Once Erik got a generator running, they pumped enough diesel aboard to make it to Guam. Alex and Mike thanked the tanker captain by radio and released the anchor cable. The consortium had already agreed to reimburse the navy for the fuel. The Magellan rose to its usual cruise height, and all electrical systems were restored throughout the ship. Alex asked the head of security about the new sabotage attempt, and he said he thought he knew who was responsible. He just needed a little more time to prove it.

The unplanned stop at Guam to refuel allowed the passengers to leave on short self-guided tours of the island. Each passenger was informed of the return deadline, so the ship could make up the lost time and still arrive in Hawaii on time. Three days and 3,950 miles later, the ship was in visual range of the Hawaiian Islands. Many cruise ships stopped in Hawaii, but none could fly over an active volcano as the Columbus could. It even circled the volcano before landing at its mooring center on Maui. Most passengers left for day tours, and Max surprised Alex by rejoining the tour. As he entered, he passed a crewman in handcuffs being escorted off the ship by two security officers. He wondered what had happened. He was even more surprised when Alex hugged and kissed him in front of the crew as soon as she saw him.

The lounge was empty, and Alex brought coffee for them as he settled into a couch near a large window. She even sat next to him and kissed him again before she handed him coffee.

"I've thought a lot about Paris."

He stared at her but didn't reply immediately. He had no idea what she was going to say. When she didn't say anything else, he replied, "So have I."

"I've missed you, Max. When you left in Vienna without saying good-bye, I realized I made a mistake. I'm really glad you're back." She put her hand on his.

After almost three years of trying to let her know he cared about her, she was suddenly telling him she cared too. He was so shocked he just stared at her until she smiled. Then it came to him.

"Do you think the crew could get along without you on the rest of the tour?"

She thought about that. "I think so if saboteurs don't finally wreck the ship."

He frowned. "Do you mean the syrup in the diesel generator's tanks?"

He didn't know about the reprogramming of the navigation system or the loosened connection spraying diesel on the generators or the attempt to make everyone ill by contaminating the shower system or the swapping of the engine fuel lines with the ballast tank lines and the dumping of most of their fuel and their mad dash to meet the navy tanker and refuel at sea. When she told him what happened, he was suddenly angry. "What! We will find who is doing this if we have to haul every member of the crew to the police station and interrogate them one by one."

"Paul Stevens said he thinks he knows who it is but needs more time to prove it."

"Let's help him then."

Max took her hand, and they went to find the head of security.

Paul Stevens was in his office when Max came in looking pretty unhappy. Right behind him, Alex was also looking pretty grim. "Hi, Max…Alex. I think I know why you're here.

I want to show you something."

He pressed a few buttons and a monitor on the wall of his office played a time-stamped video of the mechanical room.

"I put several hidden cameras in the mechanical room after syrup was found in the generator tanks. Look at this."

The video showed one of the crew looking around to make sure no one was looking and measured the fuel lines on the generator.

"There is no record of a mechanic badging into the room around this time."

"How did he get in?"

"We don't know that yet."

"Well, where is he now?"

"We have several people guarding the entrances and exits to the crew quarters. He should be in his quarters. We told most of the crew they couldn't leave the ship in Hawaii until the investigation into the fuel dumping was concluded."

Alex moved closer to the monitor. "I've seen this person somewhere."

Max and Paul both turned to her. "Where?" asked Paul.

"I swear he looks like one of the designers at the company Brad Wilson hired in Miami who said they could build an LTA vessel in two years."

"What!" That seemed impossible to Max.

"I once asked Brad about the design company in Miami, and he e-mailed me a photo of the company's design team when they kicked off Brad's project. He sure looks like the guy who was standing next to Brad."

Max was livid. "That low-life scumbag!"

"Calm down, Max. We'll turn him over to the police once we have enough evidence against him."

Paul was paged on his radio. "Yes? No!"

Alex was near Paul but couldn't quite make out the conversation. "What is it?"

Paul ended the call. "Our guys just looked in his cabin, and he's gone. The team found some of the louvers missing in a bathroom window near the crew buffet. He must have gotten out that way."

Alex frowned. "Isn't that at least a thirty-foot drop to the ground?"

Paul pulled his radio out of a holster and sent a team to find him. "He won't get far if he's hurt."

It didn't take the team long to find the missing crewman. He had broken a foot in the fall and was limping away from the mooring site. They quickly brought him back to the medical center and then to a small "secure area" in lowest level of the ship. Max, Alex, and Paul confronted him. After they took turns threatening to turn him over to the police where he would be charged with several criminal acts endangering the lives of the passengers on the ship, he finally admitted everything including making a clone of Erik's badge. No one looked at Erik's mechanical room accesses. Paul called the Maui police, who took him into custody and left for the police station to fill out a detailed report.

Max and Alex returned to her office, where he wanted to test her new attitude. He motioned her to sit down at her desk. She wondered what was wrong that she had to sit down. He sat down on the visitor's chair, hoping she could accept the deal that was finally nearing completion with Aurora.

"What's up, Max?"

"Two things. You may have heard that Lindsey and I have formed a new consortium to mass-produce a new type of lightbulb that is much more efficient than an LED bulb."

Alex nodded. "She e-mailed about that." She shrugged. "There must be a lot of money to be made, or you wouldn't do it."

Max was watching her carefully, but she didn't seem interested. He wondered what else Lindsey said in that e-mail. "Okay, I also wanted you to be among the first to know that the consortium will sell the LTA Company to one of the largest cruise lines in the world."

She jumped up. "What?"

"Now don't get too excited. I want to explain what's happening." He stood up and paced around the small room.

"I'm basically all in the LTA Company as are most of the regular investors whom I work with, along with the new investors we took on this time. We've come to the point where we need to build three or four more graphene-based ships to make the venture viable long term, and I don't think we can do it without going to the banks and forming a joint venture. Once the banks are involved, they will slowly take over control, and we would then be minority partners with little say in the day-to-day operations. So it makes sense now to sell to a company with really deep pockets that can take on the expansion and integrate the dirigibles in with their regular cruise ships. They have the necessary infrastructure to handle it." She was furious and folded her arms but didn't say anything. "I know what you must be thinking, something like, 'This is the thanks I get for getting the whole thing off the ground.'" He was glad she didn't have a Krav Maga weapon handy.

"Which cruise line?"

"The Aurora Cruise Line."

She immediately thought of Brad Wilson's first visit. Now a lot of things were making sense. Cruise line CEOs don't just show up in your office at random wanting to meet you… or offer you a job…or ask you out.

"We want to take the profits of the sale and invest in your city in the sky. With this money, we can go big and even bypass the prototype platform you had in mind if you want to."

"How will we shuttle people to and from the city without the dirigibles?"

"The new owners agreed to provide this service at their cost. We would let them rent some apartments in the new city for their guests and the condo owners get a ride to the city. It's a real win-win deal."

She felt her anxiety level fading away. At least she still had a job, and the prospect of designing and building a full-blown city floating a mile or more above the earth was exciting.

"Okay. What's the plan going forward?"

He breathed a sigh of relief as he didn't have a prayer of making the floating city work without her. He had discussed the city with Tom, and they agreed the floating city could be the biggest money-making project the consortium would ever do. Now…the hard part.

"There is one condition to the deal. They want your help to transition their ship designers and engineers to work on LTA technology."

"What? You can't be serious!"

"It's only for a year. You'll be in the same office, same lab, and the same factory as before. The only difference is you'll be directing and coordinating Aurora personnel. After the transition, you'll return to the consortium, probably in New York."

She didn't like it, but at least she would be in familiar surroundings, and there didn't appear to be anything she could do about it. "I want a letter guaranteeing I can return after a year."

"Of course, we'll get that started immediately." Max almost laughed at the thought the consortium would let her get away—that he would let her get away.

He handed her a spreadsheet. "Don't tell anyone yet, as the details of the sale are still confidential, but the ballpark price is around seven billion." Alex was so surprised she almost dropped the spreadsheet.

"That is a breakdown of the sale for each investor. You recall that the consortium awarded you a one percent ownership share in appreciation of all your efforts?"

Alex nodded as she scanned the list. Max was naturally at the top of the list as the largest investor at slightly over 40 percent. Alex found her name near the bottom and stared in disbelief that her 1 percent ownership was worth at least seventy million dollars.

"Congratulations. You are now a very wealthy woman. Personally, this is by far the biggest profit I have ever made on any deal." After all expenses, Max's initial take of $2.8 billion would still result in an after-taxes profit of over a billion. Not exactly a ten-to-one return on investment but not bad for three years of work.

Alex sat down, shocked at the turn of events. She had never had much money or ever based anything she did with the purpose of making money.

"I was thinking, you said the crew could finish the trip without you?"

"Yes?"

"How about getting off here in Maui and taking some time off. I have a house here."

She stared at him for a moment. "Vacation here, with you?"

"Yes, for a week or so. Then you could go back to Houston and work on the design of the next vessel or your sky city, whatever you want."

Her initial thought was to say no, but then she would be back to her old routine of saying no to everyone who wanted to spend some time with her. She was determined to break that cycle. It was definitely time for a change.

"Sure. Just give me a few minutes to pack."

"Can I help?"

"Yes, would you tell Mike what's going on?"

"Of course."

She kissed him, and Max watched her walk off humming to herself. He smiled and left to find Mike Hovenski and pack his own stuff.

29

Hawaiian Vacation

Max was driving a red Ferrari 458 Spider convertible on the winding coastal road near the Haleakala Volcano. Alex watched him spin through the seven forward gears with ease. Maybe he raced cars. He had the top down, and Alex tied her hair behind in a ponytail. "Nice car…"

"It sort of came with the house. I helped a hedge fund manager once, and he made a pile of money. He was so grateful he gave me the house and this car."

"Gave it to you?"

"Yes, he built a much bigger house. I don't know why, as this place is really big."

"Doesn't it cost a fortune to keep a house you only use a few times a year?"

"Normally, but I don't have a mortgage, only taxes and insurance and a small staff, and I rent it out to friends several times a year, so it's pretty much a wash on cost."

Alex shook her head. That was probably child's play for Max, but until now, she never had enough money to risk it in real estate investments like that.

Max's house was enormous and ultramodern. He handed her a tropical drink, and they strolled onto the balcony to watch the setting sun. She could get used to this.

The swimming pool temperature was perfect. Not too hot, not too cool. He relaxed in it while Alex took a call. He had to stare when she came out to the lanai, shed a bathrobe, and stepped into the pool. She could easily be a model in a swimsuit photographic shoot. She knew enough about his workday and odd eating habits that she was surprised that he was in such excellent shape (she couldn't remember very much about their night in Paris). They just enjoyed the pool and a pitcher of margaritas for a while without saying much. Max had developed a taste for margaritas, sort of.

She was feeling a little dizzy from too many drinks and almost fell as she climbed out of the pool. He caught her and held her for a moment. Their embrace naturally turned into a kiss, then a series of kisses. She tried to regain some willpower, but it was no use. They were hopelessly entangled until he carried her to the master bedroom.

The sun was shining when she woke up, and she immediately realized where she was and what undoubtedly had happened, but Max wasn't there. She heard him on the phone in the living room and started to jump out of bed, but there was a cool early morning ocean breeze blowing in through an open window, and she was warm under the blankets. While trying to remember what happened, she laid there and listened to the distant ocean waves and the sounds of seagulls until the she had to go to the bathroom. She found a bathrobe and went to see him.

Max was in the living room, on the phone completing the deal to sell the LTA Consortium with Tom Babineaux when he heard Alex rustling around and the door to the bathroom close. He wondered what her reaction would be to last night. He swallowed hard when she sat down on a sofa in front of him and waited until he hung up. She seemed surprisingly calm. He put the phone in a pocket of his bathrobe and smiled. "How are you?"

"I'm okay. So why did you really ask me to go on vacation with you?"

"We've been together in many business meetings and even had a few private moments, but it's mostly been about business, except for Paris, and I want to get to know more about you."

"I hate to keep asking this, but why?"

He sat down on the sofa next to her. "I've wondered about you since the first time we met in your office. You've proven remarkably adept at everything—with the possible exception of business. I was in a relationship at the time, and I knew that you were too—with the guy who leads adventure trips for Outbound?"

"Bill Allen. But how did you know we finally broke up?"

"He has a Facebook page…"

Alex's eyes widened. "That bastard! We broke up just before the round-the-world tour." She glared at Max. "Are you monitoring his Facebook page?"

"I asked someone to check on it from time to time."

"Why would you do that?"

He took Alex's hand. "Because I've been waiting a long time to ask you something, and I'm not used to waiting for anything."

Alex glanced at his hand holding hers, then at Max. "What?"

"Would you consider giving a relationship a try?"

It sure seemed Tom Babineaux was right. She hesitated. "Are you sure, Max?"

"Yes, I think we could have a really great time together. We could take it as slow as you like."

"Let me think about it."

"You don't have to answer now."

She stared at him while a thousand possibilities ran through her mind. How did she really feel about him? Was he serious? Could he be trusted? The physical side of a relationship wasn't an issue. She couldn't remember much of what happened last night or in Paris, but everything she could remember was good. After a few minutes, the logical side of Alex concluded the scales were tipped in favor of a relationship. After all, if things didn't work out, she could break it off. But she had a few lingering doubts.

"Could I ask you something?"

"Anything."

"You have a history of short-term relationships, mostly with models but also with some businesswomen. I know about you and Lindsey."

Max felt a sudden dread coming on. He thought about using her excuse of not remembering anything because of too many drinks. She saw the concern or anxiety on his face and interrupted his thoughts on a possible excuse.

"Don't worry. Lindsey admitted you both had been drinking some pretty strong margaritas and probably could not resist when she asked you to spend the night. By the way, she can't remember very much about that night. She found your car keys on a chair in her bedroom. That's the only reason she knew you were there."

Damn. That's what happened to the rental car keys. The next day, he couldn't find them and had to pay the rental car company three times the cost of the rental to replace the lost electronic car keys. "I was drunk, and that's not an excuse. It's just that she looks so much like you. I couldn't say no."

Alex laughed. "I guess that's a compliment in a weird sort of way, but, Max, how do I know that after I've invested a lot into the relationship, you won't just tire of me after a while?"

"I wouldn't be asking you about a relationship unless I was sure, and I don't think it's even possible for me to tire of you. For the record, I never could tell if a woman was interested in me or my money. I know for a fact you don't care about money, and now that you have a lot of money, you don't need mine."

Oh, that's right. She forgot that she now had more money than she knew what to do with. She began to see him in a different light. Maybe he was serious.

"Okay. I'm willing to give it a try."

Max jumped up and pulled her to her feet and kissed her.

After a few seconds, she kissed him back. She laughed when he picked her up and carried her into the bedroom.

Things moved faster in Hawaii than even Max would have thought. The deal to sell the LTA Consortium assets and selected patents was finally completed and awaiting his signature. Max and Alex spent the rest of the week sightseeing, eating in the finest restaurants, and not getting much sleep at night.

On the night before they were scheduled to return, they went to dinner early so the late-night fun could start earlier. While they waited for the waiter, he was watching her as she read the menu. She had spent part of the day in a beauty salon and was wearing a low-cut black dress that almost made his mouth water at the prospects for the night. He was almost at a decision point when she glanced up at him and smiled. Something about her smile made him decide to risk their newfound relationship and his promise she could take it as slow as she wanted.

He put his hand on hers and picked it up, pretending to look at it. She didn't have a clue what he was thinking.

"There's something missing."

"What?"

"This." He reached into his suit coat pocket and took out a small black jewelry box and put it in her hand. Her eyes grew wide, and she started to hand it back.

"Max…"

"Open it."

The box held a large diamond engagement ring that sparkled even in the dim lighting of the restaurant. She felt her heart racing as she knew she wasn't quite ready for that step.

"You said we could take it slow."

"I know. But you're everything I want, and it's too hard to wait. I love you, Alexandra Schultz. Will you marry me?"

Alex was so conflicted she couldn't answer. A part of her wanted to jump up and hug him; another part wanted to wait and see how their relationship developed.

"I love you too, Max. Just give me a little time to figure this out."

Finally, she said it…and she was sober. "Okay. But please hold on to it while you figure it out."

She took the ring out and stared at it. She had never seen such a large perfect diamond before, and when she glanced up at Max, he smiled at her. She put it back in the box and the box into her purse.

"I don't know if I can eat anything now. My stomach is a mess…"

He laughed and put his hand on hers. She put her other hand on top of his.

"Just out of curiosity, when did you buy the ring?"

"This afternoon while you were at the beauty salon."

He returned to the menu, and when he looked away, she smiled.

Alex woke up and slipped quietly out of bed and into the bathroom. When she came back, Max was sound asleep, and she sat on the bed staring at him. What was she going to do? The ring box was beside the bed, and she opened it and slid the ring on her finger. How did he know her ring size? Was there anything he didn't know about her? She stared at the ring for a while. Even in the low light, the large diamond seemed to sparkle. She almost laughed out loud at the change in her relationship to Max in just a week. Yes, she had known him for over three years, but their relationship had rarely strayed very much from business, except for Paris, and she wasn't expecting this. She jumped when he woke and asked her, "How does it fit?"

"It's perfect. How did you know my ring size?" She laughed when he replied, "I have sources."

He took her hand and pulled her to him. "Say yes, Alex. I promise to do everything I can to make you happy."

"Can I ask you something?"

"Anything."

"Why me? You've dated numerous models and movie and TV stars. Why would you want to marry me?"

Max had to think about that one. "I never could see myself growing old with them, and a physical relationship alone doesn't last. I'm happy when I'm with you and think about you all the time when we're apart. I've never felt that way about anyone before I met you."

She leaned over, kissed him, and whispered, "Yes."

They spent the rest of the night celebrating their engagement. On the flight back to Houston in Max's private jet, Alex fell asleep while snuggled next to him. He put his arms around her, wondering how their lives would change from this point on. As he stared at the ring on her finger, he knew he had no regrets or doubts. She was the one.

30

Dana and Mike

A few weeks later, the Columbus finished its round-the-world tour in New Jersey and Mike Hovenski returned to Houston for a short vacation. He was carrying the napkin Max had given him and, from the airport, dialed the number. He was almost speechless when Alex answered the phone. How was that possible? As directed, he told her Max sent him to help. Dana gave him the address of the shelter and said she looked forward to meeting him. Meeting him?

Mike drove directly to the shelter instead of his apartment. He was surprised that it was a school building. What was Alex doing in a school building? He went inside and asked the receptionist for Alex Schultz. The receptionist thought maybe he was confused and led him to Dana's office. Dana was filling out a grant application when Mike knocked on her open door. "Yes?"

It took a few seconds, but Mike realized she was not Alex.

Before he could introduce himself, Dana recognized him.

"You're Mike…Mike Hovenski."

"How did you know that?"

She walked around her desk to shake his hand. "Alex e-mails me photos all the time. I've seen you in several of them. I'm Dana, Alex's sister."

The resemblance was amazing, and Mike had to remind himself this was not Alex. At first, Mike wondered why Max had told him to say he had come to help until he saw the shelter.

They started a long conversation on Alex, Max, LTA ships, and his role as captain. He asked if he could take her to lunch, and she quickly accepted. After lunch, Dana showed him around, and it turned out Mike was quite a handyman. He asked if he could look at some of the systems with problems, and he fixed some simple things. Dana naturally hugged him and kissed him while thanking him for helping the shelter.

Like Max, Mike was slowly overwhelmed as Dana looked like Alex; she smelled like her and even sounded like her.

When she asked if she could cook dinner for him, what else could he say but yes, and they headed for a grocery to pick up a few things. He was hooked at this point, and Dana was reeling him in.

Aurora Transition

Max effectively moved his hedge fund management and angel investing business to Houston while Alex worked with Aurora personnel to understand LTA technology. He bought a penthouse in a high-rise condo and moved her personal things from her apartment—the rest he donated to charities.

Although their days were busy, they always found time to be together. Although reluctant at first, Alex enjoyed her new position helping Aurora design at least two more LTA vessels based on the graphene design. Jack Armstrong sold his LTA subsidiary (the original factory and the Magellan's hangar) to the Aurora Corporation at a nice profit and returned to airplane design. The Aurora Corporation also bought the new graphene factory and machines from the LTA Consortium and built a new admin building for their LTA engineering and design departments.

Brad Wilson had appeared at Alex's door soon after the sale was completed. He said he was inspecting the cruise line's newly acquired factory and graphene machines and just wanted to stop by and say hello and thank her for agreeing to the transition. Brad immediately noticed the large engagement ring and complimented her on it.

"Max?"

She nodded.

"No surprise. He's a lucky man." Alex smiled, and Brad wondered if he could ever beat Max at something. But that thought soon vanished, and he left to call Ashley to see if she knew Alex and Max were engaged.

Shortly after Brad left, a well-dressed young man appeared at her office door with two armed guards. *What now?* She stood up as he entered, followed by the two guards. "Can I help you?"

"Are you Alexandra Schultz?"

"Yes?"

He held up a picture and looked at her and the picture.

"I'm Erik McAllen of Thompson, Atkins, and Smith. I have a certified package for you."

He handed her what appeared to be a certified package with a cover document with an *x* next to her signature line.

She signed it, and he held out his hand. "Congratulations, Ms. Schultz."

She shook his hand, and as they left, she opened the package and took out a letter and what looked to be a money market account record book and an ordinary checkbook issued by one of the largest banks in the US. The letter explained the taxes taken out from her distribution share of the LTA assets. The balance in the money market account book was $56 million ($70 million minus 20 percent for capital gains taxes). She opened the checkbook, and the beginning balance was $750,000. She fell back into the chair and almost passed out. The reality of the sale finally hit her. When she recovered, she called Tom Babineaux and asked if he could help her invest the money. He promised he would stop by with some investment choices the next time he was in Houston. He also congratulated her on the success of the LTA sale.

Later that same day, Max stopped by her office. Alex was rearranging the furniture in her new office for the tenth time when he entered. He kissed her, and they hugged for a moment.

"So is this a drive-by kiss, or did you have something more in mind?"

He pulled a brochure out of his pants pocket. "I just got a call from one of my racing buddies inviting me to the qualification time trials for the Houston Grand Prix. The time trials are tomorrow. Do you want to go? He can get us some pit passes."

"That'd be great!"

"Wear something cool. It'll be hot tomorrow."

She slowly shook her head. "I grew up in Houston, Max."

31

Grand Prix Race

It was a hot sunny day, and while walking from the parking lot to the grand prix course, Alex commented to Max that she was hotter than a lizard on a sunny rock. Max laughed, and Alex took off a lightweight jacket and stuffed it into a large shoulder bag and put on a big floppy hat and Ray-Ban sunglasses. Max was looking for his racing buddies and didn't notice she was wearing a halter top, shorts, and sandals until there were some wolf whistles from nearby pit crew members as they walked behind pit row. The lead driver of the Apache Racing Team, Jake Williams, was talking to a reporter when he saw Max and Alex. He waved, ended the interview, and hurried over to shake Max's hand. He took off his sunglasses as he approached, so Alex took off her Ray-Bans.

"Long time no see, Max. Are you still driving with the Harrods's Le Mans team?"

"Yeah, but I can only find time for a few races a year."

Jake smiled at Alex. "And who is this?"

"This is Alexandra Schultz, my fiancée."

He shook her hand and glanced at Max. "It's about time, Max."

Jake had seen Max with some hot models. Alex seemed to be another one. "Are you a model too?"

Alex had some mixed emotions at being introduced to Max's racing buddies. Did they assume he would only date models? "No, I'm an engineer."

That was too incredible for Jake, and he laughed. "What kind of engineer?"

"I used to design business jets…more recently lighter-than-air cruise ships."

The incredulous look on Jake's face made Alex and Max laugh.

"No, really, what do you do?"

Max answered for her, "Have you heard of the Magellan cruise vessel?"

Jack thought for a moment. "Is that the one that crashed on an island?"

That was a downer for Alex and Max. "No, it's the one that flies all over North America."

A lightbulb came on. "Oh, yeah. I've heard of that one."

"She designed it."

Jake laughed loudly. "Right! Come on, what do you really do?"

Before Alex or Max could answer, Jake's backup driver pulled the race car in for a pit stop.

Alex had to hold on to her hat at the draft created by Jake's car. She leaned toward Jake and spoke loudly over the roar of his car and the cars practicing on the course. "You have a bad valve."

Jake and Max looked confused. So Alex repeated her comment to Jake.

"The engine's fine. Why would you say that?"

"Years of working in the pit while my father raced stock cars, I can tell a bad valve."

Jake looked at Max, who shrugged. "Let's see." He went over to his chief mechanic, and after a brief discussion, the chief mechanic motioned to the driver to shut off the engine, and he opened the engine compartment and hooked an engine analyzer to a diagnostic port. The driver started the engine, and after a few minutes, the mechanic signaled him to turn the engine off. Max and Alex wandered over as the mechanic shook his head and looked at Jake.

"The intake valve on the number five cylinder is sticking a little."

They all looked at Alex, who was standing with her arms folded and an I-told-you-so look on her face.

Even Max was surprised. "I think you should be in my pit crew in Le Mans."

The Houston Grand Prix race was less than eighteen hours away, and Jake and his chief mechanic started an urgent repair of the valve.

"Max, did Jake say your Le Mans sponsor is Harrods of London?"

"Yes, why?"

"I love Harrods! I was in London a few years ago and spent a whole day there! Why didn't you say anything about Harrods when we were in London? Would you take me shopping again—at Harrods?"

He winced. "Maybe I could combine that into a business trip to review the next race with them."

He laughed when Alex commented, "Cheapskate…"

On the way to Max's racing buddies' team, four obviously drunk guys started following Alex and making suggestive remarks. She ignored them for a while and then turned to the apparent leader.

"I'm not your type. I'm not inflatable."

The other guys laughed but not the leader. He called Alex several names before Max intervened to the leader.

"Leave her alone. Find someone else to annoy."

"Why don't you make me?"

"I won't have to. She can take care of herself."

They continued walking when the leader suddenly reached forward and grabbed Alex's rear, laughing. She turned quickly, grabbed his hand, twisted his arm, and kicked him in the rear.

He tumbled to the ground, and the others came to his defense. Alex dodged, kicked, and punched until they were all lying on the ground. Max watched, amused, glad he wasn't the object of her skills. The commotion drew a crowd, and Max handed the large floppy hat to her and urged her to come with him before security arrived. The guys got up and were still looking for Alex and Max when race security showed up and forced them to leave the racetrack area.

Max took Alex's hand and led her to his ex-racing team who were just as incredulous that Alex was Max's chief designer for the LTA Consortium.

As they were walking back to the parking lot, she commented, "I think your racing buddies were surprised you weren't with another model. They must have seen you with quite a few of them."

Max put his arm around her waist. "It just shows, eventually, you can have it all."

She thought about that and chuckled.

Max had leased a Maserati GranCabrio convertible for the year she would work with the Aurora design team and had the top down. She put her window up, and every time he glanced at her, she was staring out her window. "What are you thinking about?"

"Have you ever thought about building a Le Mans Prototype with a graphene body?"

Max almost swerved out of his lane. "Are you serious?"

"Why not? I thought that class of Le Mans cars allowed innovations."

Max thought about that. "Yes, but there is a price limitation of five hundred thousand dollars on the body and one hundred thousand dollars on the engine."

"Hmmm. That could be a problem. Building one of anything out of graphene is extremely expensive, and there is no chance we would build many Le Mans Prototype cars."

An idea came to mind. "Maybe it could be done like they blow-mold plastics?"

"What?"

"You would basically build a mold from an existing Le Mans Prototype body and then blow hot graphene fibers inside until you get the thickness you need. Then you let it cool off and remove the mold."

"Has that ever been done?"

"Of course not! Graphene is still extremely rare."

"Could you make a body for less than five hundred thousand dollars?"

"I'm not sure. Maybe."

"It would probably take a few years to get it through the FIA World Championship committee anyway." He watched her settle back in her seat and close her eyes. He would have laughed a few years ago if someone told him he would have technical discussions like these with his future wife. The discussion reminded him he needed to ask her something.

"Alex?"

She looked at him. "Yes?"

"We've had some feedback from the consortium sales organization on the graphene flyer backpack. There isn't much interest because most commuters don't want to feel like they've been in a windstorm while going to work. Most women don't like the possibility of getting soaked if they had to go to work in the rain."

She thought about the feedback. "Those are legitimate concerns. We could make a small enclosed commuter pod for about twice the price of the backpack, but then it would have to be certified by the FAA and possibly some other authorities."

"The sales team said the demand for a viable commuting alternative is enormous. We are potentially looking at millions of units."

"Okay, I'll find some time and come up with a design." She closed her eyes, and he smiled as he downshifted and wove in and out of the afternoon traffic. He needed the practice for the upcoming Le Mans race.

32

Aurora Graphene Airship

Alex was surprised at the deep pockets of the Aurora Corporation. She could ask for almost anything, and they agreed. It hadn't been that way with the consortium; she needed to review even minor changes in regularly scheduled design meetings to determine the possible cost impact. The impregnated graphene added so much lift she finally could have a small pool on the new vessel. She had almost completed a rough-draft design of an even bigger graphene vessel for 2,500 passengers when Brad showed up with Ashley. Alex was so surprised she jumped up and hugged her and Brad.

"What a surprise! Have a seat. How come you didn't call first?"

Brad was wearing a tuxedo, and instead of her usual fitness outfit or casual clothes, Ashley was wearing a designer dress and matching shoes. "We wanted to surprise you. We are on our way to a party to celebrate the Magellan's fiftieth tour."

Brad watched Ashley pulled a folder out of a large purse.

"While we're in town, we'd like to talk about a much larger graphene airship than the one you are working on."

Alex frowned. "We?"

Ashley laid out some drawings on Alex's desk as Brad continued, "I want to build the largest cruise ship in the world...out of the impregnated graphene, and I asked Ashley to make a few conceptual drawings."

"I don't know if this is even possible from an engineering point of view. I just helped Brad come up with some ideas."

Alex examined several conceptual drawings while Brad explained the details. "The largest cruise ships hold about sixty-five hundred passengers and a crew of three thousand. I'm not sure the Columbus could be scaled up to hold eight or nine thousand passengers, so here are some alternative ideas." One drawing that caught her eye was similar to a wagon wheel with a central hub and ten spokes connecting the hub to the outer wheel. A cutaway view of the wheel was elliptical like the Magellan and the Columbus.

"How big is this?"

Brad pointed to a scale on the bottom of the drawing.

"We didn't get very far with exact details. I'm not sure we even could, but I think the diameter would have to be about two thousand five hundred feet, and the ring width would be four hundred feet wide and two hundred feet tall—like the Columbus. What do you think?"

Alex sat back thinking. "I could make a rough design and let you know. How many passengers do you have in mind?"

"If we made a vessel for twelve thousand passengers and a crew of five thousand, no other line could possibly compete with it. A cruise ship large enough for seventeen thousand persons probably couldn't even dock in most ports, and tendering in from anchor would take too long and be such a logistical problem it just wouldn't make sense. This vessel, as you know, could land anywhere."

"Are you sure you want to tackle something this big? The cost could be prohibitive."

"We might have to form a joint venture with another cruise line, but let's just see if the concept is possible—from an engineering standpoint."

"Okay. This could take several days for a rough-draft design and a week for a preliminary estimate."

"That's great actually. After the party, Ashley and I are going to San Diego for a few days, so that timing would be great. I would then know if I needed to find a joint-venture partner to get it financed or not."

Brad went to make some phone calls while Alex and Ashley shared sisterly secrets about Brad and Max.

The wagon wheel design was a challenge, and Alex liked challenges. She started with Ashley's conceptual drawing with a wheel diameter of twenty-five hundred feet and wheel height of two hundred feet and width of four hundred feet.

That was equivalent to lengthening the Columbus design by almost seven times or eight thousand feet. The sheer length of a vessel like that would pose a huge structural problem just to keep it from flexing over its length. Alex liked the wheel idea with a central hub and connecting spokes as they would give the ship added structural integrity. If she made the spokes large enough, they could even contain shops or other desired features while they added strength to the structure. Graphene was stronger than steel, but there were limitations.

She was totally absorbed in the design until it hit her. There was a reason the front of a dirigible was shaped like a bullet— to slip through the air with minimal motor assist. A round vessel would require an inordinate amount of motive force from many engines to push it through the sky (and require a lot of fuel that would have to be carried from mooring to mooring). She picked up Ashley's folder and made another pass through her other designs until she found another one that seemed promising. It was basically a triangle with one side shorter than the others—effectively a wedge shape. That could work.

She started a new wedge design with the two long sides of fifteen hundred feet and the rear side at one thousand feet. Even with those lengths, she still needed at least fifteen passenger floors to provide over six thousand staterooms for twelve thousand passengers. This would be a massive ship as each floor had over seven hundred thousand square feet for staterooms and common areas (overall 10.5 million square feet in the passenger area alone). The needed common areas would have to be in the middle of each floor to provide windows on the perimeter for as many staterooms as possible. She opened up the middle of the ship to form a massive atrium with five sets of graphene escalators to move numerous passengers quickly between floors. Twenty-five restaurants would be required, as moving twelve thousand people through a few large restaurants would be difficult in the typical two-to three-hour seating allocated for each meal.

Otherwise, the passengers could always choose one of several buffets or fast-food type restaurants that would be available 24/7. She also added regular stairwells made from graphene around the perimeter as required by international occupancy codes for emergency evacuations.

At the end of the week, she had a draft engineering drawing. So far, everything was feasible technically. She had asked the LTA Consortium to help with a rough cost estimate, typically within plus or minus 20 percent of a detailed estimate that would require quotes from manufacturers. There wasn't anything actually new in terms of materials, so they just needed to add it all up—and there were a lot of materials to estimate. After she e-mailed the estimating department with her design drawings and a list of materials, she sat thinking about the design when she saw the folder with Ashley's drawings. She flipped through the drawings one last time and suddenly laughed loudly. The only thing all the drawings had in common was their origin. Ashley had based each design on some eyewitness's drawing of a UFO!

A week later, she received an e-mail from the lead estimator and closed her eyes when she opened it, hoping it wasn't outrageous. She stared at the number for a few minutes then breathed a sigh of relief. It was a big number, just over six billion dollars, but Brad must have guessed it would be that big, based on the cost of the Columbus. The Columbus was $1.5 billion and carried fifteen hundred passengers. Scaling up, a graphene ship carrying twelve thousand passengers should cost about $12 billion. This was about half that. Another way to look at it, this vessel was equivalent to eight Columbus-sized ships. She called his cell phone.

Brad was delighted. He was selling a few older ships to a new and upcoming cruise line eager to get into the business for reasons he couldn't fathom. The sale of those vessels plus the sale of a "secondary" offering of Aurora Cruise Line stock would cover most of the cost of the new cruise vessel design. He was also considering setting up a consortium if the sale of the vessels and the secondary stock sale didn't cover the cost of the new vessel. He was eager to get started on it and asked Alex to do as much as possible on it before her transitional year was over.

That was yet another challenge, and Alex was determined to finish the design before her year was done. She told Max all about Brad and Ashley's visit, the conceptual designs, and the choice to pursue the wedge-shaped design. Max was in a New York meeting with some investors, so she called him to tell him Brad's reaction to the cost estimate and her desire to finish the new vessel's design before her transition year was done. Max listened patiently, then he told her he was already working on a new consortium with Brad to fund the new vessel. He would also need her for the technical part of the presentation to the investors.

When Alex hung up, she shook her head. What was Max not involved in? She dove into the detailed design needed for fabrication and realized that it would be hard to entertain twelve thousand passengers for a week. Even if they all took day tours, there had to be a huge choice of onboard activities when they returned, and the activity areas had to be designed so that parts of the ship would not be crowded, and other parts, empty. A large central atrium with dozens of escalators would play a key role in moving passengers around and avoiding crowded areas. The bottom of the vessel required fifteen stairways that could be lowered while the ship was moored to facilitate twelve thousand passengers exiting quickly. Five sets of escalators in the atrium could bring most exiting passengers to the rear access stairways quickly, and there were fifteen elevators near the rear stairs for handicapped passengers and those who just didn't like escalators. And there were the code-required graphene stairwells spaced around the perimeter for those who preferred regular stairs. There would be ten security lines with scanners for passenger parcels for reentry at the large rear stairway.

Luckily, she could design one basic floor plan for the passenger staterooms and then duplicate it for most of the other floors. The common areas would have to be different on each floor. Some floors had a casino; others had a spa or fitness center, while others had shops or Internet cafés. It seemed reasonable to spread the twenty-five restaurants among the floors near the atrium, so they didn't look like a food court in a mall. The impregnated graphene structure was so large, and there was so much lifting gas required that Alex could finally design a decent swimming pool on the lowest common area.

The quarters for the five-thousand- member crew were also massive and required three floors on the bottom of the vessel. At least this time, there could be regular windows in many of the crew staterooms.

She e-mailed Brad several detailed design drawings, and he seemed eager to start construction as soon as possible. The design required a new construction hangar as the width of the wedge design was more than twice the width of the Magellan or the Columbus.

33

Wedge Design and Wedding Plans

Max put the "bug" in her ear. He didn't want to wait for a long time to get married. He suggested they marry when they returned to New York at the end of her transition with the Aurora personnel.

She was in no hurry. "What's the hurry Max?"

"Why wait?"

"It looks like my mother was wrong when she used to say that a man won't buy the cow if he can get the milk for free."

He was completely lost. "What?"

"Would marriage really change our relationship?"

"No, I just want to get on with that part of my life. Maybe start a family someday."

Alex stared at him. They had never really discussed children. She hadn't really thought much about children. Money wasn't an issue, obviously, and she could work anywhere on her computer, but she just wasn't sure she was ready for that. She tried to explain her reluctance but couldn't express it very well.

"All women are afraid on some level at the idea until they have one."

"I know. Let's just give this some time."

He agreed, but he didn't give up on the possibility of marriage at the end of her transition period.

Alex called Ashley to discuss Max's desire to set a date, and Ashley told her Brad had proposed, and they were also thinking about a date. Maybe they could do a joint wedding? They more they talked about it the more they both liked the idea. They agreed to discuss it with Max and Brad.

After a lot more discussion, they agreed to a joint wedding on the new graphene "wedge" ship. Brad was delighted to combine the ship's first tour with a double wedding. They could invite as many people as they liked as it would have no impact on the total passenger count of twelve thousand. Guests could leave at the next stop or continue on as long as they liked.

Design was completed in less than a year, along with the new hangar, and Alex often visited the hangar to see the ship's frame come together. Although she was intimately involved in the design, she was in still in awe of the new vessel, over six hundred feet high and fifteen hundred feet long. Even though the ship's basic structure was over 75 percent impregnated graphene, the volume of helium gas required was still enormous, at 190 million cubic feet. Tom again reminded Max and Alex their helium extraction plant had saved them almost $16 million, slightly more than the cost the consortium paid to upgrade the facility when they purchased it.

The front of the wedge was about five feet wide, but that still allowed the huge ship to slice easily through the air. The edges in the back were about thirty feet wide, to give some great views from large windows in those staterooms and to allow the company to charge a premium price for them. Alex and Max signed up for a rear-corner stateroom for the first voyage. The rear-corner staterooms were large suites with a separate living room, bathroom, and bedroom. At fifteen hundred square feet, they would be similar to premium cabins in the huge cruise ships the new vessel would compete against.

Graphene LM1 Prototype

Alex said she had a surprise for Max and asked him to stop by the graphene factory. When he walked in, Alex was talking to one of her graphene technicians, and there was something nearby under a white tarp. Alex saw Max and motioned him to come over and said something to the technician.

"I have something to show you." She motioned to the technician who pulled the white cover off and revealed a Le Mans LM1 Prototype racing car body made of graphene. It was black but had a mirror like finish that gleamed in the low light of the factory.

"Wow! It looks great. I haven't heard anything back yet from the racing committee on our application to use graphene, but it sure looks like I now have a reason to make a few phone calls to the committee members. So how does the weight of this prototype compare to a similar body made from fiberglass?"

"It's lighter, but the weight's not all that different. However, a graphene body can take a huge whack and flex back almost to its original shape. You know what would happen to a fiberglass body if it had a big impact."

"Yeah. It would be a goner for sure." Max thought for a moment. "Can you determine how much it cost to make the prototype?"

"Not exactly, but it was definitely less than the five-hundred-thousand-dollar limit."

"How long would it take to put the rest of the car together for a test run?"

"Not too long if I could borrow some of your team's mechanics."

"I'll ask them when they could fly over here. They're currently in Italy. By the way, I don't know if Lindsey told you or not, but that new bulb manufacturing plant is now in operation."

"Yes, she said sales are going great. It looks like you'll make another pile of money…"

He laughed and hugged her, and they left to celebrate the new graphene car body and the success of the new bulb manufacturing.

34

Manhattan Office

At the end of the transition, new Aurora friends threw Alex a going-away party and took turns telling her how much they would miss her. She said she would miss them too.

Max was waiting for her at home. Movers arrived and packed them for the trip to Manhattan. She wasn't sure she wanted to live permanently in New York. But for now, she would have to make the best of it, and Max would be there to help her adjust. Max had moved the headquarters of the LTA Consortium to Manhattan in a suite of offices in the same skyscraper as his hedge fund headquarters. He had high-end workstations installed for each member of the design team Alex was assembling to work on the new floating city.

She was getting settled into her new office when Max entered and reminded her that the Le Mans race was in a few weeks. He had to be there two weeks ahead for a planned "test" of each car and scheduled time trials, and they made plans to meet before the race. She handed him a folder. He opened it, and there was a detailed sketch for a graphene commuter pod.

The basic design was similar to several prototype electric vehicles. It appeared to be an egg standing on one end with four small wheels on the bottom. The non-graphene parts included a small windshield in the front and smaller window behind the passenger's head, along with the main electric motor and a small electric motor for the windshield wipers, and headlights and taillights. The main electric motor for the fans was under the passenger's seat. When the passenger pressed an On button, a large fan assembly on the top lifted up a few feet; then the passenger used a joystick to tilt the fans to control direction, and a slide switch, to control the speed of the fans.

The sketch was fairly detailed, but Max didn't see a battery compartment. "Where's the battery?"

"The whole exterior of the car is a graphene battery."

That was clever. "What's the range of the pod?"

"It's an estimate, of course, but it should carry someone weighing about two hundred pounds for about fifty miles. The battery should be rechargeable in about two hours."

He thought that might be exactly what the sales force needed. "And what's the cost—if we build a million?"

"It's probably about nine to ten thousand dollars each."

"That's excellent." He hugged and kissed her and went off to discuss the pod with the LTA Consortium staff. Besides addressing passenger safety and airworthiness certifications, any new commuter alternative would require extensive government scrutiny before any approval was given. Ironically, most certifying agencies had not considered rules on how to maintain order in the sky, when potentially thousands of commuters would undoubtedly prefer to take the shortest route to their business or to return home. A few police or news station helicopters roaming around in the sky were one thing…Thousands of commuter pods crisscrossing the sky was an entirely new problem.

Max had a vacation home in the Hamptons, and whenever they could, they spent the weekends there. Max's limo driver picked them up from the hedge fund office, and during the ride there, she snuggled next to him.

"Do you remember I once asked you how I should invest all that money from the sale of the consortium's assets?"

"Yes, I said you should find something outside the LTA area you are interested in and put some money in it."

"I have this huge windfall I never expected, and I want to help Dana's shelter with some of it."

"That sounds like a great idea. Just remember she needs a long-term solution, not a short-term fix."

"I know. I asked Tom Babineaux about setting up a trust for the shelter that would give them enough money each year to pay for full-time security guards."

"That's an excellent idea."

"I also want to paint and fix up the shelter some. They could use some new beds too."

He thought for a minute. "Okay. I'll match every dollar you spend on the shelter, but my donation has to go to fixing the utilities like lighting, plumbing, heating, and cooling."

She kissed him. "Thanks. I'm sure Dana will be excited to hear that."

He turned the limo's overhead light out, and she went to sleep in his arms.

35

24 Hours of Le Mans

Alex had never been to Le Mans, France, and thoroughly enjoyed their ornate room at a classical French hotel in the city. She arrived a day prior to the race and met Max at the course. It seemed strange to see him in a uniform. She had researched the race some and tried to dress appropriately for the June event. Several Web sites warned the temperature could be hot, and it had often rained during the event, but she had grown up in Texas and was used to it. He was pleased when she arrived wearing a colorful sun dress, a stylish hat, and comfortable shoes. He introduced her to the pit crew and the other members of the racing team. She had to go through the usual are-you-a-model routine and the usual responses when she told them she was an engineer.

Max had given her a pit pass, but she watched most of the race from one of the viewing stands set up along the racecourse. She had breathed a lot of fumes while she helped her father race stock cars, and those races were only a few hours. The 24 Hours of Le Mans race usually began around three in the afternoon, continued all night, and finished the next day. This was a different kind of race for Alex. First over the finish line didn't apply here. Winning Le Mans was done on distance; the team that completed the most laps in twenty-four hours won. The original purpose of the race was to test the endurance and reliability of the cars. No maintenance was allowed in the first one thousand kilometers of the race. There were four categories of race cars, and Max's LM1 Prototype category was the fastest as it allowed a lot of technical innovations and the largest horsepower engines.

Max was the second driver on the team. Their team was in the middle of the race cars at the beginning of the race, and teammate Sean Graham moved up in the pack in his two-hour stint. Max took over and improved their position slightly. The third-team driver Dave Green at least maintained their position. It would be a long night.

Near the end of Max's first stint, Alex put on a fire-retardant uniform provided by the team and joined him in the pit, offering him food and water. He even found a bench and took a short nap on her lap. As she watched him napping, she smiled at how her life had changed in just a few years. All those years of working at night on an idea for a new type of cruise ship had certainly paid off. Tom Babineaux had given her a lot of ideas for investing the money from the sale of the dirigibles, factory, and hangars. Now she could help her sister, and with Max's help, they should be able to put the shelter on solid financial basis. She still hadn't figured out what to do with the rest of her windfall, but there was no hurry, as Max was far richer and they had agreed to get married on the "wedge" cruise ship's first voyage. So far, she couldn't find a reason not to marry him.

He woke up, and soon they were hugging.

"Nice nap?"

"Yeah. How are we doing?"

"No change in position. But I heard it could rain in a few hours. That's when you'll be driving."

"It just slows things down a little."

He returned to talk to the pit crew, and she left for the viewing stands. Luckily, she had a reserved seat in a viewing stand with a roof over it. She watched a weather front moving in and hoped Max was right; it wouldn't make much difference when a light rain started.

The team rotation continued all night, and she yawned as Max woke up from another nap in her lap and left for the team's pit position early the next morning. She called out to him. "Be careful, Max. The fog's so thick, even the birds are walkin'."

He looked back with a confused expression until she blew him a kiss. He shook his head as he entered the pit area. When his turn ended, he was wiping his face with a towel as he entered the stands near her.

She handed him an energy drink and some pastries. "Still in third?"

"Yeah. We need a break to move up."

They got a small break when the second-place car took a long pit stop for some emergency maintenance. She breathed a huge sigh of relief when the team's car finally finished in second place for two races in a row.

Alex and Max celebrated that night. She was surprised that he had so much energy left for her after such a grueling race. Later, she watched him sleep and ordered room service.

Early in the morning, they entered the racecourse pit area. Most teams were cleaning up and putting equipment into large vans for the next race on the tour. At his team's pit area, he was excited to find the new Le Mans Prototype graphene car shimmering in the early morning light. Max had received permission to take a few laps in a section of the course that was still closed to the public. He eagerly started the new car's engine and roared off down the track to give it an actual course test. There were a few hairpin turns still blocked off from the public and a long straightaway, and Max pushed the car hard, surprised at how well it held the road in sharp hard turns and how stable it was flat out on the straightaway. When he returned, his team and Alex gathered around him to hear his summary.

"It's amazing. It holds the course fantastically, even in a tight turn, and it's super smooth on the straightaways."

Alex was smiling. "That's partially due to the new fender skirts."

"What?"

She had changed the fender skirts from the original prototype car used to make the mold for the graphene car. The new design protected the tires. "In the NASCAR and stock car races, most of the damage to race cars comes from hitting the walls near the stands. A fiberglass fender breaks off easily. Then the tire slams into the wall and gets messed up. The car spins out of control and hits other cars. If you hit the wall with this fender, it will just bounce off it, and the tire will still be intact."

Max and the team examined the new fender. The design was also aerodynamic and pushed air away from the tires. When he looked up, Alex was holding a hammer. He yelled to her to stop when she appeared to be going to give the car a "whack." She hit it as hard as she could, and he grimaced at the dent until he saw it slowly moving back to its original shape. She saw the shocked expression on Max and his team member's faces. "Graphene remembers it original shape. Some other polymers and composite materials also do this."

He hugged and kissed her. "I have an appointment after lunch with the race committee. I'd like you to come along in case they have any technical questions."

"Of course," she replied. "It should be an interesting meeting."

The Le Mans steering committee ultimately approved the use of graphene for the LM1 Prototype racing cars, but the concept was so different, Max brought the graphene car to the parking lot outside the building where the committee met to allow them to see one firsthand. The committee had many technical questions, which Alex easily answered. In the overall approval process, the committee solicited comments from the other racing teams so there would be no surprises or legal challenges to allowing a graphene car to race. Max had a video made and sent copies to the other teams, describing the properties of graphene and the LTA vessels, flyers, and commuter pods, showing the advantages of designing and building with an innovative new material. There were some questions from the other teams but no serious objections to using it in the Le Mans race. A few teams even asked if they could get a graphene copy of their racing car body. Alex really didn't want to get into the business of making racing cars, but Max convinced her it was good publicity for the consortium and could eliminate legal challenges if several racing teams were using graphene cars.

Unknown to Max and Alex, the video was forwarded to other racing committees for comments. They soon received an invitation to discuss graphene at the equivalent NASCAR steering committee. Expanding the manufacturing of racing cars to NASCAR and Formula One car races could be a huge source of income for the LTA Consortium. The possibility of greatly reducing the impact of crashes in all racing venues was a huge incentive to adopt graphene.

Several normally passive investors in the LTA Consortium convinced Max to sponsor the graphene racing car, and Harrods found other drivers for their prototype when Max and his fellow drivers moved over to drive for the consortium.

Alex and Max spent the next day relaxing as tourists in Le Mans. Over dinner, she reminded him of her original question.

"Do you remember I once asked you what you did for fun, and you said you raced cars?" He nodded and continued eating. "Was that eight hours of driving fun, Max? It looked pretty stressful."

He sat back and thought for a moment. "I think I do it for the same reason people swim across the English Channel or climb mountains or explore caves. If you really asked them, they wouldn't call it fun. It's the challenge."

"You don't need to prove anything. No one would say you can't do anything you set your mind on."

That compliment meant a lot to him. "Thanks. I could say the same about you." She laughed until he commented, "I used to climb mountains."

She didn't want to appear that she didn't believe him, but her expression made him smile. He told her that, in his early investing days, he met a mountain climber trying to form a business leading climbers on world-class mountains. He couldn't see the business return, and passed on the deal, but they still became friends, and over time, Max climbed mountains with him—small ones at first. By that time, he was becoming wealthy and caught the attention of a reporter who used to make fun of him in his column. He tried to ignore the reports, but when the reporter called him a wealthy playboy, it was too much for a serious investor. He met with the newspaper's editor and complained. The editor basically ignored him until he formed an investing group and talked to the newspaper's owner. The editor then apologized and ensured him the reporter would only report facts in the future. He even had the reporter apologize at the news conference held to announce the purchase of the newspaper by Max's investing group. At the news conference, Max accepted his apology and challenged the reporter to accompany him on his next climb. Having no viable alternative, the reporter agreed. Max treated him like any other member of his team as they climbed Mount McKinley in Alaska, but the reporter had learned his lesson. He always stuck to the facts in all his later reports.

Alex listened, fascinated at yet another facet of Max she never knew. "Why did you stop climbing mountains?"

He thought for a moment. "I started racing Formula One cars."

She chuckled and returned to her dinner.

36

Prototype Floating Platform

Alex decided to build a prototype floating platform to test the properties of impregnated graphene before they began designing the full-blown city. Ironically, the platform resembled a UFO. Calculations indicated a totally impregnated graphene–based platform could float as high as two miles, which was a little impractical as the outside air temp at that altitude is pretty cold (below freezing). Few inhabitants would want to spend much time outside on their balconies or the patios of restaurants at that temperature. At one mile, the outside temp is still cool, but with small heaters, people could spend time outside on their balconies enjoying the view of the earth below.

She asked the design team to consider all options and to bounce ideas off each other. What would they want if they had a condo in a city floating high over the earth? They also looked at the outside temp at one mile versus latitude. The outside temperature of a city floating over New York would, on average, be cooler than one floating over Miami. So where should the city be located initially? That could come later.

The first problem the team addressed was moving people to and from the platform. There would not be enough flat space on the platform for even a small airplane to land, so Alex designed a new graphene dirigible capable of carrying two dozen people and their luggage to the platform. The platform had limited means to maintain its height and required a gas bag and a reservoir of water and specific weights to keep its altitude constant. So when twenty to twenty-five people and their luggage entered the platform, a corresponding amount of weight had to be removed. This could be accomplished by transferring an equivalent weight of water between the new dirigible and the platform whenever passengers arrived or left.

The next question the design team addressed was size. This was not the full-blown-city design, and impregnated graphene was still too expensive to make the prototype any larger than needed to prove the city design concepts. Several ideas were proposed before a platform one thousand feet in diameter was adopted, and everything else was sized accordingly. That gave a potential floor space of about 785,000 square feet. The platform height was set at 100 feet, which resulted in an enclosed volume of about 78 million cubic feet.

Virtually everything that could be was made of impregnated graphene, and the platform required much less helium on an overall-volume basis than an LTA vessel. The required helium (15.7 million cubic feet) would be contained in the upper 85 feet of the platform, just above a common maintenance and utility area. This time, Alex didn't need Tom to figure the consortium's savings in having its own helium supply ($13 million).

Living quarters for 200 to 250 people in one hundred apartments were initially located on the 3,140-foot perimeter, along with two restaurants. Not all the apartments or balconies were the same size, but on average each apartment had a thirty-foot balcony. Each perimeter apartment was about one hundred feet in depth, for a total space of three thousand square feet.

There were even more and larger interior apartments for a total targeted population of about five hundred. There were a dozen large lounges around the perimeter where the residents of the interior apartments could enjoy the view whenever they wanted. A common area was established around the center of the platform with several boutique shops, a small grocery store, and a few other needed shops. The center contained several large gas bags controlled by a computer to maintain a constant altitude. To maintain a constant position over the target city, the team designed a system with four small engines controlled by a computer tied to a GPS system.

The team also answered the most basic question. Why would someone want to visit or even live in a floating city? A fabulous view was the obvious answer. If the platform could be moved around, the view would be even more amazing, further increasing the marketability of the platform; so the design team also adopted making the four small engines larger to allow the platform to be maneuvered or moved to float over other cities, if the owners collectively decided that's what they wanted.

Design of the prototype platform was completed almost the same time as the construction of Aurora's massive wedge-shaped cruise ship was completed. Brad held an online contest to name the new vessel, and the winner won a free cruise on the ship's first tour for the name "Balboa."

Alex shocked Max when she told him Lindsey was in a relationship with Tom Babineaux. When did that happen? The next day, he met Tom for lunch, and they discussed the bulb consortium and Lindsey. Tom said it was scary how compatible they were. Business was always hectic; so whenever they were together, they liked to do simple things, like bowling or tennis or sailing or camping and fishing, or sometimes they just watched movies together.

Max would never have guessed one of Alex's sisters and his best friend would get together. It was a small world.

37

New Graphene Flyer Uses

Two weeks before the first scheduled tour of the Balboa, Alex and Max drove to the Lakehurst Naval Air Station in New Jersey. She was expecting him to drive to the Hindenburg Memorial; instead he drove a little farther on the base to a small gathering of cars, trucks, and a semi-tractor trailer.

"What's going on, Max?"

"I have a little surprise for you."

She grimaced. That wasn't always a good thing when Max said it. They stopped next to the trailer where three military officers were observing five sailors trying to put on graphene flyer backpacks.

"I thought you said there was no interest in the flyers?"

"I said there was no interest in them by commuters. I didn't say the military wasn't interested."

They got out, and while Max shook hands with the air station officers, Alex wandered over to the sailors who were trying to figure out the backpack controls.

"Hi, guys."

Alex was dressed casually with jeans, a lightweight jacket, and comfortable shoes. They stared at her for a moment. The team leader replied, "Yes, ma'am?"

"Did they explain how to use the flyer?"

"No, ma'am. Are you the training instructor?"

"No, I designed the flyer."

Some of them laughed until they saw Max and the air station officers walking over. Max heard Alex's comment and reinforced it, "She really designed the flyer."

The sailors were still skeptical until she went over the controls and warned them the throttle wasn't linear so they shouldn't press it all the way at first.

The officers introduced themselves to Alex. Howard Thomas, the air station commander, was especially interested in meeting her. "I've heard some interesting things about you, Ms. Schultz, and Max provided a lot of useful information. I'm hoping we can find several uses for your flyer—in search and rescue and combat."

Alex would never have thought of that. "Thank you, Commander. The LTA Consortium is always looking for new uses for its graphene materials."

Max chuckled at that comment.

A few minutes later, five flyer-equipped sailors with radios lifted off and followed their team leader around the air station a few times while the officers watched, eventually landing back where they started.

Commander Thomas was rubbing his chin. "Pretty impressive! What is the current range, Ms. Schultz?"

"Right now, that's about twenty miles depending on the weight of the passenger, the winds, ambient temperature, and so on."

"Twenty miles…Could that range be extended some?"

"Yes, but it's easier to answer that question if you have a target in mind."

Thomas consulted briefly with the other officers before he asked, "Is fifty miles possible?"

"It's possible if we made the backpack larger."

"As long as it's not over seventy pounds, that won't matter."

"It wouldn't be much heavier than it is now, just larger."

"That's excellent. When could we have a larger prototype to test?"

Alex was hesitant to commit to a date, but Max volunteered to have a few ready in six months. That seemed to satisfy the officers. It would give them time to pass it up the chain of command and find other branches of the military that might be interested.

Max and Alex shook hands with the officers and sailors, and they entered cars and trucks and drove away.

Alex thought the meeting was over, when Max surprised her with flight-ready commuter pods. Two consortium employees opened the back of the trailer and rolled two pods out and down a ramp to the ground. The prototypes looked commercially ready with colorful designs and graphics. Max had been coordinating the development and construction of the commuter pods as a surprise to Alex.

"Wow! They really did a good job on these prototypes."

"Your sister provided the graphics." He asked about the controls. "Anything I should know about the throttle?"

"No, it's pretty straightforward." She frowned. "Max, this is an active air station. You can't just fly anything around in here."

"Commander Thomas gave us permission if I would make some available to them in a few months. They are more interested in the flyer right now."

Max would have naturally thought of that. One of the consortium employees notified the air control tower as they both entered pods and pressed the Start button. The upper part of the pods lifted up, and the fans turned slowly. Max closed the door, buckled his seat belt, and slowly pressed the throttle—just in case. The fans sped up, and the pod lifted off the ground. He was about one hundred feet off the ground when Alex zipped by him in her pod. He laughed and tried to catch her. She wasn't nauseous or dizzy from vertigo this time and had the throttle in the full on position.

He tried to catch her but couldn't. She turned as she neared the edge of the air station and headed back to the trailer. She passed him and waved. He turned quickly and tried again to catch her but couldn't. She landed first, and when he climbed out of his pod, she came over and hugged him. "I finally beat you at something!"

Max didn't care. He was just happy to be holding her. "By the way, we've made about one hundred pods and have submitted applications to several government agencies to allow us to sell them to the public. We also have some consortium employees marketing them to car manufacturers. They already have dealers, sales, and maintenance facilities. And they could easily add the commuter pod to their existing systems. There are several car manufacturers interested in becoming dealers."

Alex shook her head. "Car manufacturers and dealers aren't the problem. The FAA will have to figure out how to keep people from crashing into each other."

She was probably right, but Max hoped they could still sell millions of them to commuters.

38

The Flying Wedge

Alex and Max were eager to view the newly finished wedge-shaped ship and make final preparations for the wedding that would be held on the third day of the tour. He would finally get to meet Alex's older brother who was flying in from Washington to be with them. Alex's parents were retired and living near El Paso in West Texas and rarely visited Alex, Lindsey, or Dana. Her father was ill, and they regretfully would not be able to make the trip.

They were informed by e-mail the massive wedding cake had arrived okay. They also received e-mails from the bridesmaids and groomsmen as they arrived. There would be a rehearsal dinner the next night for everyone to meet and get to know each other.

As they entered the ship via the rear stairway, Alex reminded him the total volume enclosed in the ship was 424 million cubic feet. They took one of the fifteen elevators to the twelfth floor and found their rear-corner-of-the-wedge stateroom.

A few minutes later, their luggage arrived, and they changed clothes, eager to see as much of the huge ship as possible.

It was a relatively short walk from their stateroom to the central atrium. They gazed in amazement as the atrium was at least five hundred feet high from the lowest floor to an area near the top of the vessel. They could see the railings and platform of each floor below them, and it somehow reminded her of the atrium in a Hyatt Hotel she had stayed in. Even though she was behind a railing, she felt a little queasy looking down. He smiled at her expression.

"Nothing compares to seeing the real thing, is there?" She just shook her head.

Thousands of passengers entered and found their cabins (including members of the wedding party), then left to examine the huge atrium and its myriad collection of shops and facilities. Brad had accepted Alex's suggestion that Mike Hovenski captain the Balboa, and Alex and Max stopped by the huge control center to visit with him.

Mike was busy preparing for their first liftoff but glad to see them. They wandered around the large futuristic control center. Video screens seemed to be everywhere, and each showed a mind boggling display of information. Their navigational charts were on an even more advanced touch screen table. Confident that Mike had everything under control, she left to continue exploring the ship, while Max stayed behind to talk to Mike.

"So how's Dana?"

"She's fine. She should be on board, getting ready for the wedding. You know, Max, we're practically engaged now." He laughed. "She's something else."

Alex did tell him that Dana and Mike were in a close relationship. He put his hand on Mike's shoulder. "It's not too late to make it a three couples wedding…"

Mike shook his head. "We're not that far yet."

"Okay. See you later."

Max left the control center and headed for the mechanical room. He was sure she would go there next. She was especially eager to see the mechanical room, again located below the control center. Mike had given her his card key, and she promised to return it. Max called her cell phone, and she let him into the huge mechanical room, which was almost ten times larger than the Columbus's room. Max followed her as she wandered around the huge room. She was familiar with all the ship's systems; they were just larger or newer than similar systems on the Columbus. They saw Erik Bendorf and went to say hello. He smiled and shook their hands.

"Mike convinced me to join him on the Balboa. He said you recommended him for captain."

She smiled. "I also told Brad the Balboa needs an experienced chief engineer like you."

"Thanks, Alex."

"How are the engines?"

"Well, as you know there are a twenty-four of them, and they are the smoothest I've ever seen and more powerful."

"How about the generators?"

"There are ten of them, and this time we have a spare."

They all laughed at that comment. Max tugged on Alex's sleeve. "We probably need to let him get back to his preparations."

They let Erik return to his prep work and returned Mike's card key. It was early, so they headed for the nearest bar. Max had plans for the night.

She was drinking a margarita, and another one appeared on the bar next to hers. She saw him smiling at no one and figured him out. "Max, you don't need to get me drunk anymore. We're in the same boat now and rowing in the same direction."

He knew what she meant and laughed. Where did she get those sayings?

Alex received an e-mail from her older brother that he had an urgent meeting in Washington and had to miss the first day of the tour, but he would join them in Miami. Max wondered what he did for NASA that was so secret. Lindsey also e-mailed that she had to miss the first day of the cruise because of a big business deal. Like Robert, she would join the tour in Miami.

They left the bar at 2:00 p.m. to meet Dana, Brad, and Ashley at the "tour desk," a unique meeting place in a massive ship where most of the dozens of bars looked alike. Following the usual handshakes and hugs, they all left for a late lunch at a specialty Brazilian restaurant that specialized in Churrascaria-style meals where all sorts of meats are delivered to the table on skewers until you can't eat anymore. They chatted for hours until they noticed everyone in the restaurant leaving, and Alex reminded them the ship was about to leave New York. On every floor, there were several lounges with large windows, and they found some comfortable chairs near the large windows to watch the Manhattan skyline pass by.

Unlike the Magellan, which mainly cruised around North America, and the Columbus, which cruised back and forth between large cities in North America and Europe, the Balboa would be cruising primarily between cities in North and South America. The first voyage was a seven-day round-trip between New York City and Rio de Janeiro. There would be several stops along each way for passenger tours and to increase revenues of course. Based on feedback from the world tour of the Columbus, the ship would be traveling faster, typically eighty to one hundred miles per hour to maximize time at each stop for sightseeing and planned tours.

The gigantic ship lifted off precisely on time at 6:00 p.m. from its mooring site in Jersey City, New Jersey, circled Manhattan and the Statue of Liberty and then headed south, following the East Coast of the United States for 1,277 miles to Miami. Approximately thirteen hours later, the ship moored in Miami at 7:00 a.m., and Alex and Max were the first off, not to join a tour, but to observe how effective Alex's recommended passenger exit and reentry procedures were. At 8:00 a.m., Max watched the massive exodus from the ship's fifteen exits and told Alex he was glad he wasn't on a sea-based ship that had to unload that many passengers at each stop.

Even though it was the world's largest cruise vessel, most of the time it didn't seem crowded at all, as there were only eight hundred guests on each level in four hundred staterooms. Each restaurant could easily accommodate less than five hundred passengers during the planned two to three hours allocated for each meal. None of the common areas seemed crowded.

The only activity that required reservations were the theatrical productions. There were five theaters that held one thousand passengers each for two nightly shows, which could accommodate most but not all the passengers. Six large casinos had been almost full the first night although no one had to wait on a table game or a slot machine.

When the ship left Miami at 7:00 p.m. on the second evening of the tour, friends and family of Alex and Ashley and Max and Brad gathered in a large lounge near the front of the ship for the rehearsal dinner. Max finally got to meet NASA engineer Robert Schultz. He was a little older than Alex, with a similar slender frame and dark hair and eyes with gray sideburns. Alex had showed him a family picture when she graduated from college, and Max thought Robert looked like his father. All the Schultz women were blond and closely resembled their mother. Robert hugged Alex, Ashley, and Dana and shook hands with Max. They all started chatting with Robert, and Max saw Lindsey and Tom signing the guest book on a table near the wedding cake and went to say hello.

"How are you guys doing?"

She turned to Max, put her arms around him, and hugged him. Tom shook his hand. "We are doing great, Max. But I'm sure you knew that." Tom motioned to her to move Max to a quieter place. She pulled on his sleeve to move him away from the crowd at the cake and punch bowl. "You may have heard the rumor one of the big LED manufacturers is thinking of making an offer to buy our consortium." Max nodded and she continued, "I don't think they really want to make the new bulbs. They just want to eliminate competition."

"I know. If they want to do that, we'll make them pay through the nose..."

She laughed. It seemed almost impossible after their earlier rivalry, but she had come to genuinely like Max, and soon he would be her brother-in-law. She sometimes wondered if she met him a few years earlier, she would be wearing the wedding dress. But those thoughts quickly left as she was very happy in her relationship with Tom. If the bulb consortium were sold, her proceeds would make her wealth similar to Tom's (she was 100 percent invested in the deal).

Tom had convinced her to move her angel investing business to New York, where there were more opportunities and so they could be together. They were already living together in a nice apartment in Manhattan. If the deal went through, they would be able to afford a nice condo overlooking Central Park.

Robert had walked over to see the cake and spotted Lindsey with Tom and Max. He walked to her. "Lindsey! I haven't seen you in so long..."

They hugged, and Tom and Max slipped quietly away as they started chatting. Max wanted to know more about Tom's relationship with his soon to be sister-in-law Lindsey.

The rehearsal dinner went smoothly, and afterward, the guests broke into small groups to continue their conversations in various parts of the ship. The future newlyweds and close family camped out in one of the ship's huge lounges, and Max tried several times to find out more about Robert's work at NASA without success. He left Max guessing when he told him he would find out soon enough. Lindsey told Max she wanted to talk about some additional angel investments. Between the hedge fund, angel investing, and the LTA Consortium, there wasn't enough time for Max and Alex to be together as much as he would like. He hoped they could make up for it on this cruise and their honeymoon.

39

Troublemaker

The first sign that something was amiss on board the Balboa was largely dismissed as mischief. Someone had thrown a "cherry bomb" (a type of fireworks) in a toilet, and when it exploded, everything in the toilet was now all over the restroom—a huge and smelly mess. It was immediately reported to the maintenance staff that closed the restroom and spent some time cleaning and sanitizing everything. The mischief continued as someone stopped up a toilet and blocked open the fill valve so that water continued to run until the toilet water was all over the floor. The maintenance staff alerted Mike that someone was deliberately making it look like there were mechanical problems on the ship. Mike made a note of it in the captain's daily log but didn't do anything at first. He hoped that whoever it was would get tired of these childish acts.

He was proven wrong when several strange symbols were scribbled on a mirror in a restroom. These were quickly removed again by the staff, and Mike was notified. He asked security to be on the lookout for the troublemaker. Other troubling signs appeared in more conspicuous places until several women screamed when some graphic images were found painted on the walls in one of the passenger lounges used for bingo. The head of security examined video from numerous hidden cameras in the area but couldn't find a video of anyone doing these things. Mike felt compelled to let Brad know since he was on the ship. He also called Alex and Max for advice.

Alex, Max, Brad, and Mike met in the officer's small break room to discuss possible actions to catch whoever was doing it in the act. Unlike previous sabotage attempts on the Columbus, this person didn't seem to want to damage the vessel or hurt anyone, just scare everyone and generate a lot of bad publicity. Everything that had been learned from the sabotage attempt on the Magellan and especially the multiple attempts on the Columbus was in effect on the Balboa. The mechanical room was watched from secret cameras 24/7, and every system that might be tampered with was locked with a push button lock and a case-hardened lock, and only Erik had the keys. Strict new-badge access rules were now in place, and push button locks and card key locks had also been installed on any room with a cruise computer in it. The five thousand crew members had all passed an extensive security clearance and were not suspects—yet.

Word of the mischief and strange symbols spread quickly through the passengers and crew until Brad felt he had no choice but to assure everyone they were not in danger. He went on closed-circuit TV throughout the ship to explain what the ship's officers thought was going on and to reassure everyone the ship's systems were secure and they would catch the person responsible. Everyone was asked to be vigilant and report anything that seemed out of the ordinary, especially someone painting or spray-painting images on walls or mirrors.

Brad was identified on the video as the CEO of the Aurora Cruise Line, and feedback to his calm explanation and assurances was very positive. Once people understood it was the work of someone possibly seeking vengeance or mentally ill or just trying to get publicity, they returned to having fun on the cruise. A few more disturbing signs were found by passengers and reported to Mike, but the passengers were now mainly ignoring them.

The staff had a break when some "night owl" passengers reported suspicious activity in one of the forward lounges at 2:00 a.m. Security rushed there and caught the culprit spraying symbols on windows in the lounge. They brought him to a "secure" area in the ship and notified Mike. No one really talked about the fact that a cruise ship would actually have a holding cell on the lowest level, out of sight, as a part of the ship. Even Mike had a hard time finding the holding cell. He called Brad, Max, and Alex, who met him there.

Brad was furious as the suspect turned out to be the long sought-after former president of the design company that Aurora had used to build their only LTA vessel from Hindenburg-era materials. Tony Accardo was a small man, with dark hair and eyes. He had slowly graduated from low-level cons to more sophisticated ones, like Ponzi investment schemes. He had almost been caught a few times and decided to lay low for a while, so he used all his ill-gotten gains to buy a small respectable construction firm in Miami that was near bankruptcy and desperately needed an infusion of cash to stay in business. The biggest and shadiest deal in his life had been to submit a "lowball" bid to the Aurora Cruise Line and oversee the incompetent design and construction of a vessel that ultimately killed six people and hurt dozens more. He seemed resigned to his fate as Brad, Max, Mike, and Alex took turns telling how they would enjoy turning him over to the NTSB or FBI or any other government agency that wanted him in custody. Accardo wouldn't even look at them and just sat on a cot in the cell, shuffling his feet until they had gotten over it and were just happy to have caught him finally so he could pay for his actions. There would be no escaping justice this time.

Max laughed when Alex described Tony as a "dumbass" for his lame attempt at bad publicity for the Balboa. She said he should have stayed in hiding. But again, she pointed out that Tony wasn't all that smart to begin with.

Brad utilized the close-circuit TV again to tell everyone they had finally caught the troublemaker and he would be turned over to the police as soon as they returned to the US.

He also thanked them for their patience while they tried to catch the culprit and hoped they would enjoy the rest of the voyage.

40

Miami to San Juan

The next segment of 1,033 miles allowed the ship to travel at a more leisurely rate so that the ship would arrive in San Juan, Puerto Rico, at 8:00 a.m. San Juan was the starting point of many cruise ships, and the Puerto Rican tourism industry was eager to welcome another cruise ship and offered many local tour options. Almost every passenger left the ship for a day tour. Alex and Max rented Jet Skis and spent the afternoon with a small group led by a private guide. Brad, Ashley, Dana, and Robert rented a sailboat and sailed to popular tourist sites around the island. Lindsey and Tom seemed to spend most of the day on their cell phones dealing with rumors about the pending sale of the bulb consortium.

All passengers returned on time at 6:00 p.m., and the ship left Puerto Rico for the cruise-friendly island of Aruba.

At 8:00 p.m., the same lounge that previously hosted the rehearsal dinner now held the wedding ceremony.

In the absence of the brides' father, and in a deviation from tradition, Robert escorted Alex down the aisle, and Mike escorted Ashley. Dana served as Alex's maid of honor, and Lindsey was Ashley's maid of honor. In her discussions with Erik Bendorf, Alex discovered he was a licensed minister in his home country of Germany, and he volunteered to lead the dual ring ceremony for each couple. When they were chatting later, Brad and Max both admitted they were overwhelmed at seeing Ashley and Alex in their white wedding gowns. Ashley and Alex had coordinated their gowns so that they complimented each other while still being unique.

Each bride and groom read self-written vows, and at the end, Erik introduced both couples to the witnesses and asked them to kiss.

A nearby lounge had been set up for the reception with the massive wedding cake and a live band. The live band had actually been hired for the whole tour, something not normally seen on modern cruise vessels. The darkened lounge had large windows allowing guests to see the moon and stars and occasional boats two thousand feet below them during the reception. After a while, almost everyone was dancing and drinking champagne. After the usual cake-cutting ceremony, the one hundred or so family and guests of the two couples toasted them, wishing them a long life together. When Alex wasn't looking, Lindsey kissed Max again and wished Alex and him the best. It was so dark and unexpected that Max thought at first it was Alex and kissed her back. Dana saw Lindsey sneak the kiss with Max and laughed.

The celebration finally ended at 2:00 a.m. and all retired to their staterooms. The couples were on their honeymoons, and the graphene wedge certainly provided a unique environment.

Aruba was only 478 miles from San Juan, so the ship slowed to allow an early morning arrival and moored within walking distance of popular cruise sites on the island. The security computer confirmed that, again, virtually 100 percent of the passengers had left. Max and Alex joined an afternoon tour and went snorkeling, while Brad and Ashley joined an afternoon Jet Ski tour. Lindsey and Dana went shopping— all day. Robert and Tom just chilled out on a nearby beach. All passengers again returned on time, and the ship left for a 3,033-mile trip to Rio de Janeiro at four thousand feet and their maximum cruising rate. Rio tourism had seen a lot of ships dock in the past but had never had to deal with twelve thousand passengers and the more-than-four-thousand crew that could leave descend on them at once.

By far, the biggest attraction for most of the passengers was the Christ the Redeemer statue on top of Corcovado Mountain, one of the modern wonders of the world.

Somehow, no one was left behind, and the ship started its return voyage by stopping in San Jose in Costa Rica, then Cozumel, Mexico, then Fort Lauderdale, and finally back to New York—on time.

Tony Accardo was turned over to police in Fort Lauderdale and immediately transferred to Miami to face federal and state criminal and civil charges.

There were several reporters on board for the first voyage, and all the reports were positive. A few reports mentioned the mischief and symbols issue but said it was dealt with appropriately. There had been a few other minor glitches, but these were minimized as the main cruise had a 95 percent favorable feedback from a survey given to the passengers on the last night of the cruise. A few people complained about the security lines on reentry. Mike Hovenski was already working to double the number of security lines with scanners for carry-ons.

Brad Wilson was extremely pleased. He not only had the only LTA vessels in the world that could land virtually anywhere, he also had the largest cruise vessel by far. The next three voyages were sold out on the Balboa, and he was even considering a world tour for the massive ship similar to the world tour of the Columbus. Alex suggested a world tour of the seven modern wonders of the world: Chichen Itza in Mexico, Machu Picchu in Peru, Christ the Redeemer statue in Rio de Janeiro, the Colosseum in Rome, Petra in Jordan, the Great Wall in China, and the Taj Mahal in India. She even gave him a suggested route with flight times and days at each site. If the ship cruised at full speed between stops, there would be ample time for a dozen other stops on the ninety-day tour. Brad immediately gave Alex's proposal to his cruise development team to implement.

Brad and Ashley invited Max and Alex to visit them the next time they were in London. Alex reminded Max she wanted to go shopping at Harrods, so maybe they could combine a stay with Brad and Ashley with a shopping trip.

Max was less than enthusiastic about the shopping trip but didn't mind staying with Brad and Ashley, so he agreed.

41

New Graphene Flyers

Max and Alex met again with Howard Thomas, base commander of the Lakehurst Naval Air Station, and several officers of other service branches to deliver an improved graphene flyer backpack for testing. The new flyer was considerably larger but didn't weigh much more, and Alex had a surprise for Thomas. After general greetings and introductions, Alex helped Max put on the backpack, and he took off, hovered for a moment, then swooped down and picked up Alex and flew away with her, much like a hawk would grab a small animal while hunting. Max slowly descended with Alex and landed next to Thomas. Thomas immediately knew the demonstration was intended to simulate a rescue. All the other officers immediately thought of other possible roles for the flyer and excitedly discussed possible uses in their areas.

A naval officer mentioned using flyers to transfer personnel from one ship to another at sea.

Max also delivered on his promise as consortium employees unloaded five commuter pods for their testing.

Some of the other officers were hesitant to try them out, but Thomas quickly entered one and was soon flying all around the base. Not to be outdone, the other officers tested theirs.

They all met later in an air station conference room, and Commander Howard discussed purchasing a huge number of the new flyers and even some commuter pods for further testing. Alex mentioned the possibility of using impregnated graphene to make drones and other weapon systems. Her preliminary calculations indicated a graphene drone would have a much bigger payload capacity. That comment would eventually lead to even more orders for the consortium.

Max's limo driver was on vacation, and Max had a convertible rental car, but this time, he had the top up as the temperature in New Jersey was unseasonably cold for early fall. Alex turned the heat all the way up. "That was a good day for the consortium."

"And profitable. By the way, we've received preliminary approval to sell the pods to the public."

Alex was shocked. "How will they keep people from crashing into each other?"

"I don't know all the details yet, but a commuter will first have to get a license by passing a test demonstrating control of the pod and knowledge of some basic flight rules that are being worked on right now—sort of like a driver's license for a car. I think a commuter will be required to fly over major roadways whenever possible and only deviate when landing at a designated commuter pod landing site, like the top of a building, or when nearing their home. I think you would fly at five hundred or fifteen hundred feet if going north and south and at one thousand or two thousand feet if going east and west. I know that sounds crazy, but over the years, rules have been developed for every form of transport, from cars to airplanes—even boats. This is just something they will have to work out. I think they are planning to put out a commuting proposal for the pods and get the public's feedback for a few months before they finalize the rules."

"I didn't think they would ever be able to do that." She shifted in her chair to look at him. "Max, I've been thinking about investing the rest of my share of the money from the sale of the consortium's assets."

"And?"

"I think I'd like to put it back into the consortium. If we can find a lot of new uses for graphene, I think the value would increase even faster than it would in stocks and bonds."

Max grinned. "Spoken like an investor. That's a great idea. Now you'll have an even greater incentive to find new and profitable uses for graphene." He reminded her that he had reinvested most, but not all, of his proceeds from the sale of the LTA Company back into the LTA Consortium. He had invested the rest in the bulb consortium with Lindsey, and it looked like several companies were interested in investing in that consortium, or possibly even buying it. In any event, Max would probably double his investment in the new bulb's manufacturing. Lindsey and Tom would also make a huge return on their investments. They were slowly becoming wealthy, not as wealthy as Alex or especially Max, but Lindsey was now in a position to invest her own money in future venture capital deals. Tom liked less risky investments.

Alex thought about the day's events and the unlimited future for graphene. "I never would have thought of possible military uses for graphene. What made you think of that?"

"I once steered some military officials to Jack. They wanted to see he could engineer a carbon fiber version of some of their drones."

"I don't remember that."

Max laughed. "It was on a need-to-know basis, and I think it didn't get very far."

"Graphene would be much stronger and more effective in reducing weight than carbon fibers for that application."

"No one knew that at the time."

The heater in the convertible struggled to heat the interior, and Alex shivered. She still wasn't used to cold weather. At least their house in the Hamptons would be warm.

He saw her rubbing her arms to warm up. "Are you okay?"

"It's colder than a gravedigger's ass…"

Max just smiled.

42

Graphene Drones

A week later, Max received a phone call from a senior military officer, who invited him and Alex to a meeting in Washington DC. They flew on their private jet, and a limo was waiting to take them to the Department of Defense. They met with several low-level officials, who asked them to sign secrecy agreements then were led to a meeting with top officials. They were shown several conceptual drawings of a new type of drone that didn't resemble an airplane at all. It was about as big as a basketball and contained mainly cameras and video equipment that could transmit real-time images to a mobile monitoring station. They asked if it could be fabricated with the impregnated graphene just as the flyers were. Alex drew some sketches with the outer covering serving as the battery and a photocell on top of the fan assembly to recharge the battery. The defense department basically wanted to know if it were possible for the proposed drone to float in the air over key locations for several days at a time without the need to return to recharge. It was possible based on preliminary calculations, and if the observatory drone ball were painted white or light blue, it would be almost impossible to see during the day if the ball maintained a constant altitude of one thousand feet or more. Advanced cameras and video equipment could easily provide sharp images from that height. An embedded satellite data link could enable the video to be transmitted virtually anywhere in the world. They also asked about adding a high-power laser to the drone.

The officials also asked about the feasibility of very small observation platforms, similar in size to a baseball. Alex said she would test several sizes and report back. They would be given classified equipment to insert into the observation platforms to record data. Lastly, there was a request to test graphene missile-carrying drones, as Alex had mentioned a graphene version could carry a lot heavier payload. A shipment of rockets would be sent to the graphene factory to be mounted on a graphene drone, some live, some not. On the way to the jet, Alex expressed some misgivings as she hadn't anticipated becoming part of the military complex. Max tried to assure her they would not become dependent on military orders, but she wasn't convinced.

Occupying the Prototype Platform

LTA Consortium personnel had joined with the Aurora Cruise Line personnel to fabricate pieces for the prototype platform at their graphene factory. Aurora began to advertise a combination of a week in the floating platform as part of a cruise package, much like the Denali train tours are combined with coastal Alaska cruises. The new dirigible was completed and passed all certification testing almost as the first sections of the platform were completed. The central hub was completed first and floated to its engineered height over Houston. As each additional section was completed, it was floated to the hub and connected. Furniture and merchandise deliveries to the platform began once the platform was completed.

Near the end of construction, the first passengers arrived. Alex reminded Max the platform was starting to be occupied only eighteen months after the project was kicked off. They were among the first group of visitors and residents to arrive and occupied a large apartment on the platform perimeter. The apartment had a forty-foot balcony that gave magnificent views of the countryside below. There were even some remote control options that allowed the balcony to be enclosed with a clear plastic roof and floor when it rained. There was also a built-in heater to maintain a comfortable temperature during the day and especially at night when the lights of the city below were twinkling.

In a last-minute design change, the floors of all common areas, even the hallways, were changed to a clear see-through plastic. That took getting used to as you could see the ground far below as you walked around the platform. The design team had solicited feedback to a long list of ideas from many people who expressed interest in buying or renting a condo on the platform. The clear floors had a high approval rating.

The next day, one of the small restaurants opened for business and they enjoyed their first meal in the platform with the other residents who had arrived with them. Their apartment was not fully furnished, but it had everything they needed to celebrate the start of a whole new enterprise for the LTA Consortium. There were a number of lounges with large panoramic windows, and they watched a magnificent sunset while enjoying a bottle of wine.

The following day, they were totally surprised when Ashley and Brad showed up at their door. They all went to the restaurant to catch up and talk about the future of the platform and the soon-to-be-designed city.

Alex and Ashley started chatting about the wedding and the cruise and other sisterly things, which left Max and Brad initially to talk about the new city as the design effort would begin in a few months. Brad took the opportunity to finally ask Max about the company he had funded that bought many patents and then sued companies to collect royalties. Max seemed surprised at the question.

"That wasn't my idea. I was just a silent partner."

Brad had a shocked expression. "But your name was all over the company's Web site."

"I don't know why they would do that. One of my friends brought the idea of funding that company in a proposal to an investment meeting that we hold regularly. It didn't seem that appealing to me, but he said the return on investment would meet our criteria. He worked the deal, and I just joined in as a silent partner. All investors in that deal were silent partners except for the person who proposed it."

Brad just shook his head. "In our negotiations with them to avoid a trial over their claim that we were violating their patents, they said we had to talk to you. I tried several times, but you never returned my calls."

Max frowned. "I don't remember anyone ever calling about that company. What number were you calling?"

"I can't remember, but I think it was a Los Angeles area code. It was the same area code as our terminal office there."

"My investing company and my hedge fund headquarters are in Manhattan. I think you were probably calling their main office, and they didn't know who I was."

Max shrugged. "I was only a minor investor and a silent partner, so I couldn't have done anything about it, anyway."

Brad sat there staring at Max, who was trying to get Alex's attention away from her sister. Years of misunderstandings and his desire to get back at Max had probably cost his company several billion dollars in the lost LTA airship, damage to his company's reputation, and in paying off the numerous lawsuits that had resulted from the crash of the ship. Fortunately, in the eight years he was CEO of the Aurora Cruise Line, Brad had managed to double its revenues and increase the quarterly dividend to the stockholders considerably. That had taken pressure off the board of directors to hold him accountable, even fire him. A high cash flow had enabled Aurora to recover quickly from its LTA crash disaster. The only good thing that had come out of the whole mess was meeting Alex and then Ashley. As he watched Ashley and Alex laughing and joking, he reminded himself that he was now related to Max and that they were working together on many projects. Max had even set up the Aurora Consortium that funded the Balboa and half of the prototype platform. He laughed quietly at the irony of it all.

Brad and Ashley were planning to return to London after visiting the platform, so he invited Max and Alex to join them. Alex said yes before Max could even check his calendar on his cell phone. Max phoned his pilot to inform him of the change in plans.

Brad's driver picked them up, and they enjoyed the drive through the English countryside to the forest surrounding Brad and Ashley's home. After they settled into a large room near the master bedroom, Brad led them on a tour of the house. Max enjoyed the combination of old and modern, and Brad even showed them the part of the house that hadn't been refurbished. Alex and Ashley didn't like the dust, musty smell, and cobwebs and left to have a snack in the kitchen.

Max enjoyed the old barracks and armory and a primitive kitchen with a huge hearth and the rooms with an unknown purpose. At the end of the tour, they joined Alex and Ashley in the modern kitchen for coffee and to chat. Alex and Ashley were already planning a trip to Harrods the next day. Max and Brad opted out and decided to go horseback riding and exploring the countryside around the former castle.

Over coffee, Max asked Brad if he had ever thought about selling the house. Ashley was curious about that as well. She liked the house and the surrounding grounds, but it was really too quiet for her taste.

"Not really. I've come to love the countryside here and the solitude. Why do you ask?"

"I know an investor who's always looking for old castles and historical buildings to convert to hotels. He would pay a fortune for this place since most of it is already redone. I think you would probably get ten times what you have invested in it."

Ashley was enthusiastic, even if Brad wasn't. "Sounds like a great deal, Brad."

"But where would we live, London?"

"Yes, of course. Think of it. You could probably take the money and buy a huge penthouse in London, near your corporate headquarters."

Brad still was not a fan of the idea. He liked his house. "What about my horses?"

"I'm sure they could find a stable for them close to London."

Max was almost sorry he brought it up. He didn't want to start trouble between the newlyweds. Brad promised Ashley they would talk more about it, and they all dropped the topic.

The next day, Alex and Ashley did go shopping at Harrods, and Brad and Max did ride horses, but Max was careful not to bring up the subject of selling the estate. That night Brad and Ashley did come up with a compromise in which they would spend four days each week in a "suitable" apartment in London, and weekends, in the countryside house. Brad also gave her a budget to work with prior to her search for a suitable apartment. Once they reached the compromise, Ashley told Brad why she wanted to be in London; she was pregnant and concerned about proper medical and health care at such a remote location. Brad was ecstatic, and they told Alex and Max the next day. They hugged and congratulated Ashley and Brad and made plans to be in London when the baby was due. A few days later, Max and Alex returned on their jet to New York, while Brad invited all his friends and planned a party to celebrate the occasion.

43

Condo Cruise Ship

Tom Babineaux was waiting in Max's office when he returned to work from the platform and vacationing with Brad and Ashley. Max wondered if something was wrong when Tom handed him a folder. It was a proposal to fund a Columbus-style cruise ship that would contain condos instead of hotel-type rooms.

"I came up with this idea by combining the cruise ship aspects of the Columbus and your note on living conditions on the platform. In the proposal, we would build a Columbus-size ship with about three hundred permanent residences. There is one cruise ship that has been built for this purpose, and the owners vote on future itineraries. In our case, the sites would not be limited to coastal cities but could be anywhere in the world we have mooring facilities. And that site list is growing all the time."

Max sat thinking. He liked the idea, but he needed more information. "Can you come up with a hard estimate of the cost of the ship if we modify it to allow people to live on board and set up a Web site or something to see if people would actually want to live on an LTA cruise ship? And we would need some idea of the price of the condos to cover the consortium's costs—and make money of course."

"I have some of that already, but I think I can have the rest in a month or so."

Tom had worked on many of Max's deals over the years and invested in some of them but had never proposed a business venture before. Max wondered why he was proposing the deal.

"Do you want to be the active partner?"

"Max, I'd like to lead this activity as if your hedge fund was involved. I know it's not, but I want to manage it."

Max thought about that. Tom was asking for a 1-2 percent fee to manage the project and 10-20 percent of any profits that resulted. As the active partner in the consortium, Max could agree. That would mean the consortium would still get eighty to ninety percent of any profits. Since they were mostly duplicating the Columbus design, engineering costs should be minimal. Alex could probably do the changes required in a less than a week. The only risk at this point was not finding enough wealthy people to buy the condos. In Tom's notes, the existing condo cruise ship had staterooms that varied from $500,000 to more than $10,000,000. There would be a lot less condos than normal passenger staterooms, but it could be profitable. *Why not?*

"Okay. Keep me informed as you go. Once you get thirty to forty percent commitments from potential owners, I'll okay building the ship."

"Thanks, Max." Tom shook his hand and left.

Max wondered if Lindsey had anything to do with this.

Drone Testing

A few days after they returned from London, Alex received a special shipment of hardware from the defense department. Several basketball-sized hydrogen-impregnated graphene observation drones had been fabricated, and she inserted the small video cameras, a satellite link, a remotely controlled high-powered infrared laser, and a remote control receiver module. Much like the commuter pod, the observation drone had four small fans that lifted away from the main body and enabled it to move quickly in almost any direction. The core of the new drone was empty and filled with a remotely inflatable helium gas bag that allowed the drone to remain aloft for very long periods without using the fans or draining the battery. She even found a new commercially available photocell material that was "printed" on a flexible film and covered the outside of the drone with it. During daylight hours, the photocells recharged the drone's battery.

In just a few hours, she had a working prototype that almost floated in the air all by itself when she released it outside the building. Max watched the observation drone slowly lift into the air until it disappeared in the bright sunlight.

"I can't see it. How high is it?"

"About a thousand feet, according to the GPS."

They both were amazed at the razor-sharp images the drone was transmitting to Alex's handheld controller. She handed Max an eye chart sign and asked him to hold it up.

She zoomed the camera, and they both could read the sign's twenty-twenty letters on Alex's monitor.

Max started to comment on the amazing clarity when Alex aimed the laser pointer at the sign, and he jumped and dropped it as it looked like it was on fire.

When Alex laughed, he commented, "Very funny."

He watched her take out a baseball-size observation drone from a suitcase and repeat the same tests as the basketball-size version. Satisfied, they were ready. Max called his contacts at the defense department and asked when they could demo the new observation drones. Three days later, while they waited for a date to demo the observation drones, she told him the larger version of the drone was still transmitting video of the graphene factory's parking lot from one thousand feet. It had not moved nor required any outside intervention or a manual recharge of its battery. In a secret test, she sent a baseball-size observation drone inside the LTA admin building. Its movement was so silent as it moved slowly along near the ceiling that no one spotted it. Even Max concluded that it was kind of creepy observing people who had no idea you were watching them, especially a couple kissing behind a row of file cabinets.

Alex and Max met several army representatives from the Department of Defense at the Lakehurst Naval Air Station for a test of the new observation drones. Both the large and small drones performed flawlessly. Alex asked about the infrared laser. They said they wanted to use the observation drone to find enemy targets and "light them up" with the laser so a laser-guided bomb would find the target.

The army officials then gave Alex a concept drawing of a larger saucer-shaped drone about ten feet in diameter and three feet thick. This drone could easily be seen at one thousand feet, but it served a very different purpose and carried several mini-guns (the latest model of a Gatling machine gun) and a small rocket launcher. The operator could rotate the drone to point the machine guns or the rocket launcher. The large drone also had a fan assembly for maneuvering, a graphene battery, and a printed solar cell on the exterior to recharge the battery. This new drone would combine the ability to hover and observe with the capability to attack a target when instructed by the operator. Alex said she would look into the payload capacity of the proposed design and get back to them. Once the officials left, Max congratulated Alex on the successful tests, and they left for a short vacation in the Hamptons.

Brad ultimately bought the prototype platform from the LTA Consortium so his cruise line, and the Aurora Consortium, could claim that only they could provide the combination of a week at a hotel in the sky and another week aboard an LTA cruise ship in the sky cruising to locations not normally available to cruise fans.

Lindsey called Max to tell him the bulb consortium investors had agreed to be bought out by a large manufacturer of compact fluorescent bulbs (CFBs). Many consumers were buying their CFBs, but they knew they would lose out in the future when the LED manufacturers mass-produced enough to make the LED similar in cost to the CFB as it was more energy efficient. Buying the new bulb gave them a shot at beating the LED manufacturers on bulb efficiency and energy savings once the cost of the new bulb was comparable to the LED. Lindsey's investors made a bundle, and she personally had invested her life savings, even borrowed some money, betting on the new bulb. She made a lot of money on the sale, as did Tom, but not as much as Max. His one-hundred-million-dollar gamble had doubled in value. Not bad for a few weeks' work spread over a year.

Six months after the Lakehurst small drones demonstration, Alex and Max were again demonstrating the new larger saucer-shaped drones, this time at a secret government base in the Nevada desert. Alex led the observation team's inspection of three new drones that were now dormant on the desert floor. They were really too big to hide in the sky as the small white basketball-sized drones were. Instead of a single light blue or white, Alex had the new drones painted to look like clouds, a mixture of light blue and white. As they walked around the new drones, the observers couldn't see any weapons on them. The observer team lead even ran his hands over one of the drones' surface, feeling for an opening and couldn't find any.

"Where are the rockets and guns, Ms. Schultz?"

"Oh, sorry, the drones are currently in the standby mode." She pressed some buttons on a handheld remote, and the drones came to life. Their fan assemblies started, and as soon as the drones left the ground, several ports opened on the sides of each drone and mini-Gatling guns or the noses of small rockets appeared in each opening. It was so sudden the observers jumped back.

"We were given the Dillon M-134 mini-gun that fires four thousand rounds per minute and the AGM-114 Hellfire missiles to test the drones. Sargent Ben Willis will be conducting the live fire test. Are you guys ready for a demonstration?"

They all nodded and almost ran to a designated viewing stand where Sargent Willis was waiting. The three drones were now almost invisible in the sky with their cloud-like appearance. Willis controlled each drone separately with a handheld remote control with a video monitor. He used video feeds from the drones to control their action, just as a future trained operator would use them. The officials watched as apparently, out of nowhere, the first drone descended to within a hundred feet of a decoy truck and blasted it with more than a thousand rounds from its machine guns. The impact was so great it knocked the truck over. Just as quickly it disappeared in the sky. All this had happened in less than a minute, and even the most skeptical observers were impressed. A test of the second drone also required only a few seconds to deliver three Hellfire missiles to three separate decoy trucks from two thousand feet.

A rocket launcher one-half mile from the observers launched six rockets at the third drone. Self-defense software built into the drone turned the vessel so that it presented the smallest possible target while it dodged the rockets. The drone descended while firing its mini-Gatling cannon at the launcher, blowing it apart. It then hovered at three thousand feet and sent razor-sharp targeting-type pictures of the observers back to Willis's handheld remote.

Even the army observers were glad the drone wasn't targeting them. Willis ended the demonstration, and as the drones landed on the desert, the observers left the viewing stand to examine what was left of the decoy trucks. One official was authorized, based on successful tests of the larger drones, to order a large number of them. Max was delighted; Alex, not so much, even though the value of her shares of stock in the LTA Consortium were growing along with Max's shares.

A few days after the new drone's demonstration, Max and Alex were again invited to a secret meeting at the defense department. The subject was not disclosed, but when they arrived, they were taken instead to an unnamed building, and to Max and Alex's surprise, they were met by Robert Schultz and Colonel William Abrams of the US Navy. Robert was a member of several committees and acted as a liaison between the branches of the military and NASA. His primary role was to integrate new technology from NASA into the military when it made sense. After brief introductions, they were escorted to a conference room and given some background information while they waited for the rest of his committee to assemble. After the wedding, and the party that followed, it seemed strange to be dealing with Robert as a possible "client."

Colonel Abrams was in his late fifties, a career veteran of several wars, and straight to the point.

"I've been following your developments with graphene closely. The new drones you made for the army finally convinced us to meet with you. We've been waiting for a development like this for a few years."

"What exactly is your area?" asked Max.

"Advanced weaponry. I first have to remind you that you signed some nondisclosure agreements and a secrecy agreement with the defense department."

They both nodded, and he continued.

"The LTA cruise ships offered a new innovation to the leisure and entertainment field. The defense department would like to work with you to take that innovation to a new area. Imagine an LTA aircraft carrier that could go anywhere in the world quickly and perform the same functions as a conventional carrier."

It was hard to imagine, and Alex and Max glanced at each other in amazement. Max had to ask, "Are you serious?"

"Yes. You probably know that some of the Zeppelin Company's dirigibles and the USS Macon and USS Akron carried a number of bi-wing aircraft and they successfully launched them and retrieved the aircraft while in flight— effectively an aircraft carrier. This is a natural progression. We've also studied your prototype for a new floating city and think a larger version of it could serve as the basic platform for an aircraft wing."

Robert joined in. "NASA has some new technology that would work well with a graphene-based vessel—in the command and control area."

At that point, the remaining members of the advanced weapons committee showed up, and Abrams started a formal presentation proposal for an LTA aircraft carrier. The slides illustrated a floating platform almost two miles in diameter and two hundred feet high. There were two parallel openings through the ship one hundred feet wide and one hundred feet tall that allowed aircraft to land and take off. The latest electromagnetic launch systems being implemented on new aircraft carriers would be employed, in lieu of the old steam systems used on aircraft carriers to catapult and capture planes.

Once landed, a plane would be pulled into a huge hangar area for servicing. The whole concept was breathtaking in scope, but was it feasible or practical? What about cost?

There were many numbers on the slides that Alex scribbled on her graphics tablet, the physical dimensions of carrier airplanes, their weight, the length of runway required to launch and capture the airplanes, and so on. When there was a pause in the presentation, Alex rattled off a list of potential problems with the idea, the primary one being the weight of aircraft. A typical fighter jet fully loaded with fuel and weapons could weigh more than fifty thousand pounds. An aircraft carrier's typical air wing of sixty to ninety fighters would weigh 3 to 4.5 million pounds and, with supporting materials and crew, would require two to three hundred million cubic feet of helium to lift. Nevertheless, Robert appeared confident the LTA carrier concept could be proven. The single biggest advantage of an LTA aircraft carrier was the ability to deliver ordnance by aircraft that could be launched from anywhere in the world, not just from the sea or a coastline.

When the presentation ended, Alex left for a quick bathroom break, leaving Max and Abrams to discuss timing and mundane issues such as funding. Did his committee actually have approval and funding for such a large scale use of graphene? Abrams pointed out the latest supercarriers, the Gerald R. Ford class, cost between $12 billion and $14 billion. When she returned, Alex did some quick calculations on a spreadsheet on her laptop. A round platform two miles in diameter and two hundred feet high would contain 17.5 billion cubic feet. A platform one mile in diameter and two hundred feet high would contain 4.3 billion cubic feet. Since the impregnated graphene platforms would float to one mile or higher on their own, they only needed a little over four hundred million cubic feet of helium to lift the planes and all the ancillary equipment (and the five thousand or so carrier personnel). Maybe it could work. She needed to discuss it in private with Max before she committed to too much time in the design (regardless of how much money the consortium would make on engineering costs).

Alex left for another bathroom break, and the subject of dinner came up and Colonel Abrams and Robert agreed to meet them for a dinner that would include some additional questions and answers concerning the LTA carrier concept. When Alex returned, she answered a list of technical questions Abrams's team had prepared. The formal meeting ended, and Max took Alex to an exclusive hotel in Washington to freshen up. They met Abrams and Robert for dinner to exchange some additional ideas on how to make the LTA carrier work. They also discussed meeting in London with Robert as Ashley's due date was near.

One week later, Brad called Max and Alex, Dana, Lindsey, and Robert to let them know Ashley had gone into labor.

Max, Alex and Lindsey immediately flew to Washington to pick up Robert and then on to London. Max e-mailed a business class ticket to Dana. Robert, Max, Lindsey, and Alex managed to arrive at the hospital a few hours before her delivery and celebrated the birth of a healthy baby girl with Brad and Ashley. Dana arrived a few hours later, and they all stayed with Ashley until she and Emma Wilson were released from the hospital and went home to her new penthouse in London where several housekeeping staff from the countryside house were waiting to help her.

44

Racing the Le Mans Graphene Car

The opening day of the next 24 Hours of Le Mans race drew even more media attention than usual when several TV reporters and racing Web sites speculated on the impact of the entry of the LTA Consortium's new graphene racing car.

The reporters had done their homework and asked Max and Alex for an interview prior to the race. In their research, they identified Max as the active partner in the consortium, and Alex was identified as its lead designer. Alex didn't like interviews, but Max convinced her it would be good publicity for the consortium. When they showed up, they were shocked as word moved quickly in the sports world, and the interview had turned into a press conference.

Max answered all the business questions, like the cost of the graphene car, the approval of the FIA steering committee, and even his thoughts on the use of graphene in other racing venues. Alex answered all the technical questions, like the blow-mold process used to fabricate the car and the impact resistance of graphene compared to fiberglass. It was a friendly and a fact-finding type of press conference; and afterward, they both were relieved it had gone so well.

Based on qualifying time trials, the LTA's car was near the front of the pack at the start of the race. At the end of Max's first stint, they were in first place. Max and his racing team had been close several times but had never been in first place. Alex held her breath when another race car's tire blew out, and the car swerved and smacked into Max's car, forcing it into the wall near her viewing stand. The other car swerved off the track, crashing into a guardrail, but Max regained control of his car and sped by her. She strained to see if the car was damaged but couldn't even see a scratch on it and breathed a huge sigh of relief. TV reporters commented on the crash, which took the other car out of the race with a bent frame but apparently had no impact on the graphene car.

At ten hours into the race, Sean Graham was rear-ended in a tight turn but managed to regain control in the straightaway. The other car was not so lucky as the right front fiberglass fender shattered, and a fiberglass shard pierced the tire, causing the car to spin out of control and into a barricade protecting some viewing stands. Luckily, no one was injured.

At fourteen hours into the race, during Max's stint, two race cars collided during a turn in front of him, and he tried to avoid them but couldn't and hit them so hard one car summersaulted in the air and landed on a tall fence. The other race car actually ran up on top of Max's car when he rammed it from behind. He slammed on his brakes, and the car flew off and swerved into another car. Fortunately, no one was hurt from the incident, but Max's tires hit an oil slick, and his car started spinning. He somehow managed to straighten it out and was able to make up some lost time on the race leader before his turn came to an end.

At the twenty-fourth hour of the race, Dave Green was driving. While it wasn't a race record, the LTA team had completed almost four hundred laps and exceeded five thousand kilometers in twenty-four hours and took first place.

There was a crush of reporters and photographers taking pictures of the team and the new graphene car. Reporters tried to find scratches or dents or any indication the car had raced for five thousand kilometers and been involved in several crashes but couldn't find anything.

Max and Alex were soon inundated with requests for quotes for Le Mans Prototype cars, NASCAR, and Formula One graphene cars.

Max stopped by Alex's office to check on progress of the LTA carrier design for the navy. She had a doctor's appointment that morning, and he wanted to see if everything was all right.

As soon as he entered, she stood up, picked up a folder on her desk, and hit him on the head with it.

"You polecat!"

Polecat? "What's wrong, honey?"

"Don't honey me! Do you remember when I told you we needed to wait a few months after I stopped taking birth control pills, but nooooo. You couldn't wait. Now I'm pregnant, and the conception date was probably a week or so after I stopped the pill!"

Max was overjoyed. He picked her up over his head and then kissed her. "That's the best news I could have had."

She wasn't as happy. "I just hope everything's okay."

"Can we go celebrate the good news?"

"Yes, but no drinking…"

He laughed. "When can we tell everyone?"

"Not until the twelfth week or so. That will give me time to get a lot of tests done."

He kissed her again. "Is there anything I can get you or do for you?"

"No, just be there."

After a brief celebration and lunch, Max started shuffling his calendar to make sure he could be with her as much as possible.

45

The New City

Word spread quickly about plans for a new city floating a mile above the earth. There was a virtually endless list of people who wanted to visit and even a significant number of potential buyers interested in living there and those who just wanted to invest in the city's condos. The cost was hard to estimate, but many billions would be required to make the city come to life. The LTA Consortium was deluged with requests to join and share in the potential profits. Max and Alex's shares in the consortium had already more than doubled in value and could increase by a factor of ten by the time the city was completed. Alex asked Tom what her shares were worth, and she almost fainted when he told her $300 million.

Unlike spacecraft with strict weight and interior size limitations, apartments or condos in the new city could be almost any size, with the price based solely on square feet (in reality, volume of hydrogen-impregnated graphene required, which was still expensive). Larger units required more of the basic material, which, as it was basically lighter than air, required furniture or other accessories to provide the needed weight to maintain neutral buoyancy. The design team even found ways to make lattice-like structures that could be used on the floor of the outside balconies, allowing inhabitants to see the earth below.

Alex was in her office designing the various pieces that would make up the city when Max entered and sat down in her visitor's chair, apparently waiting to talk to her.

"What's up, Max?"

"First, how are you feeling? Any nausea?"

"I'm fine so far. You could have called to ask that…"

He laughed. "How's the city design coming along?" When she shrugged, he asked "Can you tell me something about it?"

"I've just started. You usually wait until I have a preliminary design before you want to know all the details. What's going on?"

"We're being deluged with requests for information about the city, and Tom asked me if we could share any details yet."

"I don't have an actual drawing yet, but I have a pretty good idea of what it will look like."

"Can you sketch it for me?"

"Better yet, let me show you on the whiteboard." Alex had only one request when asked about what she wanted in her new office. One entire wall was a whiteboard where she could sketch ideas and discuss them with her assistants. She started a large sketch on the whiteboard.

"I'm going to start with an idea that Brad and Ashley proposed for Aurora's massive LTA vessel, based on a wagon wheel design, and then combine it with what we learned on the prototype platform. It can be round because it doesn't have to move through the air, and as an initial starting point, right now it's a mile in diameter."

Max pulled out a small notebook to take notes as she started a list of features next to the sketch.

"The circular resident area will be about seventy hundred fifty feet wide and connected with eight spokes to a central hub that's about one thousand feet in diameter. I've played around with some ideas and generally think the condos on the outer ring should be about fifty feet wide, with large windows and a balcony. These are the most desirable, so we should give those residents some options, perhaps offer several sizes."

Max nodded, and she continued.

"The condos on the inner ring with windows and balconies are also desirable, but we may have to fix the size of those to forty feet as the inner ring is quite a bit smaller. Then we can have four rows of inner condos between the outer-ring and inner-ring condos. I'm thinking about putting an atrium between the inner condos so those residents can see the sky or the ground. There will also be a number of large lounges on the outer ring where the inner-condo residents can go to enjoy the view."

"How many levels are there?"

"At least twenty-five resident levels."

She started some calculations on the board.

"The outer-ring circumference of each residence level is about sixteen thousand and five hundred feet, and the inner ring is about twelve thousand feet. So with twenty-five levels in theory, I can have eight thousand condos, but practically, we will probably have five thousand large condos on the outer ring and five thousand smaller ones on the inner ring and another thirty thousand inner condos, for a total of forty thousand. We could make all the condos a little smaller and have fifty thousand."

Max looked up from his notes. "Forty or fifty thousand condos?"

"Yes, is that a problem?"

"That's a large city. How will we move so many people to and from it?"

"We'll need to build a large LTA vessel just for that."

"Okay. How big are the condos?"

"I'm starting with a depth of one hundred and twenty feet, so the outside condos are a minimum of six thousand square feet. The smallest inside condos would be at least four thousand square feet. All the resident levels have fifteen-foot ceilings, so all the condos will feel really large, almost like living in a converted loft."

"What about things like restaurants and shops and recreational facilities?"

"The inside of the central hub will contain computer-controlled gas bags with helium so the city can maintain its height. It will be eight hundred feet in diameter, so that leaves a one-hundred-foot space around it to the outer wall of the hub for restaurant and shops. I'll talk about recreational facilities in a minute."

She sketched five large levels on the top of the ring structure.

"There will be five levels at the top of the structure as a common space for things like recreational and fitness facilities, meeting rooms, and whatever else the residents want. The design team is recommending we use three of those for hydroponic gardens to grow most of the food the residents will need. That will greatly reduce the food that has to be transported to the city each day. The very top floor will be mostly windows and skylights to give some fantastic views."

Max was staring at her sketch and shaking his head. "What about the cost of the condos? If these are multimillion-dollar units, we'll never sell enough to pay for the whole thing."

"Based on the prototype, I would guess the cheapest inner condo would cost a little over two hundred and fifty thousand dollars to build, and the outer-ring condos would cost about twice that."

"No! It can't be that cheap." Max looked shocked, and Alex laughed.

"That's why there are twenty-five resident levels. If there were only one level, like on the prototype, the cheapest inner condo would be several million dollars. By splitting all the common costs across forty thousand or fifty thousand condos, the cost per condo drops significantly. I think we had this same discussion on the graphene flyers and commuter pods."

"Yes, but it just doesn't seem possible. That's less than one hundred dollars per square foot!"

Alex shrugged and then returned to the whiteboard to add to the features list.

"We'll get a definitive estimate once the design is done. In the meantime, the needed height of the structure looks like this."

Resident Condos: 15' + 3' x 25= 450'

Common Levels: 27' + 3' x 5= 150'

Vendor Levels: 9' + 3' x 10 = 120'

Maintenance Area = 30'

Total Height = 750'

"What are vendor levels?"

"It's not possible for the employees of the restaurants and shops to travel to and from the city every day, so there will be ten thousand small apartments for them in ten levels on the bottom of the city structure. The consortium can set up a subsidiary to manage the rentals."

"How many restaurants and shops are you planning?"

"More than a thousand altogether on twenty-five levels."

Max was copying her features and frowned. "Why are three feet added to each common, resident, and vendor level?"

"That's an access space between the levels for utilities like electrical and plumbing. So, overall, the living space of the circular structure will be a large square at seventy hundred and fifty feet high and seventy hundred and fifty feet wide. The spokes provide added strength for the structure and are about one hundred feet wide. We will utilize some of the space in the spokes for boutique shops and small eating stations, like they have in airports. That will add a few hundred more eating and shopping options for the residents."

Max sat thinking for a moment. "Why do you need such a large space for helium? I thought you once said the city could float as high as two miles but the outside temperature on the balconies would be too cold."

"I mentioned that when we were designing the prototype platform, but it's still true here. At two miles high, the outside temperature is below freezing. But to answer your question about helium, the city structure can float, but we will have very large and heavy equipment that must be lifted, like the water storage and ballast tanks, the engines, diesel generators, water and waste treatment systems, and so on. A computer tied to a GPS system will use the helium to maintain the city's height, and the engines, to maintain the geographic location."

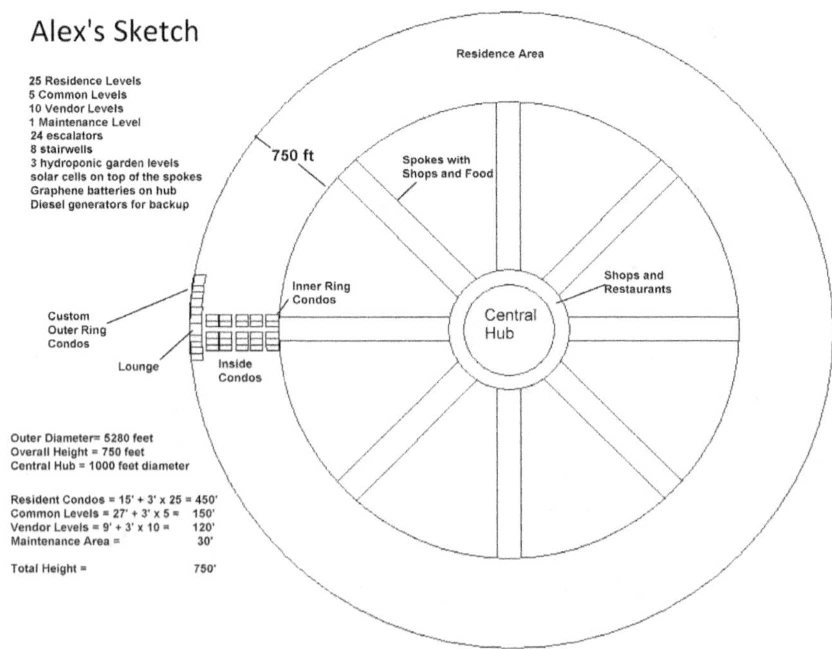

Max looked up from his notes. Alex had added a few more items to the features list:

- twenty-four graphene escalators (similar to the ones on the Balboa)
- eight graphene stairwells on the outer ring connecting all levels
- new LTA vessel to transport one hundred persons or heavy equipment
- no livestock for health reasons (meats transported daily)
- desired population is 120,000 (maximum of 150,000)
- three hydroponic garden levels for fruits and vegetables
- one level for fitness and meeting rooms
- top level mostly windows and skylights for sightseeing
- eight outer-ring lounges on each level (for inner-condo residents)
- solar cells on top of spokes provide more than 100 percent city power needs
- graphene batteries on top of central hub to store the excess power
- power during the night from the graphene batteries
- diesel generators for backup on solar cell power failures
- computer-controlled carts to transport people to and from their condos

Max was scribbling furiously to keep up with her. "Why do you want to limit the population to a hundred and fifty thousand?"

"When they're not in their condos, most people will be in the central hub or on the top floors. Too many people will make the city seem crowded even though it's not crowded based on common area square footage per resident. It will also allow a reasonable daily delivery of freshwater and food not grown in the hydroponic gardens."

Max stood up. "Okay. This is a little overwhelming. Tom and I will go over all of this and start making some promotional literature. We may need to confirm some things with you before we publish it."

"You know where I am…"

Max laughed, kissed her, and left.

As soon as the detailed city designs were completed, construction began. When fabrication of each module was complete, several weights holding it down were slowly removed, and the module began floating. Each module was then towed to the central hub by a new larger graphene dirigible specially built for that purpose (and to shuttle hundreds of workers, visitors, and owners to and from the new city daily).

Designing the city to float one mile high proved to be about ideal, as it required a reasonable amount of helium to lift the freshwater tanks, engines, and utility systems and to maintain a constant altitude. Grey water and sanitary systems similar in concept to the LTA cruise vessels were employed, and the purified wastewater was dumped periodically. Solar power assemblies on the top of the spokes provided more energy than the city needed. The huge graphene batteries on the top of the central hub stored the excess power generated during the day for use at night. Consortium personnel tested the emergency generators periodically to ensure they could temporarily provide power in the event of a failure of the solar-powered battery system.

Not long after she became pregnant, Alex moved her design work to their house in the Hamptons and, by the seventh month, was very uncomfortable sitting at a desk. Her doctor severely limited her time at a desk to no more than an hour or two a day. She didn't know which would come first, the baby or completion of the new city's design. Luckily, she had trained some assistants in their Manhattan office who could now finish the drawings she had started for each level in the city. Max was never far away as he also managed consortium and hedge fund business remotely from their home in the Hamptons.

At one mile high, the outside-air temperature is typically 41 degrees Fahrenheit (5 degrees Celsius), so only a little heating was necessary to make the well-insulated condos and the balconies comfortable. The final sections were installed, and a celebration held by the occupants who had started arriving whenever a section was completed and became livable. Alex heard condos were sold out as soon as each section was completed. That provided enough cash flow to allow the consortium to build the city without borrowing any money.

Prices ranged from $300,000 for a small interior condo and up to $5 million for a custom outer-ring apartment (although $500,000 to $1,000,000 was typical for an outer -ring condo). When Tom Babineaux showed her the sales so far, Alex was shocked as the total sales so far were in excess of $20 billion.

Even after the gigantic costs of fabrication and assembly of the graphene city components, the LTA Consortium had made a lot of money selling condos in the new floating city and would continue to profit by providing all the required services the city inhabitants needed. The consortium also made a lot of money renting the ten thousand small apartments for the shop owners and workers.

—❦—

A few months after Tom presented the idea for a residential cruise ship to Max, he updated him with the latest. Max had known Tom for a long time, and his expression indicated a problem as he sat down in the visitor's chair in Max's Manhattan office.

"It looks like the residential cruise ship idea is not panning out."

"Why? I thought it was a great idea!"

"When we looked into it a lot more, it looks like wealthy people aren't so interested in cruising all the time, even if they can remain connected to their family and friends and businesses by phone and Internet. They tend to be older, and I think the floating city appeals to them more. We had a lot of responses that they were already committed to the city."

"Not even enough for one vessel? Your proposal mentioned only three hundred or so condos."

"Over the years, there have been proposals for a dozen different residential cruise ships, but so far there is only one, and it has been around for years. Another could finally be built, but it's just lack of demand. Even on the current one, there are several condos for resale by the owners. I guess people just get tired of cruising all the time and the cost pretty much eliminates ninety-nine point ninety-nine percent of the people who do cruise."

Max was obviously disappointed. "Okay. I was hoping it would work out, but if there's not enough demand, it wouldn't make sense to build such a specialized ship."

Tom was more hopeful on the city. "It looks like the city will be sold out even before it's completed."

"That is good news. Alex will be glad to hear that after all the work she's put into it."

"On a positive note, several shipping companies have contacted us about developing an LTA vessel to transport cargo. Ideally, the cost of shipping goods should be less expensive than airplane cargo rates and more than sea-based cargo ships. We're talking about high-value goods, like electronics, not commodities like wheat or corn. If it works out, shippers could then choose the most favorable shipping method based on cost and time."

"The LTA-type cargo-ship idea has been around for many years."

"Yes, but it was never feasible from a cost and lift capacity with the old technology. With impregnated graphene, it's certainly doable."

"Okay. Let's look at the economics and build one if enough shippers sign letters of intent to use it."

"There is one more idea." He handed Max a folder. "We had a request to consider building a modern hospital ship, like the Esperanza or the Mercy or the Comfort. I've looked into it, and if it were completely built with the hydrogen-impregnated graphene, it would be about one -third the size of the Columbus and still be able to provide a tremendous array of medical services anywhere in the world, not just off the coast of a country. The ship could actually land next to a village or town with medical issues."

Max was suddenly enthusiastic. "That's a great idea. This is the kind of thing I've been looking for to show the positive side of this new technology. It would be great publicity for the consortium. It would show a balance to the military applications we've been working on."

"But it's not profitable. In fact, no charity today would be able to fund it."

"I don't care. The consortium had made so much money, we could build the basic structure on our own and then work with one or more major charities to design the rest. We could even hold fundraisers around the world, asking for donations to help finish it. This is a great idea!"

Tom was surprised at Max's enthusiasm for something that could never have a positive return to the consortium. But Tom had known Max for many years, and he had an instinct that made him successful in almost everything he tried.

"I'd like you to manage this project. I know there is no profit potential, but there could be nice bonus for you, if the publicity helps balance the occasional negative feedback we get on our military applications. If you need help with the fundraising part, let me know. I'd like to put this on the consortium's Web page as soon as possible."

Tom stood up to leave. "Okay, Max. I'll get started on it right away." He wasn't sure this would help his long-term goal of becoming wealthy someday, but it was different, and it could be fun. He would ask Lindsey to help. Maybe she had some ideas.

46
Delivery

When the big day arrived, Max called Brad and Ashley, Dana, and Lindsey and Robert to tell them Alex had gone into labor. Brad and Ashley left their daughter at the country house with a nanny and immediately left London. Max e-mailed a business class ticket to Dana, while Lindsey and Tom took a taxi to the hospital, and Robert took a commuter train from Washington to Manhattan. They all arrived in time to visit briefly with Alex before she was wheeled into the delivery room. While they were waiting, Max was chatting with Ashley and Robert when Dana wandered over. He immediately noticed her new engagement ring and congratulated her.

"When did that happen?"

"A few days ago, right before he left on his current tour. He was a tough nut to crack, but I finally convinced him he should marry me."

They all laughed as Brad returned with coffee for Ashley.

He heard the comment as well.

"How is Mike?"

"He's fine. He's on the Balboa's new 'World Tour of the Seven Wonders' that Alex suggested, so he couldn't make it. We Skype each other every day."

Brad had met Dana at the double wedding and knew Mike well after all the incidents on the Balboa. When they returned to London, he had asked Ashley about Dana, and she gave him a brief history of Dana's charity works and the shelter for battered women. She also told him about Alex and Max's help in getting the shelter on a solid financial basis.

He wondered how he could help. "Dana, would you like to work on the Balboa with Mike?"

That surprised everyone, even Dana. "Oh, sure! That would be great, I think. What would I do?"

"You probably have the right personality and experience to be the customer relations manager. It's a pretty busy job, though, as you can imagine, with twelve thousand guests and a five thousand member crew. You would have a staff to help you, though."

Dana didn't hesitate. "I'd love that. Thanks!" Brad laughed when she hugged him.

"I just need to make a few phone calls." They all watched Brad walk off, talking on his cell phone.

Robert and Lindsey hugged Dana, and Ashley told her, "I know you'll have a great time with Mike, and that sounds like a job you'd be great at."

Dana was still a little stunned when Max hugged and congratulated her.

The delivery room nurse came to collect Max, and he was in the operating room when Alex delivered a healthy boy. All went well, and soon Alex was back in her room. The staff let in two visitors at a time, and they took turns hugging her. The nurses shooed them all out but Max when they brought the baby for Alex to hold. Max mentioned Brad's offer to Dana, and Alex smiled. "That's a perfect job for her." Just three days later, Alex and Max were in their home in the Hamptons with Ashley, Brad, Dana, Lindsey, Robert, and Ryan Brita.

Now that the shelter was financially sound and had permanent security, Dana didn't mind turning over the operation of the shelter to her assistant. Mike was ecstatic when Dana called him about working on the Balboa as the customer relations manager. He didn't want to say anything, but technically he would be her boss. He briefly wondered how that would work out. Mike had a slightly larger room in the highest crew level, but he thought it would be a bit crowded if Dana moved in with him, so he moved some of his staff around to free up the room next to his.

Dana would always be on "days" while sometimes he was on the night shift. So they could still be together whenever it worked out, and she had space for her stuff.

One week later, Dana joined Mike on the Balboa in Rio de Janeiro during its stop for passengers to visit the Christ the Redeemer statue and the city of Rio, of course. It was a little awkward at first, but Mike helped her find her stateroom next to his and move her stuff in. They went to lunch to discuss her transition with the current customer relations manager. She would have the rest of the tour to learn as many company policies and procedures as possible. Aurora was building a new LTA ship for three to four thousand passengers, a size in between the Columbus and Balboa that would be dedicated to world tours. The itinerary of each tour would change, but the length would remain fairly constant at ninety days. Mike had requested to join that ship as captain as he preferred world tours over Balboa's future flights over North and South America. As soon as he found out about Dana, he put in a request to move her to the new ship as well. Dana didn't object as she always wanted to vacation in famous places but never had the time or money, and she would be with Mike whenever they were not on duty. It did take some time to get used to wearing a white naval-type uniform every day, though. Brad had kept this tradition when Aurora bought the LTA Company's assets and cruise ships since it was consistent with the rest of Aurora's cruise ships.

Tom stopped by Max's office in Manhattan to tell him the latest on the proposed cargo vessel and the proposed new hospital ship.

"We're a go on the cargo ship. In fact, technology manufacturers are coming out of the woodwork that want in on a new cost-effective and fast shipping method."

"Okay, let's build one. Have you thought about how big it will be?"

"I think we could just start with the Columbus and make a few design changes to carry cargo. Minimal engineering would be involved, and the factory already has all the forms and tools needed to make the parts. So we could be in business in six months or so." Tom laid some papers on Max's desk to sign and a spreadsheet showing various options on the cost of manufacture a cargo ship, the time involved, projected shipping rates, and gross profit margin.

Max initialed his choices on the options and signed the papers. "I hope this is the first of many vessels. How about the proposed hospital ship?"

"Several charities have agreed to work together to specify the layout of the ship, including operating rooms and patient rooms. They also agreed to undertake the fundraising necessary to furnish all needed medical supplies."

"That's perfect."

"We just need your signature on this agreement to furnish the ship at no cost to the charities."

Max signed the papers committing the consortium to furnish the basic vessel and an operations staff for the first two years until the charities could train their own crew. Most of the medical staff would be volunteers until the charities could establish a permanent medical and operational staff on the vessel. Tom was relieved to not have to lead the main fundraising effort. He had been to a lot of fundraisers with Max over the years and was not looking forward to organizing similar events. He could take care of the operations staff and would do some small fundraising for fuel and similar necessities. Since the number of hospital staff was small, they could have regular-size staterooms in the crew area.

At Max's insistence, Tom held a press conference to announce the new LTA hospital ship that was being donated by the consortium to a group of charities that would finalize the hospital design and furnish the medical equipment. Max watched the press conference with Alex in their home in the Hamptons. When it was over, she hugged him.

"That's a wonderful idea Max. How did you come up with it?"

"I didn't. A charity asked Tom about a hospital airship, and he figured out all the details and brought in the charities to make it happen."

"That's great! I know Lindsey must be proud of him too."

It took Alex only a few days to design a scaled-down version of the Columbus. More information was needed from the charities before her design team could finalize the hospital ship's functional layout. The consortium's graphene factory immediately began manufacturing the ships basic skeleton parts as they were independent of the size or location of the operating and patient rooms and it would take some time to work those details out with the charities. While she was waiting on the detailed hospital layout from the charities, she finished the design modifications of the Columbus model to carry specialized cargo. Since there were no passengers and only a skeleton crew, all four floors could serve as storage areas. She basically designed the ship to be an automated warehouse where robots operating in the central atrium loaded and unloaded shipping containers under the control of several operations staff.

47

Graphium

Construction on the new floating city was completed in twenty months. Max conducted a poll among the new owners of the city's condos to name the new city, and from a suggestion list of over one hundred names, the majority picked "Graphium," in recognition that the discovery and large-scale production of graphene had made it all possible. The consortium had kept a few condos during the start-up period to allow its personnel to bring everything online and to manage all city utilities until regular-city-functions-like utilities were established. Alex and Max left Ryan with their nanny in the Hamptons and traveled to Graphium to occupy an outside condo for a week to observe and make any needed design or operational changes. Technically, the consortium was the owner until a ribbon-cutting ceremony could be held in which the newly elected town council would formally take over the operation of the city.

If Max thought the prototype platform was amazing, he was speechless when he and Alex boarded the city from the newest transport dirigible capable of carrying one hundred people back and forth to the consortium's terminal below.

Max had studied the design drawings and knew the wheel structure had forty-one levels (owners plus common areas plus vendor apartments plus maintenance level) and was one mile in diameter, but seeing it was awe-inspiring.

To facilitate movement within the large city, Alex contacted several golf cart manufacturers and selected EZ-GO to assemble large graphene-body-based golf carts with graphene batteries to transport visitors or residents and their luggage when they arrived at the city's dirigible docking station. The docking station was on the lowest residential floor, and computers on the large transporters utilized a special GPS system with five cargo-type elevators to take the newly arrived to their condos. When they were ready to leave, residents and visitors could "call" for transport via an APP on their cell phones or graphics tablets or a security panel in their condos, and the nearest available cart would be guided to them by a supervisory transportation computer in the city.

There were also numerous small carts that could be used for transportation within the city. Users were reminded to plug in the vehicle when they arrived at their destination. Power outlets were numerous and connected to the roof-mounted solar power system during the day or the graphene battery system at night. In reality, the small carts were only used by people with limited mobility as visitors and residents could move easily between floors by the twenty-five sets of graphene escalators. Most of the escalators were near the central hub as that's where most people went to eat or shop. The rest of the escalators were spaced around the perimeter of the city. Graphene stairwells were also available if power were lost somehow and for those who wanted some physical exercise.

Although there were thousands of residents already in the city, they rarely saw anyone in the large hallways as they were transported to their condo. Their outer-ring condo was over seven thousand square feet and, with fifteen-foot ceilings, appeared enormous. Later, as they toured the city on foot, Max asked Alex how the city could be so big and still float in the sky.

"Remember, Max, the volume inside a graphene enclosure doesn't matter. A hydrogen-impregnated graphene structure made up of a floor, walls, and roof will float to its engineered height, in this case one mile. Helium provides the lift for the heavy equipment and utilities."

They visited some of the shops that were open and had lunch in one of the dozens of restaurants near the hub. They briefly visited the hydroponic gardens on the fourth and fifth common level from the top. Tiny green shoots of vegetables were already visible in the hydroponic trays that stretched far into the distance. They visited a "green space" with trees, vines, park benches, and a small pond on the second common level and finished the first day with a bottle of wine on the top floor and enjoyed a brilliant red sunset. The prototype platform had barely prepared them for the visual aspects of such a large city floating in the sky.

The next day, Alex and Max visited the mechanical equipment room. A security officer met them and swiped his access card key to let them in. The same security procedures in place to protect the mechanical systems on LTA cruise ships were in place in Graphium. Many of the functional systems in use (such as the grey water system) were similar to those on the Balboa, but many times bigger. One of the biggest "headaches" in the construction of the city was moving the massive (and heavy) mechanical equipment, such as the water storage tanks and generators, to the city. The large helium gas bags in the center counterbalanced the weight of the huge heavy equipment, but it still had to be transported to the city. When the new dirigible capable of transporting one hundred people was not needed, the lower gondola part was removed so that it could be used to lift the large equipment (or freshwater) to the bottommost level of the city.

Ironically, the first area of each new section of the city to be occupied had been the vendor apartment area at the bottom of the wheel structure. The thousands of construction workers needed could not travel back and forth from the ground each day and had to be housed in the vendor area. They were relocated to a new section when the just completed section became livable—to make room for the new shop owners and workers.

At the end of the week, Max had received inquiries from so many people who still wanted condos that he set up a videoconference with several consortium partners to consider building a second city. His list of potential owners was nearing the 30 percent mark, and most of the partners agreed that Max should pursue the idea. They would discuss the geographic location of a second city at a future videoconference. At Alex's urging, Max sent an invitation to Mike and Dana to visit Graphium whenever they could take some time off. Max was holding on to ten vendor apartments and a few resident condos for consortium staff and occasional visits by the consortium partners.

48

LTA Aircraft Carrier and Alternative

Colonel Abrams surprised Alex by showing up in her office in Manhattan to remind her that NASA and the Defense Department still wanted to investigate the use of impregnated graphene to develop an LTA aircraft carrier. He knew she had delivered a child and waited until he heard she had returned to work part-time. He asked her about Ryan, and they chatted about him. Alex then surprised Abrams with a preliminary design and rough estimate for the carrier. He didn't blink at the $12 billion price tag. He only asked when fabrication could begin on the needed sections. Alex had artificially inflated the costs, hoping the Defense Department would not pursue the idea. Feeling guilty about the cost estimate, Alex told Abrams she had some new ideas for ways to save some money and would get back to him. The true estimate was probably closer to $9 billion to $10 billion.

Abrams had started to get up to leave when Alex said, "I also have an alternative concept I'd like to discuss."

He sat back down. "Okay, let's hear it."

"I started thinking, what's the driving force in building an LTA carrier to eliminate a sea-based carrier? One of the main reasons is to allow the carrier to fly over land as well as the sea, carrying the battle to the enemy, even if he's far from the sea."

Abrams nodded, and she continued, "Why not eliminate the need for the aircraft to have to come back to the carrier to refuel. Sometimes, aircraft return with ordinance for various reasons, but mainly to refuel." She waited, and Abrams nodded again. "My idea is to make an LTA 'mother ship' that would carry hundreds of smaller LTA platforms that could remain over their targets until they complete their mission. We demonstrated some drones to the army that could remain aloft for weeks without the need to return to their base. These 'delivery platforms' could also carry a lot more weapons and deliver a lot more firepower as the platforms themselves weigh almost nothing and can lift considerable weight on their own. They would also require only minimal assistance from a few small onboard jet engines to rapidly maneuver them to their targets."

The massive firepower advantage dawned on Abrams, who suddenly became a huge supporter of the idea. "Do you have a sketch of this system?"

He laughed when she said, "Of course." She gave him a fairly detailed concept drawing of a mother ship one mile in diameter and four hundred feet high with hundreds of small platforms moored underneath.

"How many of these delivery platforms could the mother ship carry?"

"Several hundred."

"And…how big would they be?"

"They could be any size, but one hundred and fifty to two hundred feet in diameter and about twenty feet high seems to provide a solid platform to carry almost any kind of weapon, from high-velocity machine guns to rapid-fire cannons to smart bombs to cruise missiles…almost anything a fighter or bomber could carry. They would also be unmanned and controlled remotely by personnel on the mother ship, so you wouldn't be exposing navy personnel to the danger of flying over enemy missile batteries or combat with enemy aircraft. There would be far fewer personnel on the mother ship as there would be no need for the huge support staff for an aircraft wing."

Abrams stared at the drawing. "Could you present this idea to my committee in a few weeks? I want to give them a heads-up and get them thinking in a totally different way from carriers."

"Of course, that would give me some time to talk to Robert and see how NASA could help develop the mother ship concept."

Abrams thanked her profusely and said he would call her with a meeting date.

A little while after Abrams left, Max came in with some news for Alex.

"The FAA finally finished its rules around flying the commuter pods over cities and has agreed to let us start selling them. We had a number dealers interested, and a few of them have even bid for the right to sell them at their car dealerships."

Alex's skepticism made Max smile. "No, really! We think we could be selling millions in a few years. That will initially put a burden on Aurora's factory, but Brad agreed to start mass-producing them in his graphene factory as soon as we select the dealer—at a considerable profit to Aurora, of course."

Alex shook her head. "What are you going to do with that pile of money, Max?"

Even Max had a hard time answering that one...

A few weeks later, Max and Ryan's nanny took care of Ryan in the Hamptons as Alex flew to Washington to present a much more detailed concept to Abrams's committee. She began with the same basic concepts she had given him then delved into a lot more detail.

"This sketch shows the mother ship carrying three hundred delivery platforms, or DPs for short. Each DP would be equivalent to a fully armed aircraft in the carrier proposal. There would be considerable cost savings in manufacturing, as most of the DPs would be structurally identical except for the weapons they carry. Only small changes are needed for a DP to carry Gatling cannons or cruise missiles."

One DP sketch showed armament equivalent to the formidable AC-130 gunship with several mini-Gatling guns, several Gatling cannons, and several types of laser-guided missiles. The committee members immediately recognized the comparison. In another sketch, a single DP carried more smart bombs than a stealth bomber.

"Each DP could, in theory, fly at a slow rate from onboard solar-powered engines for hundreds of miles during the day, remain stationary at night, and then continue on the next day. As that isn't very practical in combat situations, NASA has recommended installing several small jet engines on each DP similar in size of those on a cruise missile. This would allow each DP to cruise at about five hundred miles per hour for several thousand miles to deliver its payload. Then if it ran out of fuel, it could use its solar-powered engines to slowly return to the mother ship. Since the mother ship is also a part of the mission, it's unlikely the DPs would need to travel very far from the mother ship."

"What type of engines will be needed to move the mother ship?"

"We have a huge choice and need your input to decide that. NASA has some recommendations for those."

Another committee member asked about the maximum number of DPs a mother ship could carry.

"Practically, three hundred would be the limit. Mathematically, you could have almost five hundred DPs underneath a one-mile-diameter mother ship, but there wouldn't be enough storage space for all the ammunition and missiles for that many DPs, and the weight of the large munitions could be an issue. Even so, think of an aircraft carrier with the firepower of three hundred airplanes that could all be launched at the same time."

"That is amazing," he replied. "Would each DP require a human operator? Three hundred human operators guiding the DPs and making decisions for them would require some high-level overall coordination."

"Luckily, NASA can help with that through software. Normally, the DPs would travel in teams of five or so. They each would have some intelligence and be capable of defending themselves or others in their team. They effectively would work together to accomplish the overall goal of destroying the enemy target. When that's done, they would regroup and return to the mother ship to be reloaded for the next mission. We also think a single DP could attack an undefended target."

Abrams asked about the mother ship, "Would you leave some DPs behind to defend the mother ship from attack?"

"It's not necessary. Since weight isn't an issue, DARPA and NASA and even the air force have developed an array of weaponry they feel could defend the mother ship from almost any attack—by ground-based missiles or enemy aircraft or even an intercontinental ballistic missile. I didn't understand it all, but they are even talking about advanced laser weapon systems and particle accelerators that can knock down almost anything approaching the ship. High-powered laser weapons on the mother ship could also attack ground targets." She showed another concept sketch in which a mother ship was destroying targets on the ground with dozens of high-powered lasers.

Several committee members laughed, and one commented that drawing could have come from a science fiction movie in which earth was under attack by aliens.

Abrams tried to get them back on track. "What about the overall cost? You said in our preliminary discussion, eliminating the aircraft should save a lot of weight—and money."

"Yes, the overall cost of this system should be less than the cost of the LTA carrier alone without the added cost of the air wing. You will also need less than one thousand personnel to control the mother ship and all the DPs, and you no longer expose navy airmen to combat or ground-based missiles."

The committee members looked to be in deep thought, trying to absorb all that until Abrams asked, "When could you have a detailed design and a definitive cost estimate?"

Alex didn't like to commit to deadlines like that but guessed she could have it ready in three months. "What about the LTA carrier proposal?"

Abrams laughed. "I don't think there will be many supporters for that now that we've seen this idea."

All the committee members thanked Alex for the presentation and went off to discuss it further. Max would be glad to know the consortium might be building the first of many major defense weapons.

⎯⟳⎯

Aurora had expanded the graphene factory and added more graphene-fabricating machines to handle the volume required by the LTA Consortium for the new floating city and commuter pods, and that capacity would now be available to build the LTA carrier or the mother ship alternative.

⎯⟳⎯

Soon after the detailed design concept presentation for the mother ship, Alex received an encrypted e-mail request from Abrams to add as many small DPs to the mother ship as possible. He suggested something similar to the ten-foot-diameter drones they had built for the army. Each small DP would only carry two or three mini-Gatling guns or a few small missiles, just like the drones they had built for the army. They also wanted to incorporate the technology and capability of the observations drones to hover and observe and then take action when needed, but they also wanted to add a small jet engine for faster maneuvering. They even requested night vision capability. Alex wondered what they had in mind but added five hundred small DPs underneath the mother ship along its outside edge. She already had detailed designs for the army's action and observation drones, so she only had to modify the mother ship to add the docking and reloading capability for them. Small ammunition and missiles didn't take up that much room in the mother ship's arsenal compared to large rockets, so space or weight wasn't an issue. Even as she was finishing the design, she was still wondering what they had in mind for all those small DPs.

Three months later, Ryan was with his nanny as Alex returned with Max to the Pentagon to present the detailed design and cost estimate of the mother ship platform. The overall design was simple, consisting of a central hub to which twenty-five nearly identical sections were connected, each capable of supporting and rearming twelve large delivery platforms (LDPs) and twenty small ones (SDPs). Eliminating the aircraft in the carrier proposal had saved over 4.5 million pounds for the aircraft alone— and much more when ancillary equipment, personnel, and spare parts were counted and, of course, money. There was a considerable cost savings in fabrication as the twenty-five sections were similar, and all three hundred LDPs and the five hundred SDPs were structurally identical, differing only in their weaponry. The mother ship, with all the DPs included, was still cheaper than the LTA carrier, not including the cost of the aircraft wing, and was now viewed as capable of delivering far greater firepower.

Alex asked about the five hundred small DPs, and one of the committee members volunteered to explain.

"When the mother ship is over hostile territory, the SDPs can be deployed 'en masse' against numerous small targets, even small enemy troop concentrations or troops hiding in cities. During the day, the SDPs could hover at three thousand feet and watch for hostile activities and then take action when needed. By adding night vision capability, the drones could hover just above a street or building and watch for enemy vehicles or troops and respond accordingly. This just adds extra overall capability to the mother ship."

Alex almost shivered at the thought of hundreds of small DPs hovering over a town during the day or at night, then blasting vehicles or troops upon command. It was getting a little too detailed for her. Robert was aware of the addition of the small DPs and was adding them to the command and control operations of the mother ship software.

Max presented a detailed estimate to Abrams that confirmed their earlier estimate. Abrams had been authorized for that amount and immediately signed a contract for delivery of the first mother ship platform to the defense department. The value of Alex and Max's LTA Consortium stock almost doubled—again. Alex was enjoying being at the center of so many new developments, and Max enjoyed collecting payments for them.

49

Visiting Graphium

In a rare break from all their busy activities, Max, Alex, and Ryan met Mike and Dana on the floating city for a week's vacation. Max bought several outside condos and occasionally rented them out to friends and business associates, much as he had done with his house in Maui. The rent pretty much covered the taxes and utilities. Six months after most of the city's apartments and condos were sold, the newly elected city council established a very small tax rate to maintain all the city's utilities and to provide a minimal amount of security (police). Compared to most cities, the tax rate was very small and the crime rate nonexistent. Power, water, and sewage usage fees were also established to recover those costs.

Mike and Dana were amazed as Max had been that a city so big could float in the sky. After being transported to their condos and stowing their luggage, they spent the rest of the day exploring the city. All condos had been sold out as soon as they went on sale, and Mike asked Max if their value had increased. Max laughed and said a new outer or inner ring condo now averaged almost two million and an inside condo almost five hundred thousand. This was based mostly on supply and demand, and Max finally set up a Web site to determine if there were actually forty thousand to fifty thousand potential buyers to justify another city.

The geographic location would make a difference, and Max suggested ten possibilities on the Web site, along with information and projected data like the average ambient air temperature at one mile above those locations. He was not surprised when commitments for condos in a city floating over Miami quickly passed New York. Max had discussed a potential city floating near New York, and city officials were less than enthusiastic citing potential terrorism issues and an already heavily congested air traffic control pattern that would have to be modified. City officials in a few other potential sites (Los Angeles, Chicago, and Boston) expressed similar misgivings, but not officials in Miami or St. Louis or Seattle.

When potential Miami buyers put earnest money deposits down for 40 percent of the new city condos, Max held one final videoconference with his partners, and they all agreed to proceed. The Web site changed to confirm the new city would be floating over Miami and provided a project schedule for completion. LTA Consortium staff personally notified each Miami buyer who had put an earnest money deposit down that construction had been approved.

Shops had sprung up in every available space in Graphium by eager vendors who really just wanted to live in the sky. The spokes were now lined with small boutique shops and small food vendor stations. The ten thousand vendor apartments had filled up quickly, and some eager entrepreneurs were even sharing the small apartments.

One night at dinner, Max asked Dana and Mike if they had ever thought about a wedding date. When Mike hesitated, Dana volunteered they had discussed a ceremony similar to the wedding on the Balboa but hadn't fixed a date yet. Mike and Dana thoroughly enjoyed their vacation and thanked Max and Alex several times when it was finally time for them to return to Aurora's latest ship, the Cortez. Dana was now quite comfortable in her role as customer relations manager, and Mike had little overview of her effectiveness other than the forms passengers were always asked to fill out at the end of a cruise. They both said the constantly changing world tours had given them many opportunities to see places they never would have been able to see on their own.

Alex and Lindsey often texted or e-mailed each other, and Alex happily told Max when Lindsey and Tom became engaged. They had used their proceeds from the sale of the bulb consortium to purchase a nice brownstone overlooking Central Park in New York and were thinking about getting married in a year or so. Max called Tom to congratulate him and Lindsey. He invited them to spend a weekend with Alex, Ryan, and him in the Hamptons.

Lindsey also called Dana to tell her the good news as the twins never kept secrets from each other. Dana was excited that her twin would be marrying soon. She wondered aloud if they could hold a dual wedding like Alex and Max and Brad and Ashley. Lindsey said she would ask Tom, and it didn't take long for them all to agree on a joint wedding.

50

Cortez Wedding

Dana and Mike and Lindsey and Tom agreed on a wedding date and invited all their family and friends to join them for a joint ceremony on Aurora's newest addition, the Cortez, which was dedicated to round-the-world cruises. Brad and Ashley flew to New York on a commercial jet and planned to start the tour in Jersey City, New Jersey, and get off in London after the ceremony. Alex and Max also joined the tour in New Jersey with Ryan and planned to leave the tour in London to spend some time with Brad, Ashley, and Emma in their countryside estate. Robert also joined the tour but would stay a little longer to leave in Venice, Italy. He apparently had a new Italian girlfriend and wanted to meet her parents. Lindsey and Tom decided to stay for the whole world tour, which would include some new sites in the Mediterranean: Madrid and Barcelona in Spain, Monte Carlo in Monaco, and Rome and Venice in Italy.

There were no mechanical glitches or saboteurs on this tour, and the joint wedding came off without incident. Brad had brought on a temporary captain and customer relations manager so Dana and Mike could enjoy the next two weeks of the tour as a honeymoon.

During the reception, Tom pulled Max aside to update him on the cargo and hospital ship projects.

"The demand for specialized cargo transport is huge, much bigger than I even dreamed. I expected some demand for fast delivery of new technology electronics, like OLED TVs, but we are receiving dozens of requests for pricing, delivery, and availability from all sorts of manufacturers. Right now, it looks like the new cargo ship will be sold out in its first three months of operation."

"What type of manufacturer is asking for this?"

"Well, for example, one luxury car manufacturer wants to lease the whole ship and deliver a large quantity of its cars directly to the dealers who ordered them, all in one trip."

Max shook his head. "That's great, but is it profitable? We still have to recover the costs to build the vessel."

"Yes, based on our latest data, we should be able to recover that cost in the first year."

"That's pretty incredible. Do you think we should start building more cargo ships?"

"I don't have enough data yet, but I'll look into it and let you know."

"How about the hospital ship?"

"We have five charities cooperating on the design and layout of the hospital area and should be able to give it to Alex to finish the design in a few weeks. Since the rest of the ship is done, we should be able to finish the whole thing in about six months."

"That's great. Let me know if any problems come along."

Max went off to tell Alex she should receive the hospital layout design in a few weeks. She urged Max to consider a hefty bonus for Tom, as the consortium was already receiving a lot of favorable press for donating the basic hospital ship. Max said he would contact the partners about a large bonus. Alex, Max, and Ryan spent a week with Ashley, Brad, and Emma at their country estate and a few more days in the London penthouse prior to returning on their private jet to Manhattan.

Luxury Commuter Pods

A few months after they returned from London, Max showed Alex an advertisement for a commuter pod offered by a luxury car dealer. The consortium, really Max, had responded to the huge demand for them by agreeing to two versions of the pods, an economy version similar to the one Alex and he had tested at the naval air station and a larger, more luxurious version that seated two persons and had more amenities—for a price of course. Ford had been awarded the "affordable" version for sale in their dealerships, and BMW would be selling the upscale version.

Max and Alex visited the nearest BMW dealer near their home in the Hamptons to see the commercial version of the larger design. Alex, of course, knew the basic structure and the engineering details, but there always is a huge difference when you see the actual product versus the 3-D design drawings she preferred to do. They entered the showroom, and large graphics directed them past the regular cars and the "Mini Cooper" area to a separate showroom where a dozen commuter pods of all colors and custom paint jobs were available for viewing and even "test flying." The rules for commuting were unfamiliar to many people, so a prequalified salesperson had to take the potential customer on a short flight around the Long Island area. The salespersons also provided a government-issued brochure describing the commuting rules and the need to pass a written and flying test prior to obtaining a license that would allow the new owner to fly solo.

A very young salesman approached them as they were examining the interior of one of the luxury pods. His name tag identified him only as "Jim."

"Quite a beauty, isn't she?"

Alex and Max couldn't help laughing. Alex wondered if he were old enough to fly one. She decided to test him. "Yes. How far can it go before it has to be recharged?"

He had that one. "It depends on the weight of the passenger, the wind speeds, and direction, but you would probably be able to travel fifty or so miles before you had to land."

Max was watching Alex and smiled as she continued,

"How long would it take to recharge the batteries?"

"About two hours."

"Where are the batteries? Could we see them?"

His expression changed. "I've never seen them. Maybe my manager knows how to find them."

Before he walked off, Alex stopped him. "Don't worry about it. The batteries are in the outer shell of the pod and aren't accessible to anyone outside the mechanics."

He was staring at her when it suddenly dawned on him. He was a big racing fan and had seen Max and Alex on TV at their press conference before the latest Le Mans race.

"You're Max and Alex Brita!" He was looking at Alex. "You designed the pods. And…you run the big consortium that builds everything out of graphene."

They both laughed and Alex replied, "Guilty as charged."

"I'm a really big Le Mans fan. I think your graphene car will permanently change racing for the better."

"Thanks, but we're here just to see the luxury version of the pod."

"Oh. Sorry. Would you like to take a test flight? We have a demo pod out back we use to take customers on test flights."

Max frowned. "Yes. Are you qualified to pilot a pod?"

"Not yet. I've passed the written test but haven't been able to schedule a qualifying flight with the aviation authority guys."

Max smiled. "Would you like me to take you on a test flight?"

Jim was surprised. "Oh, that would be great! I just have to get it okayed with my manager."

Max chuckled as Jim ran off to get an okay from his manager.

A few minutes later, Jim's manager Bill Gross came out to meet Alex and Max. Bill was in his early fifties and wearing a pin that said "Pod Certified."

"It's a real pleasure meeting you both. I've been reading about all the new graphene inventions the consortium has been coming up with, including the commuter pods. It must be really exciting finding all those new applications and being able to try them for the first time."

Max saw Jim behind Bill. "We just wondered what the final luxury version of the pod looked like, and if you don't mind, we'd like to give Jim a ride since he isn't 'pod certified' yet."

Bill realized Jim was standing next to him. "Oh sure! You must have flown prototypes many times. Just be sure you don't fly over the city. There are some hefty fines now if you fly over cities, and don't fly at the required height or follow the major roadways."

"We'll follow the guidelines."

A few minutes later, Max and Jim were buckling their seat belts, and Alex leaned over to Max before she closed the pod's driver door. "Go easy on him, dear."

He laughed as she backed up to stand next to Bill. A few other customers and even a few employees were watching as Max started the fans and suddenly zipped into the air.

Bill commented, "I didn't know it could do that."

Alex laughed as she watched the pod disappear into the sky. A few minutes later, the pod looked like it was in a free fall, but it slowed at the last minute and landed near Alex and Bill. A few seconds later, Jim jumped out and barfed on the ground.

When he finished, Max apologized. "Sorry, Jim, I didn't know you were afraid of heights."

"I'm not. I'm just not used to barrel rolls and flying under bridges and two inches over the ocean and then free-falling to the ground."

Max smiled as Bill helped Jim back to the showroom. Alex walked over to him as he got out of the pod. "I asked you to go easy on him."

"I did. I was just showing him what the pod could do. By the way, those leather seats in the luxury pod are really comfortable."

Alex chuckled as they headed back to their limo.

51

Floating over Miami

When they returned to their house in the Hamptons, Max received an e-mail from Tom concerning the new city to be built over Miami. Max was shocked as the number of commitments had passed eighty thousand. When interested parties in the other proposed cities realized they were out of the running, they decided to commit to the new city. In a note from Tom, it seemed the team that built the Web site had neglected to cut off the commitments at fifty thousand (outer-and inner-ring condos with windows plus interior condos). He was basically asking Max to decide whether the consortium would expand the city to cover all the commitments or use the time and date of each commitment and notify more than fifty thousand potential customers they could not be accommodated (because of a computer error).

The second choice was a nonstarter for Max. He showed the information to Alex and asked how hard it would be to double the number of apartments and expand the size of the city to accommodate them.

Alex was not thrilled with the expansion idea as the original city had taken many months to design. Then she realized her design team had completed all her original designs. She only needed to start the drawings for each level, and her team could finish them. That wouldn't take too much of her time away from Ryan. Max was relieved and e-mailed Tom the consortium would double the number of apartments to a hundred thousand. He also asked Tom to fix the Web site so that it would accept no more than that.

Alex played with making the diameter of the wheel bigger, but that would force the residents to find a graphene cart or walk a lot to the central hub where the stores and restaurants were located. She started a new design with the diameter of the wheel the same and doubled the number of levels. To provide more restaurants and shopping space on each resident level, she increased the central hub outer diameter to1,500 feet, leaving 350 feet of usable space around the inner hub. The weight wasn't an issue, but she laughed when the CAD program rendered a completed 3-D version of the new city: it looked more like an automobile wheel than a wagon wheel. But her preliminary design calculations confirmed it was feasible. She showed the concept designs to Max, who thought it was a good compromise and asked her to e-mail the files to her design team and copy Tom so he could start matching the commitments to the twenty thousand condos with windows and eighty thousand interior condos.

Alex also began planning twenty thousand small apartments for the shop owners and sales staff. As a preliminary design, the wheel part of the city was now one mile in diameter, fifteen hundred feet high, and seven hundred and fifty feet wide and contained fifty condo levels and ten common area levels at the top (six designated as hydroponic gardens) and twenty levels of vendor apartments (plus the large maintenance level) on the bottom. She also doubled the number of escalators to fifty and added some extra elevators and stairwells. She asked Max, and he agreed they would construct two large dirigibles to ferry so many people to and from the huge city once the city was under construction.

Luckily, all remaining details of the new city could be based on what was learned in the operation of Graphium. While they were reviewing the details of the new city, Tom asked why they couldn't make it more like a cruise ship with all the same type of amenities (libraries, Internet cafes, casinos, art galleries, and so on). Max and Alex stared at each other for a moment with matching why-didn't-I-think-of-that expressions. Alex immediately began adding these amenities to the design. The cost impact on a per-condo basis was minimal and could provide significant revenue to the consortium subsidiary that was renting vendor apartments on Graphium and would provide the same service in the new city.

Mother ship Test

Eighteen months after the contract signing, the carrier "mother ship" concept became a reality as assembly was completed high over the secret base in the Nevada desert.

Alex, Ryan, and Max were invited guests for the ship's first test and were allowed to roam about the mother ship with Robert as an escort. They were amazed at the control center in the heart of the mother ship. The control center was one very large round room containing a circle of one hundred consoles each with a human operator. In the very center, several mother ship command staff sat on a raised dais that allowed them to watch video being fed back from the large and small DPs to the operators' screens and on large monitors above those consoles. They had to leave the ship just before the test of the ship's functionality began as this would be a live fire test of many of the mother ship's weapon systems.

NASA had completed the software that made all the unmanned DPs "smart" and capable of defending themselves and attacking a target without direct human control. The DPs could also work together in concert to achieve their goals when instructed by their human controllers. The mother ship was held at a constant height of one mile as the three hundred large DPs and five hundred small DPs swarmed off the huge ship and headed for designated targets at dozens of different sites—to demonstrate the massive firepower capability of the mother ship. The sixty teams of large DPs attacked decoy ships at sea with smart bombs, and land-based targets, with missiles in several states. The small DPs used their Gatling guns to attack a training facility used to train soldiers to fight in the desert.

Ground-based observers commented that there was no real defense for troops when five hundred small DPs flew in a massive formation one hundred feet over the training facility, and all independently blasted away with their mini-Gatling guns at the same time at anything that seemed to be a target.

State-of-the-art cameras on the DPs recorded the results, and later that day, observers on nearby mountains from several military branches watched as the three hundred large DPs returned in sixty V-shaped formations of five vessels, and the five hundred small DPs all returned in twenty-five V-formations of twenty vessels to the mother ship. Overall docking to the mother ship was controlled by a dedicated mother ship computer, but, in reality, each docking port had its own computer and was in communication with its own small or large DP as it neared the mother ship.

Mother ship personnel entered some of the larger DPs and smaller DPs via loading hatches and reported no apparent damage to their internal systems or weaponry. No DPs self-reported any damage or maintenance issues. When sensors on a returning small or large DP reported damage or maintenance needed, the DP was instead flown to an open hangar on the mother ship to be repaired (and reloaded). The loading hatches on the SDPs were smaller, but mother ship personnel could easily enter a small DP to reload its mini-Gatling gun or its small missiles.

The next day, the results were summarized and surprised even the most skeptical reviewers at the Pentagon. During the test, several large DPs had been fired upon by aircraft and ground-based systems as if they were in an actual war.

The DPs easily evaded the missiles aimed at them or used onboard antimissile defense systems to knock down the incoming missiles. In a one-on-one dogfight, a team of DPs outgunned a navy fighter volunteer. It's hard to dodge five enemy ships shooting Gatling cannons and missiles at you at the same time. Fortunately, the pilot was able to bail out before the damaged plane crashed. One team of large DPs actually coordinated their firepower on a ground-based missile site when one of the DPs came under attack and had to use its antimissile defense system to knock down a missile from the site. At the end of the test, none of the DPs were damaged, and all had wreaked havoc on their intended targets.

During the test, a remotely controlled mobile rocket launcher fired a dozen rockets at the mother ship once the DPs had left. All incoming missiles were knocked down by several lasers on the mother ship, which were then trained on the rocket launcher, blasting it apart.

When the accumulated video and results were reviewed at the Pentagon, many other weapon systems under development were put on hold so that three more mother ship platforms could be built and deployed.

The Aurora corporation was becoming concerned the graphene factory had developed a backlog for the LTA Consortium, and they may not be able to start on their next graphene LTA cruise ship for some time. Brad and Max discussed the issue, and Max said he would find a solution.

There was a line of investors trying to invest in the consortium, but Max resisted as the income from the sales of graphene flyers; commuter pods; graphene bulletproof police vests; another hydrogen-impregnated graphene cruise ship (for Aurora); another floating city over Miami; dozens of Le Mans, NASCAR, and Formula One racing cars; and the defense department's three additional mother ships was forcing him to park surplus cash in overseas banks (a common tactic employed by international corporations to avoid corporate taxes in high-taxation countries).

The LTA cargo vessel rental business was booming, and Max decided to set up a subsidiary to maximize its profit potential. Three vessels were already under construction, and all were fully booked as soon as they could be available.

The consortium had received a great deal of positive publicity for donating the hospital ship, and the members agreed to a large bonus for Tom equivalent to ten years' compensation (salary and bonuses), and Max happily told him the good news. Unfortunately, there would be no management fee or percentage of profits since the vessel had been donated and there were no profits.

Max even asked Alex to find some new applications for hydrogen-impregnated graphene to make better use of their massive pile of cash. In the meantime, the LTA Consortium (really Max) decided to build its own factory for hydrogen-impregnated graphene to meet the huge demand for its products and to unload demand on Aurora's graphene factory.

52

Another Graphene Development

Alex didn't have to wait too long for the next inquiry when Abrams invited her to another meeting at the same location near the Pentagon. This time, the US Navy was asking Alex to investigate building submarines from graphene. Regular graphene is not a metal and would be invisible to most types of radar and sonar. The implications for a submarine that could not be seen or heard when underwater were huge, and she was given a large book of facts about the latest submarines to help in her preliminary design. She asked Abrams about his expectations for a graphene submarine (in addition to its potential "stealth" feature). He said he was open to any alternative she could provide, like the mother ship alternative to an LTA aircraft carrier.

If a graphene submarine had very thick walls, it could dive much deeper than the current limit of 250 meters or so (around 820 feet) of most submarines. Abrams didn't see the need to dive much deeper, so she scratched that capability off her list. Satisfied she had all the information needed, Alex said she would return in a month with some preliminary designs.

On the way back to Manhattan in their private jet, she toyed around with the idea of modifying a mother ship's large delivery platform to become a submarine. Her design team had a lot of experience with cruise missiles and other armaments on the DPs that could easily be modified for any of the three classes of submarines (attack, ballistic missile, and guided missile classes). She needed more information on how graphene would behave when submerged. Regular graphene was so light she wasn't even sure if an air-containing graphene vessel could be submerged even if they used a lot of ballast tanks. She also noted the volume of the largest submarine was about 875,000 cubic feet based on an average length of 550 feet and approximately 45 feet in diameter (subs are actually an oval, but the volume of a circle would be close enough). A typical large DP was two hundred feet in diameter and twenty feet high for an average volume of 630,000 cubic feet. However, the firepower of the large DP was much greater than a submarine as it could launch cruise missiles or ballistic missiles or smart bombs (or combinations of these). She also played around with the idea of making a small version of a mother ship and sketched a platform approximately five hundred feet in diameter and fifty feet high. This smaller mother ship would carry fifty small DPs of ten feet in diameter and four feet thick, like those on the large mother ship that primarily carried Gatling guns and cannons. The small mother ship could carry everything a submarine could carry and much more (even a number of torpedoes).

She wondered if there were any advantages of a submarine over the small mother ship and smaller DPs concept. She decided to ask Robert, and when she called him, Robert liked the idea of a smaller mother ship and said he would talk it over with Abrams. He also invited Alex to NASA's JPL in California in two weeks to discuss some ideas for graphene. A few days later, Abrams led a teleconference with his team and Alex to discuss her idea for a smaller mother ship with small DPs. Someone asked if the smaller mother ship could at least land on water even if it couldn't go under the water (he apparently understood the problem with air-filled graphene vessels being too light to submerge). Alex confirmed the small mother ship could land on water to effect sea-based rescues or similar activities, but it would put it at risk of attack while floating on the water.

As an alternative, she proposed something similar to the enclosed cargo lift employed on the Columbus. A middle section of the small mother ship would be lowered to the water with rescue personnel and rafts and raised back to the mother ship once the rescue was complete. This would allow the mini mother ship to more effectively defend itself against attack with its lasers, particle accelerators, and antimissile systems. Torpedoes from submarines couldn't reach it, and any enemy surface vessel would be detected well in advance and probably come under attack before it could attack the small mother ship.

At the end of the teleconference, with the apparent agreement of his committee, Abrams said he loved the idea and asked for a detailed design and cost estimate. When she asked whether he was still interested in a possible graphene submarine, he asked her instead to concentrate on the small mother ship idea for now.

Alex even added a few additional features to the small mother ship during the detailed design. A hundred tiny drones would leave a hangar on the mother ship and land in a grid pattern on the water with hydrophones and sonar systems to listen for possible enemy submarines. A computer on the mother ship would continuously combine the data and identify underwater enemy threats, which would be handled by the small DPs. A few small DPs would be modified to carry torpedoes, and others could drop the equivalent of modern depth charges. When their mission was finished, the hundred tiny drones would be recalled to the mother ship and refueled or recharged.

53

JPL Needs

Alex flew on their jet to the Jet Propulsion Laboratory in California for a top-level meeting with Robert and several staff scientists. She wondered what they had in mind as Robert introduced her to a special team and began the meeting with an opening slide about the future.

"So is your graphene material capable of withstanding a high vacuum?"

"How do you define 'high vacuum'?"

"The vacuum of outer space."

"Well, then yes, but only a small sphere has been tested in a lab environment. Based on internal sensors, it seemed to withstand the pressure difference without any leaks. Why do you ask?"

"We would like to build a graphene platform to explore the solar system."

Alex laughed until she saw they were serious. "You don't really expect me to believe that, do you?"

Robert started a slide show in which a modified graphene vessel, not all that different from the defense department's new mother ship design, was shown as living quarters in space. Pieces would be fabricated and transported to an altitude similar to the International Space Station and assembled. One drawing showed a gigantic piece of hydrogen-impregnated graphene on top of a rocket. A rocket lifting such a large piece of the platform didn't seem possible at first, but the graphene piece actually would be floating if not attached to the rocket, so it wouldn't take a very large rocket to lift a section of the new space platform. A high temperature protective coating would probably have to be applied to the topside of the graphene section to protect it as it blasted through the atmosphere into space.

Once completed, the new platform would become habitable, and special onboard propulsion engines would push it to Mars and beyond. The anticipated crew numbered about two thousand scientists, engineers, and support staff.

There was no sense of urgency to the ship's travels since it would be totally self-supporting and could provide many years of exploration. Robert's slides answered Alex's next question. Why was the concept possible with impregnated graphene and not conventional materials as were used in the International Space Station? The issue had always been weight. The cost to lift the required materials of such an immense vessel into space with rockets would be horrendous (typically $9,000 per pound or $20,000 per kilogram).

This was so far away from her normal designs. Alex was at a loss on how to even proceed until Robert said the sections should be designed to be assembled by International Space Station astronauts in space walks with minimal tools.

They first needed to test large graphene components to determine if they could withstand the vacuum of space. Alex was shown designs for several pieces the committee wanted to test, and she said she hoped to provide them in a few weeks.

They didn't talk about cost, and Alex assumed it was a natural progression in the space program.

Out of curiosity, Alex designed a five-foot diameter hydrogen-impregnated graphene ball with thin walls that was evacuated to approximately the vacuum of space. It contained only a GPS altitude sensor and transmitter. When it was released outside the graphene factory, it quickly disappeared into the sky, and the radio signal from it was lost when it passed ten miles in altitude.

Alex contacted Jack Armstrong, and he provided a longer range transmitter, and a newly evacuated graphene ball passed one hundred miles before its signal was lost. She wondered how well the graphene ball had survived passage through the atmosphere. Was the signal lost because the graphene failed and the transmitter burned up, or was the signal lost because its range was exceeded? At least she knew it made it past one hundred miles. Alex wondered if they could evacuate whole sections of the space platform and eliminate the need for launching them on top of rockets. That would save an immense amount of money.

Graphene Submarine Alternative

Colonel Abrams called Alex to remind her of the navy's desire to follow up on the smaller mother ship with small DPs in lieu of a graphene submarine. She sent him an encrypted file with a detailed design and a preliminary cost estimate of $2 billion, and Abrams soon asked for a definitive estimate and manufacturing timetable. He wanted to start construction immediately. Alex passed along his e-mail to Max, who personally walked Alex's detailed design and preliminary estimate to the LTA Consortium's estimating department for a detailed cost and construction schedule. At least now they had their own hydrogen-impregnated graphene factory and didn't have to rely on the Aurora's factory or worry about its huge backlog.

A few months later, Max met Abrams and some senior navy officers to sign a contract to deliver the first small mother ship and small DP package in just eighteen months. A lot of graphene could be fabricated in eighteen months in the LTA Consortium's new large graphene factory. The new vessel was immediately named LTA Sea Eagle as it combined both submarine capabilities with airborne capability.

54

Discovery Platform Development

Alex eventually learned the Discovery Platform (Robert's name) was not on NASA's funding schedule, but Robert's team had secretly contacted every member country of the International Space Station, asking if they were willing to participate. When Max found this out, he even offered to set up a consortium for the LTA Discovery Platform. When the participating countries passed ten, the project was green-lighted, and Alex began working on a detailed design based on the mother ship idea and the living arrangements of her prototype platform, while Max began setting up an international consortium to fund the project. Six months later she presented the detailed design and cost estimate at the JPL Lab for representatives of the new member countries in the LTA Discovery Consortium. Several more countries had joined the Discovery Consortium, and when the cost was broken down by percentage ownership, all members quickly agreed to fund the platform.

The LTA Discovery Consortium collectively decided to risk losing a full-size platform segment by evacuating it and letting it go to determine if it could travel into space all by itself or be destroyed by heat while traveling through the atmosphere. To avoid losing it, if it were successful, small maneuvering rockets similar to those on the former shuttlecraft were installed. Max, Alex, and Robert were among the many witnesses at the consortium's graphene factory as the evacuated platform segment was released. It quickly disappeared into the sky and was initially followed by several jet aircraft as it ascended. Later, when it reached 120 miles, the maneuvering rockets were fired to slow it down and eventually bring it into a stable Earth orbit. The witnesses were watching a data stream sent back to the JPL ground station and cheered when the platform segment achieved a stable orbit.

Sea Eagle Test

The new submarine alternative mini mother ship had its debut at the Norfolk Navy Shipyard in Portsmouth, Virginia. The new mini mother ship was assembled high over the consortium's graphene factory in Houston, then towed by several LDPs from the navy's first mother ship to Norfolk for final assembly of its myriad of weapons system. For its first test, the mini mother ship dropped to less than a hundred feet above the ocean, and the cargo hold was lowered with rafts and personnel who simulated a sea-based rescue of personnel from a sinking cargo ship. The mini mother ship then rose to its operational altitude of two thousand feet. A swarm of its tiny DPs with hydrophones landed in a grid pattern on the ocean to "listen" for enemy submarines. A few minutes later, several DPs left the mini mother ship and launched their torpedoes, destroying a retired decoy submarine. Several other cruise and ballistic missiles with their warheads removed were launched at faraway targets in the Atlantic. The tiny DPs were recalled, and observers on the docks of the shipyard cheered the successful test of their latest weapon designed to wage war at sea and provide humanitarian assistance when needed.

Discovery Assembly

One central hub and twenty-four segments later, spacewalking astronauts from the International Space Station successfully connected the last segment to the hub completing the Discovery Platform. Once the first segment successfully achieved orbit, the remaining segments were designed to contain living quarters, and most of the rest of the equipment needed for Discovery to deliver on its promise to be the living quarters for exploration to Mars and beyond. Only heavy or special equipment, like the rocket engines and the kitchen and control room hardware, had to be lifted to the platform on rockets. NASA developed a method to generate oxygen from a lightweight mineral and nitrogen from a chemical reaction, and used them to fill the platform with air.

Robert and Alex also worked on a means of transport to bring two thousand persons to the platform once construction was complete. Sending only a handful of personnel on any transport vessel would take way too long. There had to be a cost-effective way to populate the Discovery Platform. NASA had been studying the possibility of a "space elevator" for years.

The major roadblock had always been the cable, which had to be 22,236 miles long to make the upper end of the elevator geosynchronous with Earth. A cable that long made of any material would weigh so much it would exceed the material's tearing strength and make the concept unfeasible. In theory, graphene could make a space elevator possible as the elevator capsule would be fabricated from hydrogen-impregnated graphene and still be lighter than air, even with a payload of a dozen Discovery personnel. The elevator's cable could also be made of impregnated graphene to reduce its weight. Demonstrating the feasibility of a graphene space elevator would take quite some time, so an alternative transport from NASA was also investigated in which a "space plane" would be built of graphene that would be capable of flying from Earth all the way to the Discovery Platform.

Based on a series of tests with graphene for the space elevator, it was abandoned as a means of delivering personnel to the Discovery Platform. It might be possible someday, but fabrication of the graphene space plane was completed in two years and successfully tested by delivering cargo to the platform. Following more extensive tests, there appeared to be no risk to personnel, and a few volunteers in space suits were on the first manned trip, which successfully docked with the platform. The interior of the space plane had easily maintained its atmosphere and human-compatible temperature. The cost for the prototype space plane had been high ($10 billion), and it was decided there was no need for a number of them as it could deliver thirty personnel to the platform each day. Transporting all required personnel in about two months was more than adequate. When it wasn't needed for the Discovery Platform, it could be used to service the International Space Station.

55

Cargo Ship

Alex and Max attended the official launch of the LTA Consortium's shipping subsidiary first vessel at the consortium's mooring site in Jersey City, New Jersey. The "Cargo Lifter" was the first modified Columbus vessel specifically designed to transport high-value cargos quickly from the manufacturer to a dealer or the end customer. Tom Babineaux had scheduled a press conference to announce the formation of the LTA Consortium subsidiary and invite the press to tour the Cargo Lifter.

Alex and Max entered from the rear and visually inspected the new type of storage facilities and the loading/unloading robot. There were only two entrances into the ship, a front ramp for small equipment to be loaded from a larger version of the luggage conveyors used to load aircraft, and a much larger ramp in the back that allowed standard cargo containers to be transported into the large open inner space in the ship where cranes lifted the containers onto large racks. Automobiles could also be driven directly up the ramp and loaded by cranes into storage spaces. Without passengers or even passenger decking, the Cargo Lifter could transport three million pounds of containers or automobiles from North America to Europe (or Europe to North America) in less than two days (4,000 miles/110 mph = 36 hours + 10 hours to load and unload shipping containers). There really wasn't much else to see, as all internal systems were identical to the Columbus as were the reduced crew's quarters for a staff of thirty-seven (four shifts of eight persons plus command staff of five).

In the first three months, the ship would be ferrying automobiles, specialized construction machinery, and highly valued electronics between Europe and North America in twenty highly profitable round-trips.

Max wondered out loud why they hadn't thought of this sooner. Alex commented that without the discovery of the hydrogen-impregnated graphene, it would still not be possible.

Hospital Ship

Max and Alex attended the ribbon-cutting ceremony for the "New Hope" LTA hospital ship in New York. The New Hope was much smaller than the original Magellan at five hundred feet long. The hydrogen-impregnated graphene provided so much lifting capability a larger ship just wasn't necessary.

They walked up an entry ramp at the back of the ship and were impressed at the clean white interior. The hospital volunteer staff was making final preparations for their first tour to Africa to address a recent outbreak of malaria. Alex and Max even put on protective suits that enabled them to visit the operating rooms and other areas not normally on the tour set up for officers of the participating charities and politicians who just wanted to be photographed in the newest weapon in the fight against diseases all over the world.

Alex had incorporated the cargo lift feature into the new vessel. This would allow the ship to lower hospital staff and equipment to the ground without the need for mooring facilities. It would also provide some isolation for the onboard staff if they were trying to combat a highly infectious disease. When it was raised, everything on board the lift could be decontaminated before allowing patients or the returning staff access to the rest of the ship.

After the restricted area, Alex and Max toured the control center and met the captain of the New Hope and its officers. They knew some of them from the Columbus and Balboa. Brad was a huge supporter of the hospital-ship idea and had volunteered them (and paid their salaries) for the first two years. Alex, of course, had to see the mechanical room. It was very similar to the Columbus's mechanical room but quite a bit smaller. The systems were state of the art, benefitting from the experience of the consortium and the Aurora Cruise Line systems.

They ended their tour in the patient area. There were five levels of patient care that ranged from common wards for patients who did not have infectious diseases up to extreme isolation rooms for patients with highly infectious diseases.

Alex and Max thanked their tour sponsors and left the ship to discuss whether the consortium should sponsor or donate more ships like this. While Max wanted Tom to investigate a second ship, Alex wanted to wait until there was some feedback from the charities on the effectiveness of the hospital vessel in treating illnesses in remote locations, and Max finally agreed to wait for the feedback.

Miamium

Alex and Max were among the first visitors to the new city floating over Miami. Even before it was completed, the new residents set up a city Web site and held an online vote to pick a name. The vast majority picked "Miamium" to recognize the home location and to continue to make graphene-based city names unique. While it was similar in many ways to Graphium, the new city had a "vibe" that made it unique. The condos were a little smaller than graphene condos, but this freed up space for every form of entertainment imaginable. The state of Florida approved the establishment of several casinos; and there were literally hundreds of nightclubs, movie and Broadway theaters, and several sports venues for jai alai and tennis, and possibly a basketball team in the future.

While most of the activity on Graphium was concentrated on the central-hub restaurants and shops, the 240,000 residents of Miamium seemed to be everywhere (but their condos). There were no lines, but all the common areas were always very busy. After a few days, Alex and Max returned to New York to discuss possible changes to Graphium with Tom. A consortium marketing person immediately began contacting Graphium residents about the possibility of adding similar amenities. The consortium subsidiary managing the three hydroponic levels reported they only needed half the allocated space to supply fruits and vegetable to the residents, which would free up enough space in the common areas to provide many of the entertainment facilities. Making structural changes to an existing graphene structure would be a challenge, but Alex liked challenges.

56

Discovery Platform Journey Preparation

Robert invited Alex and Max to visit the Discovery Platform. Almost all personnel were on board, and the last remaining systems were being brought online. The platform would leave for a mission to Mars as soon as everyone was on board and everything was ready, so their visit was timely. They left Ryan with his nanny and flew to the Cape Canaveral Air Force Station in Florida, where the space plane was based.

Luckily, there was no need for space suits as the interior of the space plane was pressurized and temperature controlled, much like a regular passenger airliner. As they neared the boarding ramp, Alex didn't seem impressed at the final product, as she had spent countless hours in the design of the plane, and its length was only a little larger as airplanes go, only a little longer than two hundred feet. Max admired the sleek futuristic lines of the black plane, thinking it looked somewhat like the famous Lockheed SR-71 Blackbird spy plane. Over 90 percent of the plane was fabricated from hydrogen-impregnated graphene, which gleamed in the early morning light. Two huge dual-purpose engines would lift the thirty passengers all the way into space.

The interior was small and reminded Max of the interior of the now-retired Concorde. There were no windows to look out to provide maximum strength for the walls of the plane, but there was a monitor on the back of each seat with a GPS-style map to show their location over Earth. After settling in, Alex soon drifted off to sleep, and Max was still reading his e-mail. After the usual announcements about buckling their harnesses, the plane taxied out to the runway. A few minutes later, the passengers were pushed back into their seats, and the plane roared off the runway and maintained a forty-five-degree angle of ascent until they were at eighty thousand feet. They seemed to be leveling out, but Max knew they had to switch the engines from air-based mode to rocket mode.

They were suddenly pushed back into their seats again as the plane nosed upward and accelerated into space. Too bad there were no windows. At least the monitor in front of him was now showing a video feed from a camera mounted in the nose of the plane, and he watched the blue sky fade away into black, and soon the stars were burning brightly. Data on the monitor gave speed and altitude information, and within a few hours, the Discovery Platform was finally in sight. Max nudged Alex so she wouldn't miss the magnificent views of space and the approaching platform. It was exciting watching the huge vessel grow in the monitor's screen until they were approaching an open hangar near the bottom of the platform.

When they finally arrived in the hangar, there was an announcement that the hangar was being pressurized and the door would be opened as soon as it was safe. There wasn't anything to carry off the plane as there were no luggage storage compartments in the passenger area, and they had been told their luggage would be waiting for them in the cargo bay.

It didn't take long for thirty passengers to disembark and find their luggage. Most of the other passenger's luggage had NASA stickers or a special sticker indicating the person was a member of the crew and representing one of the Discovery Consortium's member countries.

Gravity on most of the platform was low as it revolved slowly while in Earth orbit. During a voyage through space, they would speed up the rotation to more accurately simulate Earth's gravity.

Max and Alex found their rolling suitcases and followed colorful graphic signs to an elevator and eventually to their assigned quarters. In a week or so, their quarters would be occupied by a permanent member of the platform crew. It would take a few more weeks for all the staff to be ferried to the platform by the space plane. Max wasn't sure what he had expected the interior of the platform would look like. Each crew's quarter was pretty sparse, containing only the minimal furniture needed. The room was a little larger than he thought it would be, but there were no windows, which made it a little claustrophobic. However, there was a huge flat screen OLED monitor showing a view of Earth below. He didn't expect the light pastel colors in the living quarters or the bold blue and gray tones in the corridors. He would soon find out about the control center. After a while, Max admitted to Alex the pastel colors had a soothing effect. Max had never been afraid of climbing mountains and racing cars, but he was subconsciously anxious about going to the platform. He knew his fears were unfounded, and the pastel colors helped soothe his concerns.

Alex was not concerned at all about visiting the Discovery Platform and enjoyed reconnecting with some friends she had made while the platform was being designed.

Robert met them in a lounge and gave them a short, effective tour. The tour was short because most of the sections of the platform were alike. Crew's quarters were built in units of one hundred apartments, and the units were spaced around the platform, much like crew's living quarters on an aircraft carrier.

Robert enjoyed acting as host in the control center as he played a large role in the design and installation of some of the platform's control systems. At least there were a few large windows in the control center, and Max and Alex enjoyed the view of Earth from 120 miles.

Robert then led them on a tour of the engine room and spent some time explaining the new Variable-Specific-Impulse Magnetoplasma Rocket (VASIMR) engines from NASA. These rockets were small yet powerful as they converted various types of fuels to a type of plasma that pushed the platform through space. The platform would provide the first real test of a large system in which a nuclear power plant would provide the needed power source for the VASIMR rockets.

Alex knew a great deal about the platform from her design team's work. Many ship systems were similar to those on the navy's mother ship, but some were unique.

Robert then showed them a pair of smaller space planes in the platform's hangar deck where they had landed. The smaller version would be used to ferry explorers to the surface of planets or asteroids or the moons of a planet—wherever they needed to explore with personnel. There were also a number of escape pods around the platform that could shelter personnel for a brief period if something catastrophic happened on the platform, and it became necessary to temporarily abandon it.

The tour ended in the cafeteria, so Alex and Max could enjoy several types of food that had been especially treated to last for a long journey in space. Alex noticed there were about an equal number of men and women on the crew and wondered whether that was by design or just the random result of individual crew members volunteering for a long journey in space.

Max wondered about resupplying the platform and asked Robert, "How long can the platform be away from Earth before it has to be resupplied?"

"I'll be retired before that happens. We are working on an unmanned supply ship that would be directed toward the platform. We hope to have it ready in a few years, long before it will be needed for the Discovery Platform."

"What about food and water for so many years?"

"We have enough water for at least five years right now, and one of the primary missions of the platform is to find water and, hopefully, life on other planets or their moons. Otherwise, the platform will have to rendezvous with the resupply ship. Let's go look at the hydroponic gardens that will be supplying the crew most of their food needs."

A significant portion of the Discovery Platform was designed to be a huge hydroponic garden that could supply fruits and vegetables for a crew of two thousand for many decades. NASA also set up a large experimental 3-D printer to "print" meats and other foods the garden couldn't produce, from basic minerals and bio-inks. Robert showed the early results to Alex and Max, who thought it was a great concept, but it would take some time to overcome someone's natural resistance to eating something that looked like a steak but was totally artificial (even if it was tasty).

Max would have thought water would be a problem for short or long-term space exploration, but the platform utilized redundant monitoring systems as it recirculated, cleaned, and purified every water source that was used by the explorers. Most of the water on the platform had to be lifted by conventional rockets as it was too heavy for lifting just by evacuated hydrogen-impregnated graphene structures. The platform carried the huge quantity of water in tanks located next to each crew's apartment units.

Two days later, Alex and Max had seen just about every unique part of the platform and said good-bye to Robert and returned on the space plane to Cape Canaveral in Florida.

They then flew on their private jet to New York and looked forward to returning to their home in the Hamptons and playing with Ryan.

57

What's Left to Do?

When Alex and Max finally returned to their Manhattan offices, they reviewed the status of all their graphene initiatives to plan a path forward. Alex began a summary of all the new things they had developed with graphene that changed the way people lived, worked, and played (actually, the way they vacationed). The LTA dirigible cruise ships continued to be sold out even as Aurora was building more with the consortium's hydrogen-impregnated graphene. Two LTA cargo ships were now in operation and generating a huge cash flow. Many graphene bulletproof vests had been sold to police departments all over the world and had undoubtedly saved many law enforcement officers' lives, commuter pods sales had passed a million sold, and their graphene factory could barely keep up with the demand. The success of the graphene Le Mans Prototype was changing auto racing as deaths on the NASCAR, Formula One, and Le Mans circuits was now very rare. Lessons learned from the prototype platform had resulted in two huge LTA cities floating over major cities. The military applications had far exceeded their wildest dreams with the graphene flyer, the unmanned army drones, the LTA mother ship and its delivery platforms, and finally the Sea Eagle submarine alternative. Alex was especially proud of the consortium's role in the Discovery Platform, which would soon be on its way to Mars and then Jupiter. Lastly, for Max, the most satisfying development of all had been the LTA hospital ship, which was already having an impact on a malaria outbreak in Africa.

He also thought about the huge pile of cash he had parked in several overseas banks and wondered out loud if there was anything left to do with graphene. Alex just shrugged, and they both were at a loss until Tom knocked on Max's open office door and entered carrying a stack of graphene proposal folders.

LTA Consortium Developments								
Vessel or Item	Construction	Length (ft)	Width (ft)	Height (ft)	Volume (MM ft3)	Passengers or Residents	Crew or Vendors	Helium (ft3)
Prototype Dirigible	Titanium	210	60	60	0.565	up to 10	None	500k
Magellan	Titanium	1200	400	220	80.68	1000	300	73MM
Columbus	60% Graphene	1300	400	250	94.6	1500	400	42MM
Balboa (wedge)	75% I. Graphene	1404	1000	600	424	12000	5000	190MM
Prototype Platform	80% I. Graphene	1000D	Round	100	78.5	250	None	15.7MM
Graphium City	90+% I. Graphene	5280D	750	750	9330	120,000	10,000	933MM
LTA Mother ship	90+% I. Graphene	5280D	Round	400	2800	None	1500	280MM
Sea Eagle	90+% I. Graphene	500D	Round	50	3.1	None	300	310k
Miamium City	90+% I. Graphene	5280D	750	1500	18660	240,000	20,000	1866MM
Discovery Platform	95+% I. Graphene	5280D	Round	500	3480	None	2000	None

Bibliography

Figure 1 "The Golden Age of the Great Passenger Airships," by Harold G. Dick with Douglas H. Robinson, Smithsonian Institution Press, Washington, D.C. 1985